Emerson Dunn Mysteries
by Roy Maynard

.38 Caliber
.22 Automatic
A Quick 30 Seconds
The Old Man

(more to come)

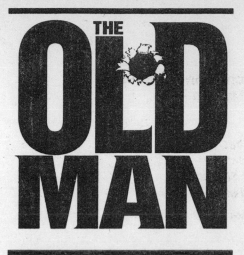

THE OLD MAN

AN EMERSON DUNN MYSTERY

Roy Maynard

CROSSWAY BOOKS • WHEATON, ILLINOIS
A DIVISION OF GOOD NEWS PUBLISHERS

The Old Man.

Copyright © 1994 by Roy Maynard.

Published by Crossway Books
　　　　a division of Good News Publishers
　　　　1300 Crescent Street
　　　　Wheaton, Illinois 60187.

Cover illustration: Keith Stubblefield

Art Direction/Design: Mark Schramm

First printing, 1994

Printed in the United States of America

Library of Congress Cataloging-in-Publication Data
Maynard, Roy.
　　The Old man : an Emerson Dunn mystery / Roy Maynard.
　　　　p.　　cm.
　　1. Dunn, Emerson (Fictitious character)—Fiction.
2. Journalists—United States—Fiction.　I. Title.
PS3563.A96387042 1994　　　813'.54—dc20　　　　　93-43218
ISBN 0-89107-772-3

02		01		00		99		98		97		96		95		94
15	14	13	12	11	10	9	8	7	6	5	4	3	2	1

*To
the memory of
my father*

1

The bailiff watched me over his newspaper for nearly twenty minutes before he spoke.

"This your first time in court?" He asked the question pleasantly, almost as if we were waiting for a ball game to start.

"I've been in courtrooms before," I said.

"Watching, though, is my guess. Not participating."

"You're right."

He smiled and nodded. For the third time in as many minutes, my hand went to my collar, almost without thought, to loosen my tie. But again I stopped myself; juries probably like to see snug ties. They're like girlfriends and mothers that way.

The old bailiff casually leafed through his newspaper — my newspaper, in that I was the editor. We sat on similar folding metal chairs. The small, windowless waiting room had nine of them; I'd counted. They weren't arranged in any sort of pattern; two together here, three facing each other there, the rest scattered about in the 25 foot by 25 foot room. The walls were painted yellow. A wall hanging commemorated the nation's bicentennial in 1976. A small rectangular table stood against one wall. It had a telephone on it. There was also a clock; it read 2:42.

"Relax, son; they'll get to you soon enough." The old bailiff must have caught me watching the clock.

I just nodded.

"And when you go in there, son, you don't want to go in looking all glum, like you just went to a funeral."

I frowned. "But I did."

The bailiff raised his eyebrows; after a moment he smiled. "Well, I sure put my foot in my mouth this time, didn't I?"

"Don't worry about it," I said.

"Did you lose someone close?"

"Yes. A friend. A good friend. The ceremony was this morning. I came straight here."

"Makes for a long, hard day."

"Yes, I guess it does." The clock read 2:44.

"What do you do for a living, son?"

"You're holding it," I said. "I write for that newspaper."

The bailiff nodded. He was an aging black man, with big, meaty arms and a wide, relaxed girth. His coarse, close-cropped hair was graying. He was still in the uniform of the county sheriff's department, but I guessed he had been retired for at least five years. The uniform looked as if it had been adjusted a few times to accommodate a broadening of his horizons. He wore black tennis shoes instead of the patent-leather uniform shoes.

"What's your name, son?" He was looking at last weekend's issue of the paper, probably at the staff box on page 4.

"Emerson Dunn."

"Well, here you are right here," he said, sounding pleased. "Managing editor. That sounds like a nice job."

"It's not bad. The pay is about the same as a deputy sheriff's, though. You and I didn't pick our professions for the money."

The old bailiff chuckled. "Well now, I guess that's right. But my wife and I raised three kids on my pay, and our house is paid for. I made a good living — not so awfully good that working part-time now doesn't help, but a good living just the same."

He leaned toward me a little. "Plus, working part-time gets me out of the house. If I stay at home, my wife finds things for me to do. She read somewhere that you live longer if you stay active in your retirement. I told her she can be just as active in her retirement as she wants, but I earned a rest. You married, son?"

"Engaged."

"Oh, now, that's nice. I highly recommend marriage. Been married nearly forty years myself. The same woman the whole time." He chuckled a little more. "Now my oldest, he's already gone through his second. Yessir, married and divorced twice. He's not even thirty-five yet. This your first time around?"

"Yeah. Her first time, too."

"What's the young lady's name?"

"Aggie Catherine Remington."

"Pretty? No, forget I asked. Of course she is. And you know what, son? She'll stay that way. I'll tell you something: I haven't seen my wife since the night I proposed — not really seen her, if you know what I mean."

"I think you lost me."

"You won't see her with an objective eye, son. That's what I mean. When you look at her, you'll be looking at the girl you fell in love with. She'll only get prettier. You won't see the wrinkles or the gray hair. Of course, that only happens if you let it, if you want to see her that way. My oldest boy, now, he's Mr. Objectivity. He was always comparing his wife — both of them — to other women. You can't do that. Because what you haven't got will always look a little better than what you have got. It's human nature. So you have to concentrate on what's important. She's the girl you fell in love with."

Lowering his voice a bit, he continued, "What if they noticed every extra pound on us? Not that you have any to spare yet, but you will someday. You just take my word for it."

"I'll do that." The clock read 2:49. "They've been in there a long time."

"Now, son, don't go worrying. These things take time. They've got a lot of questions to get answered. Now, tell me about your girl."

I shrugged. "She's complicated."

"Aren't they all? It's been forty years, and I still haven't figured out Eleanor. That's my wife's name — Eleanor. Few days ago, all of a sudden, she don't like carrots. I do lots of cooking at home; comes from back when I pulled the night shifts. Back then, she worked at the church most days; so in the afternoons I cooked dinner. She'd come home, and we'd have a meal together before I left for patrol duty. Well, when I retired, I just kept cooking. Getting pretty good at it. But like I said, a few days ago I was cooking up a pot roast, and she told me to leave out the carrots. I asked why. She said she doesn't like them. After nearly forty years. Now explain that to me."

He looked at me expectantly. I shrugged again. "No telling," I said.

"Son, you're thinking about it too much." He sounded concerned. He wasn't talking about his pot roast. He put down the paper.

"It's hard not to," I said. "There's a lot at stake here."

"I'm not going to talk about the trial with you; wouldn't be proper. But I can give you some advice. When it's your time, just go in and tell them what you know. When one of the men in the suits asks you a question, answer. When the man in the black robe tells you that you can step down, step down. If he says you can go home, go home. And trust that the jury will do what's right. There's no better system — at least not in this world. You a churchgoing man?"

"Yeah. I'm even pretty regular about it these days."

"Then you know you don't have a thing to worry about. Not much that we can mess up here that He can't fix later. That's not to say the system messes up often. I think our system has a pretty good track record. You hear about the bad cases now and then — the guy that goes in and is later proven innocent, or the guy who walks out of here when he's as guilty as they come. But for every one of those, there are dozens of cases decided correctly. You can count on that. Now tell me, when's the wedding?"

"We haven't really decided yet; we think in June of next year. Maybe later, though."

"That's good. Long engagements are best. It gives all your female relatives a chance to put in their two cents on the wedding plans. You like weddings?"

"Sure."

He chuckled. "You won't when it's over. I highly recommend marriage, but weddings are another matter. If me and Eleanor was to do it again, I think we'd elope. Yessir, I'm sure of it. We'd elope. Make the decision, then get out of town. Maybe Vegas. Do it in half-an-hour there."

"I thought you said long engagements are best."

"I did, but I didn't say best for who." He chuckled again.

I smiled.

"That's more like it," he said. "You're starting to relax some. You know the secret words to a happy wedding? These two: 'Yes, dear.' That's all. 'Yes, dear.' Say it with me, son."

"Yes, dear," we said in unison. I was grinning. The man knew women.

"Now we're going to practice some. You'll thank me for this someday." He cleared his throat; then in a soft falsetto he said, "I think the colors should be blue and orange."

"Blue and orange?"

"Wrong!" He was back to his deep, chesty voice. "You was supposed to say 'Yes, dear.' Son, I'm trying to save your life here. Let's try it again."

Again in falsetto: "Honey, my sister's children want to be in the wedding. I know Little Maurice throws up a lot, but he'd be such a cute ring-bearer."

"Yes, dear."

"And you know how Little Maurice has reactions to heavy perfumes and colognes; I think it would be best for you to tell your brother to lay off it a little. Our wedding isn't a singles bar; he can't be trying all night to pick up one of my bridesmaids."

"Yes, dear."

"And if you want, we can invite your old girlfriend to the wedding. I don't mind. Do you want to?"

"Yes, dear."

"Wrong!" he boomed. "Double wrong! That's how to get yourself killed, son. I've seen men crippled for life for making a mistake like that one."

"You told me to just say, 'Yes, dear.'"

"That don't mean stop listening. That's how you slip up; you get sloppy and stop listening. Once that happens, you'll go home one day and there'll be a new, red Chevrolet Caprice in the driveway. It's gonna have shiny spoke wheels and a fanny-heater built into the seat. You'll say, 'Honey, what's this doing in my driveway?' and she'll say, 'But you said I could.' And then you'll notice your fishing boat is gone."

"She wouldn't sell my boat."

"That's what they all say." He shook his head sadly. "I'm still paying for that Caprice. Take my advice: never stop listening. Of course, my daddy never listened to my momma. And she knew it, too. When he got old, he went deaf, but that didn't stop her from talking to him — all day long, about everything in the world. One day she was talking to him and I said, 'Momma, you know he can't hear you. Why are you still talking to him so much?' She laughed and said she knew he never did listen; she said no one should have to listen to her prattle all day anyway. She laughed about it. They were married sixty-five years before he died. I figure out of sixty-five years, he listened to about eight months' worth of talk from her."

He grinned and leaned a little closer again. "That's how I got the name Percival."

"Percival?"

"Everybody calls me Percy. Momma liked to read stories almost as much as she liked to talk. Coulda been worse; coulda been Gawain or some such like that. Percival was salvageable. Once my daddy found out what she named me, he started calling me Percy and wouldn't let her call me anything but that."

"Percy's not a bad name," I said. "Now, with the name Emerson, there's not much you can do. My parents called me 'Sonny' when I was growing up. I put a stop to that as quick as I could."

"I see what you mean," he said. "Tough for girls to take you seriously with the name Sonny."

I grinned. I was starting to feel good. Or at least I was starting to feel alive again, which is often a passable substitute for feeling good. I should have known it wouldn't last. The single door to the waiting room opened, and a man in a suit entered.

"Emerson, we've recessed for fifteen minutes," said the man in the suit, a guy named Fielder. Fielder was a lawyer. My fiancée wanted to be a lawyer. She'd look better doing it than Fielder did. Fielder looked tired, angry, and frustrated. I hoped he looked better to the jury.

"We'll be ready for you in about an hour," he said. "It may be a little longer than that. The prosecution has its ballistics guy on the stand. He's got a great voice — deep and confident. He's good at this. The jury likes him. I'll have to take it easy on him. But that's fine. He doesn't have much to do with my case or even the prosecution's case. He's just there to confirm which shot went where. He's their last witness, and you're one of my first. I'll start with Walter Schmidt, and then I think I might put the photographer on. Then you."

I nodded. Percy was watching Fielder now; Fielder was a hotshot Dallas lawyer who came down to Brazoria County at the expense of the Police Officers Association. He specialized in defending cops. His suit wasn't expensive, and his briefcase was plain old cow leather, nothing exotic. His hair was short and conservative, his face clean-shaven. Every aspect of his appearance was thought-out, I knew. He did everything he could to seem a good ol' boy just down here to defend a friend. I might have believed it if I hadn't seen him drive up to the courthouse in a late-model Mercedes 500 SL convertible.

"Emerson, as we've discussed before, what I'll need you to do is to tell the story," Fielder said. "Just like it happened. I'll ask you a lot of questions, something like 'And what happened then?' and you just tell me. Don't try to slant anything; don't even think of leaving something out just because you're worried it might hurt our case. I've had witnesses do that, and I've watched the prosecution eat them alive. You just answer the questions."

"Fine."

"It might be best if you go over everything in your mind again, while you're waiting. That will keep it clear, make your answers come quicker. A jury likes that. Not a one of those jurors can tell you what he had for breakfast yesterday, but he'll want you to remember every detail of what happened months ago without hesitation. So don't rehearse, but think back a little now. Go over it one more time."

"Okay."

Fielder nodded, put his hand on my shoulder, and squeezed.

"Cheer up, Emerson, we've got this one in the bag," he said. "Nothing to worry about." He winked at me and left.

I closed my eyes and leaned back in my chair. I heard Percy's newspaper rustle again. I thought back to an afternoon four months ago. Anger began to pool in my gut, anger at myself for not seeing the signs, the small indications. But at the time, I wasn't even looking.

2

I t was July 30. You're supposed to look back on days like that
fondly, so I did my best to commit the details to memory. July
30 was a bright day, a hot day. The Dallas skyline was hazy
with smog and heat by 8 A.M., when my photographer (and best
friend) David Ben Zadok and I drove south from the city. We
were in separate cars. I don't know what David thought about. I
thought about marriage. I had made an appointment to see a
man about some jewelry. The thought of the unbreakable bond
of matrimony wasn't unpleasant, but I was still having a few second thoughts. And when I wasn't having second thoughts, I was
having thoughts about remote South Seas islands with weak
extradition treaties.

I had been dating Aggie Catherine Remington for seven
months. It was time to do something about it. I knew it, she knew
it, and my dog knew it. The day before the drive south from
Dallas, David and I were offered jobs with the Dallas newspaper.
I also had learned that A. C. Remington had been accepted to the
Southern Methodist University Law School, which is also in
Dallas. It seemed we were being led north from our Houston-
area homes to the Dallas prairies and a bright new future.

Now it was time to define that future a bit. I was going to ask
Aggie Catherine Remington, affectionately known as
"Remington," to marry me. If David and I accepted the jobs in

Dallas (and at that point there was little doubt that we would), David and I could room together for a few months while Remington went to school and planned the wedding.

As I drove, my mind would occasionally drift to the details of when and how we would get married. I put those thoughts out of my head and concentrated on the real crisis at hand: purchasing jewelry and finding out if she was even interested in the idea of marriage.

Actually, the subject had been broached. We had talked about it (though not by name) on the telephone the night before. At no point did she laugh audibly, and I was taking that as a good sign.

Near Huntsville, David turned on his blinker, then changed into the right-hand lane. He pulled off at the next exit and found a gas station. I was getting a little low myself, so I steered my overly large '73 Ford to a pump near David's Toyota. We refueled with little more than a smile passing between us. David seemed to know I was deep into my thoughts and didn't want to talk much.

We hit the highway again, and in a little more than two hours we had passed through Houston and its outskirts and were starting to see trees again. A few minutes later we neared the small town where we both lived; he drove through it toward his home, and I drove south to my rented farmhouse.

It was after noon when I found myself on the small farm-to-market road leading home. Remington and the aforementioned dog, Airborne Ranger, were waiting inside for me as I pulled into the driveway of my country estate. You're allowed to call it a country estate if you can smell cows. I could, so I did.

I parked my decaying Ford and closed the door softly as I got out. I wasn't trying to cut down on noise; rather, I was worried about some rust around the door hinges. Rust and an inconvenient pothole had already claimed a large part of my muffler somewhere near Madisonville. Maybe I could squander all that extra money I'd be making in Dallas on something frivolous such as a car that worked.

I was getting my bag out of the trunk when the front door of the house opened. Remington and Airborne emerged to greet me. Airborne bounded off the porch and ran up to me with his big golden retriever tail wagging wildly. He licked me in the face when I knelt down to scratch his ears.

Remington did none of the above. She stayed on the porch and looked nervous. I didn't blame her.

I could tell her mind was on matters other than her wardrobe; she had taught me enough about clothing to know that you shouldn't wear conflicting plaids. She was wearing a light-colored, subtle plaid skirt with a blue plaid blouse. She stood on the porch with her hands on the chipped wooden railing and just smiled at me. Just smiled.

"Do you have the whole day off?" I asked, closing my trunk. She nodded. I realized all over again that Aggie Catherine Remington was a beautiful woman. She was tall, with long black hair and deep blue eyes. "I guess we ought to talk," I said.

She nodded again. I walked with suitcase in hand onto the porch. As I neared her I wasn't sure whether to kiss her or mention the plaids. I took the easy way out.

"Your plaids are a little at odds with each other," I said.

She looked down at herself for a moment. "This is something I'd expect to find *you* wearing," she almost whispered.

"What a terrible thing to say. You know I hardly ever wear skirts."

I thought I had successfully avoided the kissing situation when she struck. I was standing at the door, about four feet away from her, and without warning she pounced. Before I knew what was happening, her arms were around my neck and she was squeezing.

But that wasn't the worst part. Then she started crying. I looked down at Airborne for help. He just looked up at me with his tongue lolling about and his tail swinging slowly from side to side.

"Did she pull this with you?" I asked him. He didn't answer.

"Pull what?" Remington asked, sniffing a little. The grip around my neck loosened.

"I was talking to my dog," I said. "Never mind. What's wrong?"

"Nothing's wrong." She let go and fumbled with the handle of the screen door. I helped, and together we succeeded in getting it open. We then worked on the larger problem of the front door itself, which was mercifully ajar. Remington held the door as I walked into the house. She had very nice manners for a journalist and future law student. I walked into my living room and put my bag down by the couch.

I looked around at my home; it was cleaner than when I'd left. Remington and one of her girlfriends house-sat for me while I was in Dallas on sort of a working vacation; they took care of Airborne and had obviously improved upon my standard of housekeeping.

I turned to Remington, who had followed me in. She was getting a tissue from the box on the end table.

"If nothing's wrong, then why are you crying?" I asked.

I thought it was a perfectly reasonable question. She apparently didn't. She just sniffed and reached down to pet Airborne, who had taken up his position on the couch.

"Are you upset? Angry?" I asked.

She shook her head without looking up at me. She sat down beside Airborne so she could better scratch his ears. He didn't argue. I wouldn't have, either.

I sat beside Remington and took her other hand. On closer inspection she looked tired.

"Remington, did you sleep last night?"

"No. I was up all night talking to your dog."

"I figured as much," I said. "What did you guys talk about?"

"Things."

A one-word answer, and just when I thought we were going to have an actual conversation. I took another stab.

"This isn't easy for you, is it?" I asked.

"Of course it's easy for me. The question is, is it easy for you?"

"Sure."

She was looking at me now through eyes reddened by tears and fatigue, but eyes that held a hint of amusement. "Well, then, let's hear it."

My throat seized up. I knew what she was alluding to. I knew what I should say. I thought about that South Seas island one last time before I took a deep breath and said it.

"Remington, do you wanna . . . ?"

"Do I wanna what?"

She said it so innocently.

"You know," I mumbled.

"No, I don't. Do I want to what?" There was a little hostility in that last sentence. Maybe I wasn't going about this in the correct manner. Maybe I needed to try a bit of that old Dunn Romantic Magic.

"What I mean is, Remington, do you think we should . . . ?"

Her eyes were narrowing to the point where they were dangerous-looking, squinty little red things. Hardly any blue was visible at all. "You're not going to get too many more shots at this, Dunn," she said.

"Okay. Fair enough. What I'm trying to say is this: Remington, you wanna get married or what?"

She laughed. It sounded good. "Smooth, Dunn, that was smooth. The delivery needed some work, but you communicated the message. So what now?"

"Now you answer. You're not getting out of it any easier than I did."

"I guess you're right. Okay, I'll answer. Sure."

"That's it? The biggest romantic moment of my life and you answer, 'Sure'? Maybe we should start over."

"Maybe." She was still holding my hand.

"Aggie Catherine Remington, will you be my wife?"

"Why do you ask, Emerson?"

Pushy. I always said this dame was pushy. "Because I want to build a life with you. Because I want to get old and cranky with you. Because I want my dog to have a proper mother."

"It *would* be more fun to get old and cranky together, wouldn't it?" she asked.

"Yup."

"Emerson, I would love to be your wife."

Not having anything more to say, I kissed her. It was one of those long kisses you get when you've said the right thing.

3

Ablinking neon sign was the first indication that something was wrong. Not wrong with us — Remington and me and Airborne — but with some friends of ours. It was nearly 4 P.M. Remington and I were driving north on Commerce Street to a jewelry store owned by a man named Mordechai, David's uncle.

As we passed Zarape, a Mexican restaurant owned by German brothers named Walter and Gunther Schmidt, we saw a bright, new neon sign in the window. The sign said *Open*. I didn't think anything about it. I was busy thinking about other things, such as holy matrimony.

Had I thought about it, I would have realized that little would be more out-of-character than a bright, new neon sign in the window of the Schmidt joint (and it was most definitely a "joint," having been converted into a restaurant from a gas station). Their restaurant was an understated wonder; they put their effort into their cooking, their money into ingredients. For as long as I'd known them, they'd had a simple hand-lettered sign hanging in the door that said *Open* or *Closed*.

But again, I didn't think anything about it. I drove Remington's Volvo, with Remington beside me, to Mordechai's store and parked in front of the brick building on the north side of town.

Mordechai knew I might be by; I'd called and discussed it with him the night before, while I was still in Dallas at a friend's place.

Before we got out of the car, Remington took my hand. "Emerson, are we really doing this?"

"I think so," I said. "At least I hope so."

She gave me a smile that told me I'd said the right thing again. Twice in one day. I was on a roll. We got out of the car and went into the jewelry shop.

In my gut there was a controversy raging: should I have bought a ring first and presented it to Remington as I popped the proverbial question, or was I doing right in letting her choose her own? Martin, a friend and reliable counselor, recommended the latter. He said Remington would probably appreciate helping pick it out, since I have abominable taste and she'd be stuck with it for the rest of her life. Martin often gave me that sort of tip, whether I wanted it or not.

Mordechai and his new assistant, Maggie, were sitting on stools behind the counter; they smiled in unison when we entered. Maggie (who had helped Remington house- and dog-sit while I was in Dallas) giggled a little. Mordechai, who had been a colonel in the Israeli Defense Forces, refrained. You get that sort of training in the IDF.

Mordechai was wearing a white shirt over his ever-present prayer shawl, and even though he was inside he still wore his hat. Mordechai was a round, dark man with a thick, full beard and a passive frown that was betrayed by eyes that always smiled. He worked with a minimum of motion; he spoke with an abundance of it. To point to a jewelry case, he might motion with his eyes. To explain his recipe for broiled fish, he would pantomime the building of a boat. The incongruencies didn't end there. He was the jolliest, most open man I've ever suspected of being in the Israeli secret service, the Mossad. A veteran of three wars, the former colonel was still gentle and optimistic.

Mordechai now lived with his sister (David's mother) and her husband Carl, Mordechai's cohort in mischief. He'd been staying on their couch since his recent immigration. He said he was look-ing for a place of his own, but I think he'd have been lonely, and besides, the idea of extended families living together isn't unusual in Israel, or even in the Bible. So he stayed put. No one seemed to mind, despite the grumblings his sister made.

Maggie — a.k.a. Margaret Sullivan, a former exotic dancer — was wearing a new business suit; she looked a little different. It took me a moment to realize that her formerly blonde hair was no longer blonde. It was a chestnut shade of brown; it was a lit-tle less attention-grabbing than the Marilyn Monroe look she for-merly sported, but she was still attractive. Maybe more so. She seemed content now, happy to sit and listen to Mordechai's sto-ries all day as she worked. I bet Mordechai would have paid her just to sit and listen, but she wasn't bad with jewelry; she mounted stones, replaced watch batteries, and even made a few pieces herself.

Mordechai had told me recently that the jewelry store wasn't intended to turn much of a profit; the real money was being made by importing and exporting diamonds through his con-nections in Tel Aviv. That required a good bit of travel, and with Maggie he had someone whom he could trust to keep the store open. "She is a blessing," he told me, but I knew it worked both ways; Maggie needed a secure job and an employer who didn't ask too many questions about her past.

Maggie had spent the week with Remington house-sitting for me, so she knew what was coming. She had probably talked about it all day with Mordechai.

"My friends," Mordechai said, "this is a social call?"

"Business," I said.

His eyebrows went up. "Then, Mr. Dunn, Ms. Remington, what may I help you with this fine day?"

Maggie and Remington exchanged a look. I didn't exchange anything with Mordechai; in fact, I was trying to ignore his grin.

"We want to look at some jewelry," I said. "You know what kind."

He nodded, then looked over at Maggie, still behind the counter. She stood, then walked a few paces over to a display case.

"I think we have a few pieces you'll like," she said to Remington. I figured I had a choice: either stand beside Remington and nod at the appropriate times, or shoot the breeze with Mordechai — thereby admitting to the world that I had little or no say in this matter.

Better to at least appear involved, I decided, so I went and stood by Remington.

She was looking at a tray with about a dozen rings stuck between folds of velvet. She made the appropriate noises, and after about twenty long minutes of my life, she had narrowed the field to two wedding sets. She asked which one I liked better.

I took a deep breath and tried not to think about the ramifications of answering wrong. "I like the pointy one," I said.

"Ah," erupted Mordechai, who had been watching the proceedings from a distance, "the marquis set. Maggie sized the ring just this morning." In a lower voice he added, "We used Miss Remington's college graduation ring."

Maggie looked a little embarrassed. "It's in the back," she told Remington.

"I thought I left it by the sink or something," Remington said with a smile. "Well, that explains why this one fits so well."

"Do you like it better than the other one?" I asked, wondering if I had, by some strange twist of fate, again made the right choice.

"Yes."

"Well, then, I guess we'll take it, Mordechai," I said.

He nodded. Looking at Remington (who was still staring at her hand), he said softly to me, "We shall haggle later. Come back tomorrow, or next week, or when you feel like it. But not now. You two go, have a nice dinner, let her show off the ring, and we'll work out the details later."

"Fine," I said. "I'll stop by first thing in the morning."

"You will come by the house tonight, yes?" he asked. "My sister will want to know everything. I cannot tell her, because of professional confidentiality."

"Professional confidentiality?" I asked. "You're a jeweler, not a doctor."

"I would have been a doctor, if I had listened to my mother. But why do you bring up painful regrets? Take your future wife and feed her. She is too skinny. And so are you. Come over later, for coffee, and I will feed you dessert, yes? And you can pacify my sister."

He waved me away and turned back to his work. Maggie leaned over the counter and gave Remington a quick squeeze — Maggie's eyes were getting wet, and then she waved to me as Remington and I left.

Outside, I noticed that Remington was still staring at the ring. "You like it?" I asked.

"Yes."

That's all I got out of her. I had no idea what was going on inside her head, and she was giving me no clues.

I drove south, toward the restaurant. Remington and I hadn't gotten around to eating lunch, so we decided on an early dinner.

Several months before, we'd had our first unofficial date at that same restaurant, and when things got serious it was at that restaurant I'd told Remington I was in love with her. I was also in love with the restaurant. Although the boys served mainly Mexican food, they made a few select German dishes, including a phenomenal strudel. The boys also had a habit of sitting with their customers and passing the time of day. As often as not, they forgot to bring me the check; I always paid anyway.

Remington said nothing as we drove into the parking lot. There were a few more cars than normal, which appeared to be a good sign. The boys had taken a gamble opening up a restaurant in that particular location; at least three eateries had failed in that building since it was converted from an old gas station. The most recent restaurant (besides Zarape) had been a catfish

joint; the boys spent more than a month cleaning the place, trying to eradicate the smell of grease before they opened again as
a Mexican/German restaurant.

Usually the parking lot had one or two cars in it, rarely more
than five. The lunchtime crowd was a little larger, since the
restaurant was so close to City Hall, but the dinner crowd was
never so big that we had to wait for a table. So now, at 4:30 P.M.,
after lunch and before dinner, we were surprised to see three
cars in the lot. One belonged to the Schmidts.

"I hope things are looking up for the guys," Remington said as
we chose a parking space next to a dark blue Lincoln. "They've
worked so hard; I'd hate to see the business fail."

"If it fails, they'll go cook for someone else until they have
enough capital to try again," I said.

"It wouldn't be the same," she said after a moment. "*We've* got
a lot invested here, too. Time — emotions."

"Yeah," I said. I knew the boys had a lot more than that
invested. To be honest, I'd been getting a little worried about
them. I wasn't sure business was picking up fast enough. I wasn't
sure how they'd managed to keep the doors open. But they never
complained about money, and I never asked.

Maybe I should have.

I turned off the engine and looked at the building. The large
picture windows that lined the restaurant were spotless; most of
the mini-blinds were drawn up so patrons could watch the world
go by on Commerce Street.

I got out of the car, then went around to open Remington's
door for her. She had returned her attention to the ring. She
emerged from the car, then hugged me before we started for the
door to the restaurant.

"I love it," she said. "This is the right thing to do. I know it is."

I nodded. I opened the door to the restaurant for her; she
went in, and I followed. We stood for a moment waiting for
either Walter or Gunther to notice us.

Gunther spotted us first. He was to our left, down a row of

booths, taking an order from a group of older businessmen. Three of them, all wearing suits. Their coats were on despite the fact that the bank clock across the street said it was 97 degrees outside. With all those windows, the restaurant tended to warm up a bit during summer afternoons.

I didn't recognize any of the three businessmen. After a couple of years in a small town, you get to know at least the faces — if not the names — of almost everyone. It heartened me a little that I didn't recognize these mugs; I assumed it meant the boys were attracting out-of-town customers.

Gunther shot me a quick, nervous glance; that was a little peculiar. Gunther would usually at least greet us verbally and politely tell us he'd be with us in a moment.

Remington frowned a bit.

"He's trying to impress the suits," I said. "Don't sweat it. Or maybe he's heard that I proposed. He's had his eye on you for months."

"Don't be silly," she said. "Let's just grab a booth."

I followed her to one against the front window, three down from the suits, and we took our seats facing each other. The booth had high-backed seats, so we had a little privacy; we could still hear the men at the table, though.

"When should we go talk to my parents?" she asked.

"This weekend, I guess. Is that soon enough?"

"Yeah. Do your parents know?"

"I called my mother and father before I left Dallas this morning. They know."

"How did your mother take it?"

"As expected," I said. "She started crying. But not bad crying. Just crying. We're supposed to drive up within a few weeks. Labor Day at the latest."

"Okay. Shall we do my father first or my mother?"

Remington's parents had divorced some years ago, so it was going to be twice as much effort to inform them of our intentions and to ask their blessings. Not that we had any doubts about their blessings; her father was an easygoing man who seemed to like me, and her mother had apparently taken to me as well, though we'd never met. Remington was a smooth talker, I guess. My parents liked Remington, and I had the all-important approval of Martin Paige and his family. Martin was the pastor at our small church; I valued his opinion highly. He would probably suggest we go see Remington's father first, so that's what I told Remington we should do.

"Fine," she said. "Nice and traditional."

Remington was being remarkably agreeable. In fact, it was so remarkable that I started to remark on it when I saw Gunther appear above her shoulder.

"Waiter, is it true you use only the finest of horses in your fajitas?" I asked.

Gunther's eyes got wide, and he motioned with his head at the table full of neckties. In a loud voice he asked, "May I take your order?"

"What order?" Remington said. "You know you don't take our order. Just bring us what's good today."

Gunther nodded and went back to the kitchen.

"What a grump," I said. "He had his chance at you, but I was too smooth. He couldn't compete. I don't blame him for feeling grumpy."

Remington shook her head. "That's not it. Look behind you . . . by the door. We walked by it on our way in."

I turned around and looked at the door; just to the right of it I saw a chest-high cigarette vending machine. It hadn't been there a week or so ago, the last time I'd eaten at Zarape.

"You know what Walter says about putting in a smoking section," she said. She frowned and lowered her voice in an awful imitation of Walter: "I will not contribute to the ruining of a customer's taste buds. If they have no taste buds, then how will they taste my cooking? Then what joy shall they have in their lives? Their lives will be dismal, and all of my training will be wasted."

"He does think rather highly of his cooking," I said. "But if they were losing customers because they didn't have a smoking section, maybe . . ."

"Maybe not," Remington said. "I don't think he would. And even if he did, would they put in a cigarette machine?"

"I don't know. Maybe they're trying to make a little extra money."

Gunther reappeared with two cups of coffee on a tray. "Enchiladas will be out soon. I hope you will like them."

He never met my eyes as he put our coffee cups down on the table, then turned and marched back to the kitchen.

"Something's up," I said to Remington in a soft voice. "I'm going back to ask Walter what's wrong with his brother."

Remington nodded. I got up and walked back to the kitchen. Six eyes from three suits watched me. I ignored them.

I followed Gunther back behind the main counter that held the coffee maker, the silverware, and the napkins. I went through the double doors leading to the kitchen, and I started to smile when I saw Walter, dressed in his uniform whites, leaning over a skillet.

But then he looked up at me. His right eye was swollen shut, and other parts of his face bore signs of a recent beating. He quickly looked back down at his skillet; before he did, I glimpsed his fear and shame.

You should not be in here, Emerson," Gunther said. "Not now. Go back out and sit with Remington."

I ignored Gunther. "Who hit you, Walter?"

No answer. I tried again. "Why is there a cigarette machine by the door?"

"We will talk later," Gunther said, moving toward me and toward the door. He took my arm when he reached me. "Not now. Please, Emerson."

Gunther's voice was strained. I hesitated a moment before I obeyed and let him lead me out of the kitchen. As soon as we hit the door, Gunther began to smile. "You see, we have left the jalapeños out for you, Emerson. You know we take good care of our customers. Now, you wanted decaf? Wait a moment, I shall find you a cup."

The cups weren't that hard to find; they were in a neat stack beside the coffee maker. Gunther poured me a cup of decaffeinated coffee, then handed it to me with a stern expression on his face. His back was to the table full of neckties.

I nodded and thanked him, then went back to my booth to sit with Remington.

"Report," she said softly.

"Victim is one Walter Schmidt, chef extraordinaire, with multiple contusions," I said. "Only he's not talking. He didn't say anything."

"The suits weren't as quiet," she said, even more softly. She passed me a napkin with some writing on it. "They got talkative and a little annoyed when you went into the kitchen. I have two first names and one last name. If we watch when they pull out, I bet we can get license plate numbers. Then we can go see Bill Singer."

"Aggie Catherine, my dear, you're the best," I said. "I'm sure Detective Sergeant Bill Singer will agree with me."

"And your dog already has," she said sweetly.

We continued talking for a few minutes. At 4:52 the suits got up and left; one dropped a fifty-dollar bill on the table. They marched through the door without saying a word to us, but one of them called out to the kitchen, "Lunch tomorrow, boys, 2:00. There should be four of us. Howsabout that schnitzel you make so well?" Without waiting for an answer, they left.

"License plates," I said a moment or so later as I was squinting through the glare of the picture window. "Texas, BBL 324C, and Texas, RHR 190M."

"Got 'em," Remington said, making a few more notes on her napkin. "Now get the boys out here, and let's find out what's going on."

"Anything you say, my dear." I smiled. Since we were the only ones left in the restaurant, I raised my voice. "Gunther! Walter! Howsabout some food?"

"Yes, yes, it's coming," Gunther called from the kitchen. He emerged with a tray; it contained two plates. "Walter is busy; he's sorry he can't come out and talk now. And I must go back and help him. Yell if you want something."

"We want something," I said. "The story. What's with Walter's face? What's with the vending machine? What's with the suits?"

Gunther, a young, dark-haired, clean-shaven German, started wiping his hands on the white dish towel tucked into his apron.

"It's just business," he said, not looking at either of us. "*Our* business."

"Business isn't done with punches to the face," I said gently. "Who were those men?"

"Men," Gunther said. "Just men. Customers. One is our investor."

I nodded. "How bad is it, Gunther?"

He shook his head. "It's not your worry. We shouldn't be talking about this. You eat. I must work."

He walked back to the kitchen.

"That wasn't very informative," Remington said when he was gone.

"Informative enough," I said. "It looks as if we've got your basic, run-of-the-mill loan sharking going on here. I didn't think there was much of that still around. But in a tough economy, a risky business venture . . . Banks might be a little reluctant to talk to our boys. That creates a void, and nature will fill that void . . . With a loan shark."

Remington frowned.

"Look at the table the suits just left," I said. "Wine glasses. You know this place doesn't have a license to sell alcoholic beverages."

Remington turned to look at the table; she rose from the booth and went over to it. Among the plates and napkins and silverware were three wine glasses. She found one with a little liquid left in it; she raised it to her nose, then nodded at me. She came back to the table frowning even more.

"Maybe the customers brought the wine with them," she said.

"No — there's no empty bottle on the table, and the men didn't carry one out with them," I said after a moment. "It's pretty clear what this investor is doing. He loans a little money, the boys have some trouble keeping up with the interest payments, and he eases his way in. He says a cigarette machine — and a little wine with dinner — might help make a little more money. And the boys aren't in a position to argue. Maybe Walter tried."

Remington thought for a moment, then nodded. "So let's finish eating and go talk to Singer."

We ate in silence for about fifteen minutes. When we were done I took twenty dollars from my wallet and left it on the table. We left without saying good-bye to the boys.

"You're mad," Remington said when we were outside. "You're mad at Walter and Gunther."

"They should know better," I said. "We could have helped. There were other options."

Remington didn't respond. We got into her car and backed out of our parking space. As I pulled out onto Commerce Street, I caught sight of Walter watching us from behind the blinds.

"And maybe I'm mad at myself," I said. "We should have seen this coming."

"How? The boys don't talk business with us. They would rather talk politics," she said. "Emerson, we wouldn't have had the money to solve their problems even if they had come to us. So maybe they were just being considerate, not bothering us with their problems."

I didn't say anything. We drove to the police station and parked in the *Visitors* spot. Detective Sergeant Bill Singer's maroon unmarked was there; our favorite cop was in.

We walked into the shabby police station and into the overly bright waiting room. Remington waved at the dispatcher, who was sitting behind a wall with a window of bulletproof glass. When the dispatcher saw it was us, she hit a buzzer, which tripped a latch allowing us through the door and into the rest of the building.

The police station smelled like most aging cinderblock structures: old, musty, with the remnants of cigarette smoke and stale coffee. The narrow halls were lined with warping wooden paneling, as if a long-ago chief had tried to give the building more warmth than the walls could take; the inadequate fluorescent lights added shadows that made the dark paneling just seem dismal.

Through the halls we could hear — as always — the jokes, the curses, the confessions, and the lies that drift through a police station. We passed an open door leading into the squad room; two Hispanic officers were laughing. A black cop with a torso like a Volkswagen squeezed by us. We found our way through one last corridor to Singer's office at the end of the Criminal Investigations Division room. His door was open, and he was on the phone. Singer, a burly, dark-haired, mustached cop — who counted among his talents the ability to insert in-your-face insults between syllables of words — was being polite to someone.

"No, ma'am, I don't know why someone would want to spray-paint your mailbox," he said into the phone, motioning for us to sit. "No, I'm not going to dust your mailbox for fingerprints, Mrs. Webster. No, I'm sorry, but I've already told you, I can't stake out your mailbox either. I'll tell you what I *can* do. I'll send an officer by to paint it silver. If the kids do it again? Then I'll paint it again."

He hung up the phone and looked at Remington. "Some cases can only be solved by being nice," he said. "I hate those."

He picked up his phone again and dialed a four-digit extension. "Richards, go by the city barn and find a can of silver spray paint. Then go to Mrs. Webster's house and repaint her mailbox." He paused. "Because if you're not busy doing that, I might have to give you a couple of barking dog cases. Yes. Thank you."

He hung up again. "Ms. Remington, it's wonderful to see you. Is that a ring on your hand?"

Remington beamed. "You're the first to notice. Yes."

"Is there a date yet?"

"Not yet, but we'll let you know."

"Congratulations." Singer turned to me. "I never thought you'd have the nerve."

"Did you know you look sort of green in fluorescent lighting?" I asked.

He turned back to Remington. "Is this a social call?"

"Not really," she said, smiling sweetly. Singer almost smiled in spite of himself. "We're here about some friends. You know the Schmidt brothers? The guys who own Zarape? We think they might have gotten themselves into a little financial bind."

"In a financial bind with guys who like to hit people," I added. "We've got some first names, one last name, and some plates."

Remington handed Singer the napkin. He stared at it for a moment, frowning. "Jim, Tommy, Mr. Ciotti . . . Fuzzy," he said, starting to grin.

"What's fuzzy?" I asked.

"Fuzzy Ciotti is Fuzzy," he said. "Dad should hear about this."

"Dad?" Remington asked.

"Yeah. My father. He was a Galveston cop, back in the '40s and '50s. Back in the bad old days . . . Before Galveston was cleaned up. He would come home from work and tell us stories. He still likes to tell me stories. He likes the names. Names like Francis 'Fuzzy' Ciotti."

"Who and what was Fuzzy Ciotti?" Remington asked.

Singer put down the napkin and smiled at her. "He was muscle for the Maceo family. You ever hear of the Maceo family?"

"No," she said. "I don't think so."

"Sicilian brothers, Salvatore and Rosario, or 'Sam' and 'Papa Rose'; they came to Galveston around 1910, I guess. Went to barber school and had a barber shop. On the side, they also controlled the largest gambling and bootlegging syndicate in the Southwest. It was shut down in the '50s, but it looks as if there are still remnants. Like Ciotti."

"What kind of a mob name is 'Fuzzy'?" I asked. "And a big mob family? In Galveston?"

"Look it up in the newspaper archives," Singer said. "Or just talk to a few old-timers in Galveston. It was Vegas when Vegas was still a dry spot in the desert. Fuzzy got that name because of his hair; he was bald by the time he was twenty-five."

"So what's Ciotti up to now?" I asked.

"Last time we talked about the old days, Dad said Ciotti was still in Galveston; he has some sort of vending machine company. That's not out of character for him. He ran the slot machines operation for the Maceos for years. He had slots in every restaurant in Galveston County. I guess it was natural for him to move up to candy and soda."

I looked at Remington, then back at Singer.

"Like we said, we think the boys are into Ciotti — or someone — for some money," I told him. "Walter was beaten up. What can be done?"

Singer shrugged. "They can fill out a report. My guess is they probably won't want to."

"You're right," Remington said. "They wouldn't even talk to us about it."

"So what do we do?" I asked.

Singer paused and leaned back in his chair. "They're in debt, and we can't do much about that — at least, I can't. And I don't think either of you two have enough cash on hand to pay off a loan shark."

"Right," I said. "So again, where does that leave us?"

"I'll do what I can to keep the boys intact," Singer said. "But if we're dealing with an old-time mobster, we'd better call in an expert. How about dinner with my dad later this week?"

"Great," I said. "Do you think he'll know what to do?"

"To hear Dad talk, he taught Eliot Ness everything." Singer laughed. "Actually Ness predated him by a few years, but Dad will at least give us a little insight."

"What are you going to do to keep the boys whole until we get this figured out?" Remington asked.

"I'll make a simple traffic stop," Singer said slowly. "When I hand Mr. Ciotti a warning notice for going too fast, I'll casually mention that I enjoy eating at the restaurant, and so does the rest of the police department — and that we'd all be real disappointed if any bodily injuries were to prevent Walter or Gunther from cooking. That will let Ciotti know that we're aware of present financial arrangements, and while we don't approve of someone going into debt with a shady character, we approve even less of the shady character using assault to collect on such a debt. Can you find out for me when Ciotti will be back in town?"

"Lunch, tomorrow, 2 P.M.," I said. "They already made their reservations."

"Then I'll be out on Commerce Street at 1:55," he said. "Now about dinner with my dad . . . How's Friday?"

"Fine," Remington said. "Is that okay with you, Emerson?"

"Sure. We can work that in."

Singer smiled nicely at Remington as we stood, then turned to me. He wasn't smiling as nicely. "Now try to keep out of trouble, Dunn. I'll expect you two here at 6 P.M. Friday. We can ride over together. If you're good, I might even let you play with the lights and the siren."

5

By 8 P.M. I was exhausted. I had driven from Dallas, asked some dame to marry me, bought a ring, met (or at least encountered) a loan shark, and talked for a total of eight hours about weddings and marriage. Remington, dear that she was, seemed convinced that she should tell me all about the weddings of her friends, so I could decide (from her verbal descriptions) what sort of wedding I wanted. I didn't mention Vegas; I didn't even mention that the Chapel O' Eternal Wedded Bliss has a half-price special on Tuesdays.

Remington wanted to talk, so I listened. We sat around the farmhouse until about 8:00, when it was time to pop over to David's house for that dessert Mordechai had promised us. It took a few minutes for us to drive through town to the part where the cars look nothing like mine. As we pulled into the driveway, Rebecca was waiting for us at the door.

"Lots of squealing, I bet," I said as I parked. Remington nudged me. "Well, I'm ready. Maybe I'll get lucky and be ignored the whole evening."

"You'll live," Remington said. "You just sit and talk to Mordechai and David and Carl. And remember, no cigars."

"Of course," I said.

We got out of the car and walked up the driveway to Rebecca's waiting arms. She was crying when she squeezed Remington; she'd gotten over it when she got around to me.

"You will be a good husband," she said more forcefully than I thought was absolutely necessary. Her Mediterranean accent was particularly thick, so it sounded as if she said, "Joo weel be a goot hosbant." Her English wasn't as good as David's, but she made herself understood. "If A. C. tells me different, you will answer to me."

"Yes, ma'am," I said. "I'll treat her like a queen."

"Yeah, sure," Rebecca said with more than a hint of suspicion. "Like you treat her now? You must do better than that. But it could be worse. You should see my sister's husband. He's a bum. No head for business, or for taking care of my sister."

I knew full well that her sister's husband was a successful businessman, but in prior conversations I had gathered that he once lost a little money — not much, as far as I could determine — in a venture Rebecca had warned him against. Mordechai said that despite the setback, the sister in question was still well-provided for, and the husband was still grossing six figures. But Rebecca usually couldn't be swayed with mere facts.

Not that I didn't love Rebecca, flaws and all. She kept her arm around my neck as she led us into the dining room. Places were set for dessert; coffee was on the table. Carl was at the head of it, looking on with amusement. Mordechai was next to Carl, looking at us with a frown. David was still eating. He sort of looked up and winked at me to acknowledge our existence.

"Come sit down," Rebecca said. "I will bring the cake."

"I'll help," Remington offered. Rebecca released me, and I found my way through the opulent dining room to the table. I sat beside David as Carl poured a cup of coffee. The women were safely in the next room, so I relaxed a little. I think I even sighed when I heard them talking to each other and not to me. Then Carl grinned.

"We heard," he said.

"Not from me," Mordechai added.

"These things happen," I said.

"Yes," Carl replied. "These things do. To the best of us."

"Not to me," Mordechai said.

"Not to me yet," David added, talking with his mouth full. How rude.

"*Mazel tov*," Carl said.

"Watch your language, pal," I said.

David snickered.

"I have something stronger if you need it," Carl offered. "I still have half a bottle of that arak Mordechai brought from Israel."

"No thanks," I said. "I need to be alert. If I let my guard down, who knows what could happen? I could agree to almost anything. Blue tuxedos. Binding vows involving sickness and health. Who knows?"

"You might as well get used to the idea now," Carl said. "In a few months you'll have that ring on."

"I know. But give me these few months at least."

"He's right," Mordechai said to Carl. "Give the boy a break. He can deal with his mortality later."

"Mortality? Who's talking about mortality?" I asked.

Mordechai shrugged. "I am sorry to have brought it up. Forget I said anything."

"Fine."

"But in my years," he went on, ignoring me, "I have observed that nothing brings a man closer to his own mortality than marriage. You will now have a family to support; when you are gone, who will provide? But these are serious matters, matters not to be discussed at a time of celebration. So let us eat cake and sing. You have life insurance, do you not?"

"I'm not going to talk about life insurance."

"Never mind, then," Mordechai said with finality. "But still . . . well, never mind. I was only thinking of your beautiful fiancée.

And, of course, your health. How are you feeling? Any dizziness, any shortness of the breath?"

David came to my defense. "Emerson is fine. He will live to a ripe old age. Unless Remington shoots him."

"She won't shoot me. She promised."

Carl nodded. "It's good to get that in writing, though."

The future lawyer — Remington — emerged from the kitchen with a cake. "Get what in writing?" she asked, carefully placing the cake on the table in front of Mordechai.

"That you won't shoot me, dear."

"Oh." She sat down, nonplussed that we were discussing my mortality. "Cut the cake, Mordechai. Rebecca will be out in a minute. She's calling someone's cousin's accountant's daughter to see if she can get a good deal on fabric. I didn't have the heart to tell her I can't even sew buttons."

"Ms. Remington, that wouldn't stop her. Take it from me. Better yet, take *her* from me. Please."

He roared with laughter; the evening wasn't getting any better. Rebecca came out of the kitchen, drawn by the sound of fun being had by her baby brother (he was easily fifty, but that didn't matter to her).

"I heard what you said, and I think in the morning you can make your own coffee and lunch," she said, sounding casual. "Let's see if you really don't need me. Just like last time."

"Last time I was seven years old," Mordechai said to us. "I was being bothered by a bully. I didn't want my sister to defend me, even though she wanted to punch his lights out. I said, 'No, I'm going to face him myself.'"

"You could have been sent to the hospital for weeks," Rebecca said.

"I wasn't, though, was I?" Mordechai said. "No — I got a bloody nose, but I kept my pride."

"That's okay, Mr. Smart," Rebecca said. "I pounded that little boy Simon later. No one picks on my brother."

"Except you," Mordechai pointed out.

"You can cook your own dinner tomorrow night, too."

I leaned over to Remington. "This family thing . . ." I whispered. "Are we sure we want to get into it?"

6

On Thursday morning I found myself standing in my office, staring at my desk. It — my desk — was clean. That's an eerie feeling.

Sharon the Receptionist saw my confusion.

"We cleaned it," she said. "Me, Sherri, Robert. We used a match."

"A newspaper office shouldn't look like this," I said. "Not a *real* newspaper office. Where's the stack of unopened mail? Where are the rude notes from staff members? Where are my staff members?"

"They'll be in soon," Sharon said. "They've worked out a schedule. Sherri comes in at about 10:00, and Robert comes in at about 11:00. They write their stories, and while Sherri is developing the film at 5:00 sharp, Robert is editing Sherri's stories. When she goes home, he lays out the pages. But they'll be in at their normal times now that you're back."

"You see?" I said, plunking down in my chair, staring at a clear desk. "I knew they would do just fine in my absence. But they'll never make it in this profession if they stay that organized. Any word from David yet?"

"He stopped at a house fire on his way in."

"Good. Some front-page art."

"I think Robert has the front page about laid out," Sharon said. "It's in the back."

I grunted. Robert, my City Hall reporter, was showing signs of initiative, foresight, responsibility, and good news judgment. Despite those qualities, he might make a good newspaper editor. I think he wanted my job. I smiled to myself; soon he could have it. I'd be heading north to Dallas, with a fiancée and a photographer and a dog. What more can a man ask for?

"How about some coffee?" Sharon asked.

"Oh, yeah, that."

"What?"

"Nothing. I was talking to myself. Yes, some coffee would be nice. Thanks."

"On the printer table next to your desk, there's a stack of the papers Robert and Sherri put out while you boys were galavanting through Dallas."

"Yeah, thanks," I said.

I rolled my chair over a few feet to the left, toward the table that held our laser printer. I found the newspapers and wheeled back to my desk. We put out two newspapers per week, a Thursday edition and a Sunday edition. We put together the Thursday paper on Tuesdays, and the Sunday paper on Fridays (Robert seemed to have gotten a jump on me, but I didn't really mind). I had left two weeks ago, so there were four papers without my personal stamp on them.

They didn't need it, I decided after perusing the front pages of the four issues. No major natural disasters, no political scandals, not even a decent crime to speak of; still, they'd put out some interesting issues. Sherri ran a three-part series on getting new classrooms built and furnished before school started. Robert had an editorial on the new bleachers being put up at the junior high football field by some boosters. The front pages were clean, with no glaring errors, and the art was good. Sherri was becoming more and more proficient with her camera.

"They didn't even miss us, did they?" I asked Sharon as she returned with coffee.

"Not a bit," Sharon said. "Except Robert had to buy the pizza Friday night, since you weren't around to do it."

"Good. I hope they overcharged him."

As if summoned by my ill sentiments, Robert walked into the office, at his normal reporter time no less. He wasn't wearing a sport coat, but he was still wearing a tie. "Hi, chief," he said.

"Hello, Mr. Christian. Is the *Bounty* still on course?"

"What?"

"Literary reference," I said. "Ignore it."

"I get it," he said, sitting at his desk. "Captain Bligh, Fletcher Christian, *Mutiny on the Bounty*, right?"

"Right."

"Don't worry about a mutiny. I haven't had a night off since you left. You're safe for now — I've got a social life to salvage."

"I feel better," I said. "Tell me about the Sunday paper. How are we going to fill it?"

By the time he finished outlining his stories for me, Sherri had come in. She outlined her stories for me, and I nodded my approval.

"Sherri, that was a good series you did," I said, looking at the strawberry-blonde, fresh-from-college reporter.

"Thanks, chief," she said, blushing. She never did take compliments well. "But we sure missed you."

"Bless you, my child. I'm doubling your Easter bonus for that."

"We don't get Easter bonuses."

"Another mutineer for you, Mr. Christian," I said to Robert. Sherri didn't bother to ask.

I went back to the newspapers, and when I was through with those I started reading the papers from surrounding communities.

By 11 A.M. David was in the office. He offered up the same sorts of compliments to Robert and Sherri as I had. Sherri blushed again. Robert didn't. David came to my desk with an expectant grin.

"Does it feel any different?"

"What?"

"Being engaged?"

From another sector of the office I heard a squeal. It was Sherri. "Engaged? That's so sweet! What a sweet guy!"

"Ready the plank, Mr. Christian; we'll make her walk it if she calls me 'sweet' again."

"Aye, aye, sir."

"You're changing the subject," Sherri said. "When did it happen? How did it happen?"

"Well, it just sort of occurred."

"What was it like?"

"Well, I dunno."

"You were there, weren't you?" Sherri was losing patience.

"Take down this number," I said. "555-7406. That's Remington's desk. Call and ask her. She'll be glad to talk about it."

"Fine, I will." Sherri reached for the phone. I turned back to David.

"We're taking a late lunch today," I said. "We need to be at Walter and Gunther's place at 2 P.M. Just in a corner, eating. They have a little trouble."

David thought for a moment. "Okay, but I'll need to run this film now. Come into the darkroom with me while I do it, and you can tell me what kind of trouble we're getting involved in this time."

I nodded and rose from my seat. Robert was on the phone hunting up the mayor, and Sherri was on the phone hunting up my future mate. "We're in a high-level conference meeting," I told Sharon. She smiled and waved us away.

I followed David back through the small newspaper office. It smelled of coffee and ink and perfume and darkroom chemicals.

The darkroom was open, and when David flipped on the light I noticed that Sherri had kept it as clean as David did.

"The boys seem to be in a little financial bind," I said as I closed the door. "It's kind of complicated."

David grunted as he checked his equipment. He looked to make sure the chemicals were where they were supposed to be and that his wire spools were clean and dry. "Douse the light," he said.

To transfer film from the canister to the spool and developing tank, total darkness is required. The red "safe light" can only be used when you're developing the prints. I turned off the lights, and after a moment I heard David deftly transferring the film. "So, go on."

"Well, it seems the boys are in hock to an old gangster."

"Like in the movies?" he asked.

"I guess so. Anyway, the boys seemed to have missed a payment, and the bill collector came calling. Walter was beat up. The boys are pretty scared."

"That's complicated? That's not complicated, Emerson. Complicated is trying to figure out why you chose that tie, for example. Complicated is trying to understand females. But dealing with a criminal who is threatening a friend, that is not complicated. There are things I'm good at, and those things to me aren't complicated."

I smiled in the darkness. David was a veteran of Israel's 1982 invasion of Lebanon. He spent three years fighting in the best army in the world. He was a tank commander but had cross-trained as a paratrooper. With his disarming grin and agreeable nature, one might tend to forget how deadly he was. But one would be making a mistake.

"Let's just go and have lunch," I said. "I think the perps are going to be there at about 2 P.M. Singer's going to make a traffic stop and warn them that he's fond of the boys, but I want us to be there in case the bad guys get upset with Walter and Gunther."

"Okay, Emerson, turn on the light. I'm loaded and sealed."

I turned on the overhead light; I had to shut my eyes for a moment. I heard David humming something that sounded vaguely Israeli. "So we're on for lunch?" I asked.

"Sure."

I nodded and let myself out of the darkroom. David was still humming when I left. I wandered back to my desk. My staff still had telephones coming out of their faces, so I sat down and started looking through mail. When I was through with that, I started trying to come up with an idea for an editorial. Within a few minutes I was elbow-deep in a treatise on a proposed bond sale to finance some street improvements. Who says I don't lead an exciting life?

David had to clear his throat twice before I looked up from my computer. "Yes?" I asked.

"It's 1:45," he said. "Hungry?"

"Starved. Let's go."

I followed my faithful photographer out of the office with a quick word to Sharon about lunch at the restaurant. We took David's car the half-mile to Zarape; we smiled in unison when we saw the flashing red-and-blue lights of a police cruiser a few blocks ahead. A dark sedan was pulled over, and a cop who looked at a distance quite a bit like Singer was standing with one foot on the sedan's bumper writing out a ticket on his knee.

"Perfect timing," I said. "Let's go in and have a bite to eat."

We went into the restaurant to find the boys. Walter wasn't in sight, but Gunther was standing at a table full of little old ladies. "We'll seat ourselves," I said to his back.

We walked down the row of booths to the last one, the one in the corner. We sat down, and after a moment Gunther approached. "Just bring us some lunch," I said. "And some water. Maybe some antacid for later."

He bowed and left without speaking. He didn't even insult my tie in response to my request for antacid.

"He's nervous," David said.

"I picked up on that."

A few moments later Gunther reappeared with water and some coffee; we hadn't asked for coffee, so maybe he was trying to make up for being curt with me the day before. He hesitated as he placed our cups and glasses on the table. "Walter says the rouladen is good today. You want some?"

"Sure," I said. "Whatever he says is good. We trust you guys."

Gunther again bowed and left. That was a bit formal for him; it was expected from Walter, but Gunther normally would have sat down with us for a few moments, asked about our work and families and such.

A moment later the door jingled; three men entered. One was an older bald guy. The other two looked like well-dressed long-shoremen. They were the same three guys. They stood just inside the door. The goons had on suitcoats again. Awful hot for that sort of wardrobe, I thought to myself. I glanced at David, who was facing the door. He looked alert, interested.

"Schmidt!" one longshoreman called out.

Gunther reappeared, straightening his apron. "Lunch for three?"

"Mr. Ciotti doesn't have time for lunch on account of a delay we just experienced," the suit said amiably. "You got friends here in town. That's nice for you. We got friends all over. That's even nicer for us. We don't like you bringing third parties into this business transaction. Remember that. And remember a payment is due one week from Saturday. We'll be going now."

The older bald guy spun on his heel and marched back out into the summer afternoon's heat. His goons followed. The door closed, and Gunther started breathing again.

"You might be wondering what he's talking about," I said. "The part about the third party."

Gunther looked at me sharply. His dark features showed confusion mixed with fear and anger. "You are involved?"

"Well, not much," I said. "Detective Sergeant Bill Singer might have made a traffic stop a few minutes ago and warned your loan shark that the cops here sure like your cooking."

Walter emerged from the kitchen; the bruises on his face were yellowing. "What have you done?"

"Bought you some time," I said. "And a measure of protection."

I got up from the booth and approached the boys. I studied their faces. There was a certain measure of relief — maybe even hope — showing.

"Guys, friends come in handy at a time like this. We can help. Tell me how much you owe."

"This time one thousand dollars," Walter said. He reached up and brushed the blond hair out of his face. "That's interest only. The total is twenty-two thousand dollars."

"How did you get into that much debt?" I asked.

"I am not good with business, Emerson," Walter said weakly. "I came here to cook. But to cook I need ovens, I need ingredients, I need the rent and the electricity paid. A few months ago Mr. Ciotti offered us a loan. We took it. It was either that or close down. What would you have done?"

"You knew what kind of loan it was."

"Yes. The payments were high; five hundred dollars per week. We got a little behind, so the principal grew. The original loan was fifteen thousand dollars. We now owe more than that."

"How much have you paid?"

Gunther snorted. "We have paid fifteen thousand and seven hundred dollars. Can you explain this math? That we owe more than that, even though we have paid more than we borrowed?"

"I don't need an explanation for that," I said. "Ciotti's accountants were carrying guns. That means their math counts, not ours."

"But we don't know what else to do," Gunther continued. "If we don't keep paying, they will take the restaurant. We signed an agreement. A contract."

"That contract was signed under considerable duress," I said. "I don't think a judge would hold you to that, especially since you guys have paid more than you borrowed. And then there's the factor of Walter getting beat up."

Walter turned his head in shame. Gunther came to his defense.

"Ciotti wanted to put in a cigarette machine," he said. "Walter didn't want it. He stood up to them. I wasn't here, but if I had been, it would have been different."

"I doubt it would have been much different. Look, guys, I'm not here to gripe at you. I'm here to help. So is David. I'm not an expert on dealing with mobsters — and that's what this Ciotti is — but I'm going to talk with an expert, and we're going to find you guys a way out of this mess."

"You make it sound simple," Walter said.

"It is. And it starts with some simple steps. First, you get the beer and wine out of here. I know it's in every restaurant in Germany, but to sell it here you have to have a license. You guys know that. If Singer stops in for lunch and finds you selling it, he'll have to act."

"And the cigarette machine?"

"Leave it for now, but put an *Out Of Order* sign on it," I said after a moment. "Let's keep Ciotti from making any money with it."

David, who was now standing just behind me, spoke. "I think it would be wise if you stayed close to home. I don't know what that man meant by them having friends all over, but it might be smart if you stayed within the city limits. After what Singer said to them, they'll know not to bother you too much around here."

"That's good advice," I said. "Now, are we going to get some lunch or what?"

An hour later we were back at the newspaper office. I called Remington and told her that all was well, that Singer had warned off the goons and the rouladen was indeed good.

"They even sent home a plate of schnitzel for you," I said. "They feel really bad about not realizing we got engaged yesterday."

"How bad is the financial situation?" she asked.

"It's bad, but not so bad it can't be straightened out. The boys have already paid more than they've borrowed, but due to some questionable mathematics on the part of the loan shark, they still supposedly owe twenty-two thousand dollars."

"That's a lot of money. How could they ever pay that off?"

"That's the point, my dear. They can't — not at the interest rates that Ciotti is charging. See, they can only ever afford to pay the interest, and they can't always even afford that. So the principal keeps growing, and Ciotti has a reliable source of income. And if he ever wants to, he can foreclose and take the restaurant."

"So what do we do? We don't have twenty-two thousand dollars."

"I'm not worried about the twenty-two thousand dollars," I said. "That's a fictitious number. What matters to me is that they've paid more than what they originally borrowed. So Ciotti could walk away from this, financially unhurt. All we have to do is convince him that he ought to do that."

"We could threaten his life. Or run him over with a train, maybe."

"That's not a helpful suggestion, dear Aggie," I said. "It's a long-established theological doctrine that Christians shouldn't go around bumping people off by running over them with trains. Also, the boys have signed an agreement. They put up the restaurant as capital. Now what does my favorite future lawyer have to say about that?"

"I haven't had contracts class yet. Check with me in a year or so."

"Until then, let's talk with Singer's dad and see if he knows how to do business with these guys."

"Okay. No trains?"

"No trains."

"You're no fun."

I hung up after saying the obligatory mushy stuff to my

sweetie-weetie. I looked up from my desk and saw Sherri grinning.

"Sooner or later it's the plank for you," I said. "No doubt about it. Don't you have a story or two to write?"

There was a note on my desk when I got into the office on Friday. It was from Singer. "Call," it said. So I called.

"Dinner with Dad will be a little later, at about 9:00," he said. "I'll come by your office at 8:45 and pick you up. Ms. Remington is going to be joining us, right?"

"Sure. Should we bring anything?"

"No. He's cooking. Pork chops, I think."

"What have you told him?"

"That you want to talk with him about the old days. I outlined the problem. He seemed willing to talk."

"Good. I'll see you tonight."

The day passed slowly. Robert's and Sherri's articles were clean — they needed very little editing. David and Sherri shared front-page photo space; David's fire went above the fold, and Sherri's pictures of the high school ag department's new calf went below the fold. By 8:30 P.M. we had the headlines pasted down, and I was giving the paper a final proofing. I had sent everyone else home. Remington walked in through the unlocked door and made her way back to where I was going over the pages.

"Hi," she said. "We're on for my dad at 6:00 tomorrow night, then Sunday lunch with Martin and his family. Everyone's excited."

"About what?" I asked absently.

A stone-cold silence followed. I made an effort to smile. "Just joking," I said. "They can't be any more excited than I am."

"Close, Dunn, really close. Need some help proofing?"

"Yeah; take Section B. Thanks."

A few minutes later Singer knocked on the office door, then let himself in.

"I hope you're ready for a long night," Singer said as he entered. "Dad's gotten out his clippings. Mostly old stuff from the *Galveston Daily News*. All the old murders, the shootouts, the busts, the getaways. Ah, Ms. Remington . . . Had any second thoughts about your engagement yet? There are at least five young police officers who would gladly arrest Dunn just for the chance to take you out on a date."

"Sorry, detective," Remington said sweetly. "Tell those boys in blue that Emerson has already handcuffed my heart to his."

Singer suppressed a grin. "They'll be sorely disappointed to hear that. They might arrest him anyway."

"I'm sorry, but there's no explaining the ways of love."

Singer looked at me and grunted. "That's for sure."

"Can we leave now?" I asked. "I'm hungry."

Singer turned and held the door for Remington. I thought he might even hold it for me, but he didn't. He followed her out, and I had to get the door for myself. What manners. They also made me sit in the backseat of Singer's maroon unmarked car — the doors didn't open from the inside. When I got in and got buckled, Remington was telling Singer about our preliminary wedding plans. Served him right.

We drove through town to South Street, then took a left and went east for a couple of miles. In a subdued subdivision, Singer wound his way through a few streets until we reached a red-brick house with a Ford LTD Crown Victoria in the driveway. The Crown Vic is a common cop car; this one was several years old, but it had new black paint.

"Did your dad pick that up at an auction?" I asked Singer.

He grunted. "Dad likes the police suspension and the bigger engine. But the city's no longer paying for the gas for that monster. I've been telling him to get rid of it."

Remington was the first out, and she opened my door for me. Good thing she has manners. We followed Singer up the drive to

the concrete walkway leading to the front door. Singer's dad —
a somewhat shorter, thicker version of Singer with a head of
thick, wavy gray hair — was waiting for us. He took Remington's
hand for a moment, then shook mine. "Ms. Remington, it's good
to meet you. And, Mr. Dunn, you too. Just call me Harry. I hear
there may be wedding bells? Congrats. Sincerely. My boy's told
me a lot about you two. You're good folks. And I don't mind
telling you, that's why I've invited you here. Good folks don't
need to be bothering with the other kind, like that thick-headed
Fuzzy Ciotti. I musta busted him ten times, and he walked away
from every charge. But that's business, and it's rude of me to
make you stand here listening to me go on. Come on in — the
table's ready."

I was out of breath just listening to Harry. Singer let loose a
grin. "It's going to be a long night," he whispered to us. "Dad's
in fine form. The stories he'll tell . . ."

We followed Harry through a hallway papered with citations
and plaques. On a little shelf below a mirror was a trophy; I
glanced at the inscription as we passed by. It said, *First Place,
State Marksmanship Finals, 1964.* I was impressed. There was
also a picture of a pretty blonde woman — Singer's mother, I
thought. I recalled vaguely that she'd been dead for a number of
years. Singer never talked about his parents (plural); he always
spoke of his dad. I wondered if she'd died when Singer was a
child.

We were led into a dining room with a table laid out with a
fine Southern meal. Pork chops, mashed potatoes, okra, butterbeans, and a pitcher of iced tea.

"The rolls are in the oven," Harry said. "I'll be just a sec."

He left the room as Singer motioned for us to sit at the large
rectangular table. Singer sat to the left of his father's place at the
head of the table, and Remington sat to the right. I sat next to
her. I looked around the room; more family photos. The ones
with Singer as a teenager showed only him and his father. His
mother must have died when he was about ten or so.

"You're an only child?" Remington asked.

"Yeah," Singer responded. "Just me and Dad. But we had it pretty good. I didn't have much cause to complain."

Harry emerged with a small wicker basket heaped with hot rolls. He laid the basket beside the platter full of pork chops and sat down, taking his napkin and putting it in his lap. "Son, would you ask our blessing?"

Without hesitation, Singer bowed his head. We did the same.

"Lord, thank You for this food, for another day of sunshine and safety, and for Your Son, and for each other. We give the night and the next day over to you. Amen."

I looked sideways at Remington, then over at Bill. He hadn't exhibited many signs of religion before. I guess I was a little surprised at this near-public display. Bill saw my expression and raised his eyebrows, as if to ask if I had a problem with that. I grinned. It was somehow comforting to know that Bill Singer would be among those who will come rejoicing, bringing in the sheaves. I bet he'd bring them in handcuffed. Wait a minute — can you handcuff sheaves?

Harry spoke. "That's been our blessing ever since I started out as a cop. Nothing fancy, but it gets the food blessed and keeps us in mind of the fact that it's not always safe in this line of work. To tell the truth, I didn't really want Billy going into law enforcement, but there was no stopping him. Pass your plate, Miss Remington. You, too, Mr. Dunn. No, he's had his heart set on this since he was six. It was six, wasn't it? Well, anyway, he started school with mean old Miss Ryland, but she really wasn't that mean. The first week he ran away from the first grade. Just up and left. Two pork chops for you, Emerson? Fine. Yup, he just walked out. Nine blocks later a squad car slows down and asks what he's up to. He tells them he's quitting school. They recognized him as my boy, so they brought him to the station. I get called in on the radio, and I come to find my Billy sitting in the chief's office discussing the crimes of the day. He tells me he's ready to go back to school, since the chief told him he had to graduate to become a police officer. No problems at all after that."

"I wouldn't say no problems at all, Dad," Singer said, taking his plate, which Harry had heaped with food. "But you're right. This is all I've ever wanted to do."

"So, Mr. Dunn, Miss Remington, when is the wedding?" Harry asked.

"Next summer," Remington said. "And just call me A. C. By next summer I'll be through with the first year of law school, and Emerson will be settled in his new job."

Singer's eyebrows went up slightly. "New job?"

"Oops," Remington said. "I guess that's not public information yet."

"It's okay," I said. "It's no big secret. I start at the Dallas paper at the first of the year. David, too. It's working out well, what with Remington going to school at Southern Methodist University in Dallas. I'll room with David for six months, then trade him in for Remington."

"Hmmmm," Singer commented. He seemed more interested in his butterbeans.

"But we're not here to talk about us, Harry," I said. "We need some information; some help, really. Tell us what you know about Fuzzy Ciotti."

"Well, my boy, that's quite a request. I can tell you when I first met Ciotti. He was covered with blood and was trying to convince the captain there had been no shenanigans. And do you know what? The captain bought it. He let him walk. But maybe that wasn't such a bad thing. That was right after the war started, early 1942, I guess. I was a beat cop then, but being a beat cop in Galveston in the '40s wasn't what I figured on when I joined up. Anyway, it was 1942. There was a nightclub — and what a nightclub — called the Balinese Room. It was out on the pier on Seawall Boulevard and 21st Street. It had fine dining, top-name entertainment, and gambling in the back. Did we know about the gambling? Sure, we did. Did we do anything about it? Not a thing. And you know why? Because the mayor was a regular. We wouldn't want to risk catching His Honor in a den of iniquity, would we? No sir.

"But back to Ciotti. We get a call about a shooting outside the club. So I go in code three — lights and siren, the works — and what do you know, but when I get there the captain's already on the scene. It's only a few blocks from the police station. So he's grilling the short, balding man about the blood on his suit. I get closer, and I see where the blood — at least some of it — is coming from — his lip. So the captain, he's in control, and he tells Ciotti to go back into the Balinese Room and stay out of trouble. Then he winks at me. The captain winks. 'Papa Rose,' he says to me, 'Papa Rose will take care of this.' So I'm still confused, being a rookie and all, and I ask what happened. Seems that Ciotti was in an argument with a man named Dutch Voight — one of Papa Rose's trusted friends. Dutch takes him outside and tells him to cool off. Only Ciotti doesn't cool off. He pulls a gun. It discharged once before Dutch took it out of Ciotti's hand and busted his lip with it. Then Dutch walked back inside. Ciotti probably hoped we would arrest him — just so he didn't have to go back in and face Papa Rose. But go back in he did, and as I hear it, it was only the Old Man's juice that kept him from swimming with the fishes that night."

"The Old Man?" Remington asked.

"Verini. Alberto Verini. He was a second cousin to the Maceo family, I think, maybe by marriage. But he was a top lieutenant to Papa Rose Maceo. Came over from Sicily a few years later than they did. Verini had a heart, and an awful lot of influence with the Maceos. If he took a liking to you, you were safe. Even if you took a shot at Dutch Voight."

"Tell us more about Papa Rose and his brother — was it Sam?" I asked.

"Salvatore — also known as Sam. Right. Born in Palermo, Sicily. Sam was four years older than Rosario — Papa Rose. They came to the States around the turn of the century. They arrived in Galveston in 1910, according to the local history. They had a barber shop, but Dutch Voight knew talent when he saw it, and he decided to recruit the two into his bootlegging. They were cutting hair by day and running rum from Cuba by night. That led to gambling — they bought an old bar, the Hollywood Dinner Club, and turned it into a casino. That's where the empire started. Sam was the charming one. He was good-looking, and he liked living the good life. He had friends — friends like Sinatra and Burns and Allen. I remember 1947. In Texas City, on the other side of the causeway from Galveston, there was a big explosion and fire. Sam Maceo had everyone from Sinatra to Jack Benny to Gene Autry come down for benefit performances for the disaster victims. The Balinese Room was really his baby. He went all over, New York and L.A. and Hollywood, to find talent to book for it.

"Papa Rose was another matter. Some think he was the brains behind everything, but he had the muscle as well. It was never proven, but that doesn't mean he didn't kill his share of people. Papers say he once shot a pilot whose last word was 'Rose.' Papa Rose was still acquitted by a Galveston jury. His English wasn't so good, but he had the smarts to keep the businesses up and running. A little money here, a little muscle there, always the right balance."

"What did the police think of all this?" I asked.

Harry paused. He didn't seem the least bit interested in his food. "I'll tell you what the police thought — at least the ones I talked to. Because, let me assure you, I was a little disturbed by what I saw. I wanted to know why we didn't shut these guys down, run them out of town. But, Emerson — you too, A. C. — things were different then. There wasn't any discussion about running the sin out of town, because sin *was* the town. It was the economy, it was the major employer, it was the drawing card. For the most part, our job was to contain the bad elements to one part of town, and keep the other part peaceful. That wasn't always easy, with hotheads like Ciotti around. But that's what we focused on. Every so often, the state troopers would come down from Austin, but it seems that Mayor Herb Cartwright always got a warning beforehand, and that was enough time. The slot machines and the gambling tables were stashed soon enough. That's one reason the Balinese Room was out on a pier — things could be dumped over the side if the Rangers were on their way."

"But you're not saying you approved of all that, are you?" Remington sounded a little worried.

Harry laughed. "No, ma'am, that's not what I'm saying at all. Maybe I just sound a little livelier when I talk about it because that was when I was young and fast and good-looking. Christy — that was Billy's mother — and I moved there when we were both nineteen years old."

I stole a glance at Singer. He was looking at his plate.

Harry went on without pausing. "It was different then. Galveston was wide-open, and everyone knew it. It was bad for business for Papa Rose to permit too much goings-on, and he usually policed his own businesses. We just made sure everyone else behaved. The higher-ups — well, they were another story. The sheriff was Frank Biaggne — I'm not making this up — and he never once raided the Balinese Room. When he was called to Austin to explain himself, he told the committee that the reason he never raided the joint was that he wasn't a member. He would go up to the door, he said, but they wouldn't let him in."

7

The courthouse waiting-room clock said 3:22. I was getting restless. The break was over, and the hearing had resumed. I was waiting to be called by Fielder, the attorney from Dallas. The bailiff, Percy, was waiting for his shift to be over so he could go home to his wife. I was tired of sitting in the hard metal chair, tired of waiting. Percy must have noticed me getting antsy.

"Come on, son, relax a little," he said. "That lawyer said it was going to be okay. Not that you should go around trusting everything a lawyer says, now."

I smiled. Percy was good at his job. "How long you been with the county?" I asked.

"Oh, about sixty years," he said. "Graduated from high school here, got married here, spent most of my career with the Brazoria County Sheriff's Department. Spent a little time in the '40s in Galveston County, after some windbag got himself elected here. Lot of us deputies spent that four-year term in Galveston, then came back when the windbag got himself un-elected."

"You remember the bad old days in Galveston, then," I said.

"I remember."

"Was it so bad?"

"God isn't mocked, son. We'd all do best to remember that.

God isn't mocked by no gangsters, no gamblers, no prostitutes. They reaped what they sowed."

"Including your old boss? Sheriff Biaggne?"

Percy laughed. "Sheriffs come and go, son. Some get themselves into political trouble and go faster than others. I don't worry much about that. Us lowly deputies were only in Galveston for the short haul, anyway."

"The bad guys were in it for the long haul, from what I've heard. They had the run of the town for years."

Percy nodded. "I'll grant you that, but who's around today? Who's in as good shape as me? Tell me that."

I smiled, but it was without humor. "You outlived the Old Man. He died a few days ago."

"Yes, sir, I know that, but pay heed to this: the only reason the Old Man was around so long was because he'd changed his ways. That's no secret, son. It's quite a story in itself."

8

arry Singer told us the story of the Old Man the night we had dinner with him. Over dessert — he'd made a lemon meringue pie — he told us what we needed to know about Fuzzy Ciotti, and about perhaps the only man who could talk Ciotti into walking away from our friends.

"Your problem is that this isn't crime to Ciotti, it's business," Harry said. "He doesn't think what he's doing is wrong, so he's not afraid to do it. You can't scare him off with threats of prosecution. Chances are he has a signed paper saying he gets his money or he gets the business. Am I right?"

"Right," I said.

Harry nodded his gray head. "Right. And Billy said one of the German boys was assaulted? That's nothing to Ciotti. He thinks he can take their business, and they know it, and they all know they won't press charges."

"So what do we do?" Remington asked.

"You might try working within the system — his system."

"How?"

"Well, think hard about what motivates a man like Ciotti to do anything. Money, sure. Also, though, a guy like that — especially being from the era he's from — is motivated by other things. One is influence. He's done favors and been done favors, and those count for something. You could find a way to call in a few markers."

Harry leaned toward us. "I've been thinking hard myself, since the other day when Billy told me about the problem. I believe your best bet is to go see the Old Man."

"Verini? Was that his name? The guy who kept Papa Rose from killing Ciotti?"

"That's only one example. Ciotti was always getting into jams when he was young, and Verini got him out of most of them. Ciotti owes the Old Man a lot, and if the Old Man wanted to, I bet he could tell Ciotti to leave the German boys alone. That night outside the nightclub wasn't the first such incident, and it certainly wasn't the last. I remember when the Old Man saved Ciotti's life by shooting Ciotti's own brother. Nasty business, but the brothers had been fighting for months, and Nicholas — the older one — was obviously drunk the night it happened. Anyway, that's another example. Ciotti owes the Old Man big."

"And he could help us if he wanted to," I said. "But why would he want to?"

"Billy tells me you're a religious man," Harry said, leaning back in his chair and appraising me. "Is that so?"

"Depends on your definition of religious," I responded. "I have most of the basics down, though. Yes, I guess I'd say I am."

"So is the Old Man."

"Verini is religious?" Remington asked somewhat incredulously.

"He wasn't always, of course," Harry said. "It wasn't until late in the 1940s that it happened. Verini was kept pretty busy. He helped run most of the Maceo nightclubs and bookie joints, so he never spent much time with his family. His wife, though — she was religious. Spent most of her time at St. Mary's Catholic Cathedral, volunteering some and praying even more. Right after New Year's Day in 1949, she made a novena — that's a prayer every day for nine days — for her husband. She took ill about that time, and by the end of January she was dead. At the funeral the priest went up to the Old Man — he was always called 'the Old Man' because his hair went gray early — and told him about his wife's prayers. Well sir, that did it. The Old Man broke down right there. He's been a faithful Catholic ever since. He didn't go to the nightclubs or the bookie joints anymore, and he started investing in real estate. I always thought that was something of a gamble itself, but at least he wasn't breaking the legs of people who didn't make good on their markers."

"So he's still around?"

"Sure, and so is the priest. In fact, that's who you'll have to see first. For ten years Verini tried to keep his nose clean, but his old life kept coming back to haunt him. The Maceos, not just Sam and Papa Rose, but also Vincent and the other relatives, kept coming to him, asking advice, asking him if he wanted back in. And he slipped back into his old ways a few times — nothing violent, but a bet here, a few dollars to a campaign there. But the priest didn't give up. Father O'Donnell believed that the Old Man's soul could be saved. What's more, they became friends. After a few years of trying to stay on the straight-and-narrow, the Old Man asked the priest to help him make a break from his past; so, to get to Verini you had to go through Father O'Donnell. I think that's still the case."

Harry smiled. "There aren't many of the old gangsters left. A few — Ciotti, maybe one or two others. The Old Man isn't bothered by anyone anymore. In fact, he and the priest are both ancient now; they seemed old to me even back then. But they spend their days together, I hear — two retirees enjoying each other's company. I hear they pray together, read the Bible, talk about spiritual things. Sometimes they just sit together in that big old house in Galveston, talking about what Heaven will be like. Some ending to a gangster's life, huh?"

Remington smiled. "It sounds like a *nice* ending. So to see the Old Man, we have to see the priest?"

"Yes," Harry said. "On Saturday afternoons he goes into the church to hear Confession. That's about all he does now that he's retired. You can find him then. Go in and confess."

"But I'm not Catholic," I said.

"Well, then, I think that would be the first thing to confess," Harry said with a smile.

9

I was awake before dawn on Saturday morning; no real reason, I was just awake. I fired up the coffee maker and took a cup out on the back porch to spend some quality time with my dog.

"We're not going to be here much longer," I told him as I scratched behind his ears. "We'd better enjoy it while we can."

I was sitting in an old wooden rocker; the blue paint was chipped and faded. The chair had spent most of its life out on this very same porch. It sort of came with the house. The farmhouse was built before air conditioning, so it faced the northeast. That kept any one wall from bearing the brunt of the full summer sun or the cold winter winds from the north. The back porch faced the southwest, so the sun was coming up from behind me and to the left. There was a little bit of mist rising from the pasture. The dozen or so cows out past my backyard fence were already becoming active — at least as active as cows get in a Texas summer.

Airborne had eaten his bowl of diet dog food — his one bowl for the day — and seemed ready for an early-morning nap. He was content to take it on the porch beside me, where Remington had left a blanket out for him. She was worried he'd get splinters from the aging, weathered wooden surface. I thought she was spoiling him, but he didn't seem to mind.

Airborne sighed a little, as big dogs will do, as he got comfortable on his blanket. "It's not a bad life for you out here, is it?" I asked. "No, I guess it's not. I don't know what kind of house we'll have up in Dallas, but it's not really time to worry about that now. We have a few more months here."

My coffee was warm, and the cool air of the night was beginning to lift. I glanced down. Airborne was already asleep. I felt a million miles and a hundred years away from gangsters and loan sharks and crooked sheriffs and gambling dens. The quiet of the morning was something almost holy; I knew in a while I'd begin to hear the rumbling of cars and farm equipment in the distance, but I felt sure the quiet wouldn't be broken until God had His say.

I took another sip of coffee. Maybe that's why I was awake; maybe God had something to say to me.

"I'm listening," I said quietly. But all I heard were the sounds of a pasture waking up — the crickets, the mockingbirds, the quail, the call of some cattle a hundred yards off.

I got my answer in a moment, though; I heard a familiar car approaching. I heard it stop in front of my house; I heard the door slam. I winced at the harshness of the sound as it broke the quiet, even if only momentarily. Then I smiled.

"We're in the back," I called out, breaking the quiet myself. God had had His say.

"Good morning," Aggie Catherine Remington said a minute later as she rounded the corner, carrying a grocery bag. She smiled at me as she climbed the wooden steps. She approached and leaned to kiss me. "You're up early."

"I wasn't sure why until just now," I said. "Aggie Catherine Remington, you are beautiful."

She smiled. "I was going to surprise you with breakfast. Interested?"

"Soon. But first get some coffee and just come sit with me for a while. What time is it, anyway?"

"About 6:30. Let me put these up."

She carried her bag inside, then emerged a moment later with a cup of coffee, properly doctored. She didn't sit in the chair beside me; she opted for Airborne's blanket. He didn't seem to mind. She sat cross-legged beside him, and with her free hand she began to pet him. She was dressed in what was becoming her Saturday uniform: jeans and one of her dad's old oxford shirts. Her hair was pulled back again; I liked that. I liked her face. Her white leather sneakers looked new.

"It's nice out here," she said. Airborne rested his head on her leg and tried to resume his nap. "You get the feeling that everything is going to be all right. All the questions you have, all the doubts."

"Do I have questions and doubts?" I asked.

"Don't you?"

"Mostly, no," I said after a moment. "I don't. And I do believe that everything is going to be all right. You, Aggie Catherine Remington, are one of the best answers I've ever received."

She smiled and kissed the dog — and he hadn't even said anything. Without looking up at me, she pushed a little more. "But don't you ever worry?"

"About what?"

"I worry about the old me," she said. "The old Remington. I'm awfully hard-headed, awfully stubborn. I know that since becoming a Christian, there's a new me, that I'm a new creature. But that doesn't mean the old me is all gone. And the old me isn't very pleasant to be around all the time. Are you sure you want to risk it?"

"I really didn't think the old you was that bad," I said. "I think I started having feelings for you before there was a new you — in the sense you're talking about. And you've seen plenty of the old Emerson, too. The most visible sins are gone — the substance abuse, most of the rebellion — but the subtle ones stick around. The pride, the selfishness. There's a little of that in all of us. But you accept it in me, I accept it in you, and everyone's happy."

"Do you think we will be?"

"Happy? Married? I think so," I said, reaching over and touching her face. "I know I will be. I am now. I just hope I can keep you happy."

She kissed the dog again. The dog was getting the better end of the bargain. I got the questions, he got the smooches. And they say dogs add affection to your life. Ha!

"I think I'm looking forward to being Mrs. Dunn," Remington said. "Most of my friends from college didn't change their names when they got married. They think the idea of taking your husband's name, especially after you've started your career, is old-fashioned."

"The idea of staying married forever is old-fashioned too," I said. "Maybe the whole idea of marriage is old-fashioned. I don't mind being old-fashioned."

"Me either." She paused. "But it's still not that simple, Emerson. When I've talked to Martin, he says we've got to be able to put each other ahead of ourselves — our old selves and our new selves."

"And any other selves there might be."

"Emerson, I'm serious. Do you think we can do it?"

Something was nagging at Remington. "Tell me what's bothering you, love of my life," I said.

She took a deep breath. "It's my parents . . . You know . . ."

"I know. They divorced. But that was them, not us."

"Do you think that might be . . ."

"No," I said firmly. "As long as you choose not to view that as an option, then it's not even a question. And I've watched you and listened to you; I think you deeply feel that your parents made a mistake. I don't think you'll make the same one."

She nodded, still looking out at the pasture. "All I really want is a home, with you, where I'm not always scared that someone is going to leave."

I thought about that for a moment. "Did you know before it happened that your parents were having problems?"

"I was eleven; I knew what was going on. Dad would come home later and later, Mom would nag him more and more. I just knew he was going to leave. Then he did. After the divorce, it wasn't much better. For a few years Mom was looking to sell the house — she was ready to dump it. I always had the feeling that the house — the only house I'd ever lived in — was on the verge of being sold out from under me, that we'd be in an apartment any day. I guess that's why I want permanence now — that's why I'm always doubting myself and my ability to find permanence."

"Let me put it this way: you ain't getting rid of me, sweetie, so don't worry yourself about it. I'm here to stay."

She smiled. "How about this mangy old dog? Is he permanent?" She leaned over and kissed him again. He sighed a little at being disturbed. I wouldn't have minded being disturbed like that. "We'll have to find a nice house for him, Emerson. A big yard. Maybe outside of Dallas. It would be worth a commute."

"Let's see what bureau I'm assigned to, or if I'm kept downtown," I said. "But maybe we can find something just outside town. I'd like that."

"Me, too. Emerson, where do you want to live?" she asked. "I mean, once I'm done with school and we can go anywhere?"

I thought about it. "I think Texas is home, and always will be. I wouldn't mind spending a little time seeing the rest of the country, or the rest of the world, but Texas is where I'd like to come home to."

She nodded. "It sounds a little old-fashioned, but I'll follow you, Emerson. Just take me along."

At 3:00 that afternoon I was in Galveston, winding my way through the numbered and lettered side streets, looking for St. Mary's Catholic Cathedral and hopefully a cooperative retired priest. Galveston is an island full of extremes; the architecture that has survived the successive hurricanes is ornate, splendid, and usually well-maintained. Most of the rest of the island is plywood and cinderblock, ramshackle and rough. The shabby structures simply aren't meant to last through the next big storm; they were built cheaply so they could be rebuilt quickly and at low cost.

Some of the wealthiest people in Texas have summer homes in Galveston; the island also has one of the state's highest unemployment rates. There are opulent hotels on the beach, and dangerous slums and drug wars in the inner city.

Any priest at St. Mary's during the last half-century would have seen Galveston's slide into economic hardship. In the newspaper clippings that Singer's father had loaned me, I learned that some in Galveston — not all — want a resurgence of the "Bad Old Days." Some feel that once the town was cleaned up, the economy went sour. Others felt that perhaps the island was getting its due; it had prospered on the misery of others — someone had to lose at the gaming tables in order for the island to win. The debate was still raging.

I drove through town along Broadway Boulevard, which cuts across the island in a series of ill-timed stoplights. On the left and right I saw the subtle indicators of poverty — the homeless, the Salvation Army, the men in front of liquor stores. Galveston has much of the feel of a poor Caribbean island — the mild weather, the laid-back pace, and a sense of despair in the background.

At 21st Street I turned to the left, heading toward the old downtown district. This was the area the Maceos ruled by night fifty years ago. I passed the Galveston County Courthouse on my right one block before I reached the church; the courthouse is a three-story structure with plain, uninspiring architecture and imported palm trees (palm trees aren't native to Texas, I was once told).

At 21st and Church Street, I found St. Mary's Cathedral. Since no one was looking, I made a U-turn in the intersection and parked on the street in front of the impressive Gothic building — a congregation of buildings, really. More imported palms lined Church Street, while the cathedral's 21st Street frontage was softened a bit by the native oaks spaced evenly in front.

I put a quarter in the parking meter, then crossed the street and trudged slowly up the paving-stone walkway. A statue of Mary looked down at me from atop a tower. When I reached the door, I found it closed and locked. Beside it was a historical marker. The church had been built in 1847 by Texas' first bishop, the Most Rev. John Odin. It was damaged by the 1875 flood, the plaque read, and afterwards the congregation erected the statue of Mary. Since then, no storm has touched the building, the marker attests.

Another marker said that Saturday mass was at 5 P.M. and Confession at 4:15. I checked my watch. It was 3:50.

For fifteen minutes I wandered around the outside of the building, looking at the stained-glass windows and the spires. My own denomination tended to build plain, functional buildings at little expense and with even less style. Perhaps we were missing out on something by sacrificing reverent buildings.

At 4:00 bells started to ring out; they played a tune I didn't recognize. A few moments later an older woman approached slowly. She wore a black-and-maroon dress; despite the heat, a red scarf was covering her head, and another was wrapped around her shoulders. She smiled at me when she realized I was waiting for the cathedral to open.

"The father will open the doors soon," she assured me. "He's always a little early, never late."

I nodded. As if summoned by the woman, someone opened from the inside a small door beside the big front entrance. We heard the latch slide back, and then we saw it swing open. A dark, black-haired Hispanic man smiled at us. "Come in," he said. "The father will be ready in a moment."

The Hispanic man didn't appear to be a priest; he wore slacks and a simple, white, short-sleeved shirt. I assumed he was a deacon or something similar.

It took a moment for my eyes to adjust to the lack of light in the cathedral. Gorgeous stained-glass windows filtered a little light in, but compared to the bright sun of the Galveston summer, it wasn't much.

The lack of light was a small blessing, I decided. My first impression of the church was its smell. The cathedral smelled like old wood, varnished and rubbed with devotion and hope. Throughout the good times and the bad, the cathedral had stood. And through it all, someone cared enough to varnish the wood. Maybe this was what faith smelled like.

As I waited for my eyes to adjust, I thought about my Protestant beliefs and wondered about the Protestant aversion to the notion of saints. I had asked Martin about it once; he reiterated what I knew about the sainthood of all believers. Then he smiled and told me that even we Protestants have our own versions of most devout saints. He told me about Katie Moore, a little old lady he considered one of the most spiritual people he knew. When he had a problem, he said, he would call Katie and have her praying on his side.

"According to some, there's not much difference between that and asking Mary or Joseph or St. Patrick to intercede," he told me. I recalled his words as I stood just inside the door of the big, old cathedral.

Since I wasn't sure how to fax Mary to ask her to pray for me, I just went straight to the One whose assistance I needed anyway. "I could use your help, Lord," I said softly in His sanctuary.

Gradually, I was able to see more and more. The entryway in which I stood had four beautiful marble statues of Jesus; each showed a different stage of His ministry and His life on earth. The ceilings were easily thirty feet high and were supported by broad wooden beams arching up and weaving an intricate, beautifully functional pattern above.

The front of the church was a study in white marble, from the steps to the statues of seraphim. Latin inscriptions across the front of the steps, just below the marble altar railing, said something that sure sounded holy.

To each side of the entryway were confessionals — rich, dark wooden chambers with black curtains for privacy. And in a pew at the back, near me and near the confessionals, I saw an older priest — at least he was someone dressed in black — reading a small prayer book. I walked up the aisle quietly; when I reached his row I could see his collar.

"Father? Father O'Donnell?" I said.

He looked up and squinted at me for a moment. "Yes?"

"May I have a moment of your time?"

He nodded and rose slowly. "Right over here," he said. He pointed to a confessional, then went in one side. He saw I wasn't following, and he smiled. "Come on, son, right in here."

He closed his curtain. I knew what I had to do, but it was a little awkward. I went into the confessor's side of the confessional, knelt down, and closed my own curtain. My weight on my knees reminded me why I was no longer a runner. A small window, blocked by a screen, opened, and I could feel the father waiting for me to begin.

"I don't . . ." I started. Then I stopped. I wasn't sure what to say.

"That's all right, son," the priest said. "It will come back to you. You begin with, 'Bless me, Father, for I have sinned.'"

"Bless me, Father, for I have sinned," I said. "That's true enough. But that's not really why I'm here. To tell you the truth —"

"I certainly hope that's what you'll do, being that we're in God's house," the priest said. I could almost hear a smile.

"Right. Well, I'm not here to confess, although I'm sure it would do me good. I'm here to ask you to intercede for me — for my friends."

"Intercede?"

This time it was me who was smiling. "Wait . . . I didn't mean it in that sense. Sorry. I'm not a Catholic, so I'm not very good at this. What I mean is, I need to talk to the Old Man — Mr. Verini. You're his friend, I believe?"

"Yes, I am," the priest said slowly. "And because I'm his friend — and his pastor — I must ask you what the nature of your business is, and what your name is. Remember, you're in the house of God."

"My name is Emerson Dunn," I said. "That doesn't mean anything to you; I'm not from around here. I'm here for some friends. You see, they've gotten themselves involved with the wrong sort of people. An old associate of Mr. Verini's has loaned them money. They've repaid it fully, with interest, but you know how these kinds of loans are — you never really pay them off."

The priest considered this for a moment. "And what do you want of Al — Mr. Verini?"

"I want to ask him if he'll use his influence to convince Ciotti to back off, to leave my friends and their business alone."

The priest paused again. "Francis Ciotti, is it? I see. Are you a religious man, my son?"

"You're the second person to ask me that lately," I said. "I think so . . . Yes. I believe that Christ died for me."

"Easy words to speak, son. But do you seek God? Are you looking for Him around every corner — for that's where He'll be, you know. Have you set yourself apart? Have you been baptized in the name of the Father, the Son, and the Holy Ghost?"

"Yes," I said slowly, considering the rapid-fire questions. "I have done those things. I was nineteen when I came to Christ. I can't say I've lived for Him every moment since then; I've fallen back a time or two. But I still seek Him. And it seems that when I'm not seeking Him, He'll usually find me."

"Good enough, son," Father O'Donnell said. "The reason I ask is this: the Old Man, as you and everyone else refer to him, is a changed man. He has been for many, many years. Still, his past comes back every so often. You don't know it yet, but you're part of that past now."

"We need his help."

"Perhaps. And perhaps I can take you to meet him. But, son, my job isn't an easy one. It's a man's soul at stake here; in light of that, how do worldly troubles count for much? That's not to say I'm not sorry about your friends. But you see, for me it's a delicate balance. Tell me, son, who sent you to me."

"A man named Harry Singer."

"And how do you know the good Captain Singer? He's retired now, isn't he?"

"I know him through his son — they're still in the area. Harry is retired now, but his son's a cop. A good cop."

"He would have to be, wouldn't he, being Harry Singer's boy," Father O'Donnell said. "You came with good references, Mr. Dunn. I'll tell you what . . . I'll allow you to meet with Al — Mr. Verini. But I won't tell him what to do. If you can convince him to go into the abyss one last time, then fine. But realize that in his way of thinking, it *is* an abyss — a dark, powerful one. Many years ago he lost his life in it — he watched it slip by him as he pursued worldly gain. So he's found for himself another life, a life devoted to the Lord. He fears his old nature, as we all should. Many is the morning I've come into his house and found him alone, saying a Hail Mary — self-imposed penance for past crimes only he knows about."

"Do you think he'll help us?"

"I don't know, son. All I can ask him is that he meet with you. But we can pray about your troubles, and better help than that you can't ask."

"Amen, Father."

"Go home now, son, and I'll speak to Al tonight. I'll call you when he's ready to meet with you."

"I have a business card with my number," I said. I opened the curtain of the confessional and stepped out. Wait. That makes it sound easy. In reality, I pulled myself off my knees and stumbled out, hoping my legs would soon begin to work properly. When Father O'Donnell emerged a moment later, I handed the card to him.

"Thank you, Father."

"Bless you, my son, in the name of Christ Jesus, our Lord."

The old woman in the plaid dress was in a back-row pew, apparently waiting patiently her turn in the confessional.

"Hail Mary, full of grace," I heard her saying softly. "The Lord is with thee. Blessed art thou amongst women, and blessed is the fruit of thy womb, Jesus. Holy Mary, mother of God, pray for us sinners, now and at the hour of our death. Amen."

I admired the woman's devotion and faith. I again marveled at the grace of God that so wonderfully reaches the hearts of all who truly call on Him.

The woman rose from her seat, then knelt before the cross above the altar. She turned and smiled at me as she passed. She went into the confessional and closed the curtain. I wondered if her knees were in any better shape than mine.

I turned around and walked out the same side door through which I had entered. My soul, Protestant that it is, nevertheless felt the priest's blessing draped over me like the scarves the old woman had worn.

I stopped by the office on my way home; when I tried the door,

I found it was locked, with no sign of any reporters or ad sales people. I didn't bother to unlock it and go in to check for messages. I drove on to my house, another ten minutes past the office. Before long I pulled into my unpaved driveway and parked.

I could hear the telephone ringing as I unlocked my front door. It was on at least the sixth ring by the time I opened the door and ran across the living room to the phone on the kitchen wall.

"Hello?" I said.

"It's almost 6:00," Remington said. "Remember . . . dinner? Tonight, with my father?"

"Right," I said. "I remembered. Really. I was just getting changed. I'll be at your apartment in half an hour."

"No, I'll be at your house in fifteen minutes. We'll take my car."

Pushy. The dame was still pushy. "Tell me how bad it's going to be."

"Not too bad," she said. "You'll meet the stepbrother, and maybe the trophy wife."

I'd met her dad once, briefly, when he dropped off a new microwave he'd decided his daughter should have. It had been just after Easter — a weeknight, I think. He must have dropped it by on his way home from work. He'd been cordial, but more concerned with the fact that the security guard at the apartment gate looked a little sleepy. That was typical of him; in the time I'd known Remington, her father had swung like a pendulum between bouts of intense protectiveness and indulgence (the new Volvo, for instance) and months of showing no visible interest in her life (he forgot to call on her birthday). I'm sure guilt spurred both extremes.

The guilt might have been well-founded, but I tried not to think about it in those terms. Remington's dad was someone I'd always considered a product of the times. His professional life always took precedence over his personal life. Still, his relationship with Remington was beginning to heal, after some rough years when he left her mother. He was tall, which is something

Remington inherited, along with her father's dark hair and blue eyes. He had a salesman's smile and a job with an oil company.

Her new stepmother — only about fifteen years older than Remington — had a now-teenage son from her first marriage. Remington referred to him as the Stepbrother of Death, due to his propensity for black clothing and heavy metal songs about suicide. "He'll off himself any day now," she'd often predicted. I didn't worry about the kid much. At that age I'm sure I was listening to something equally senseless — if I recall correctly, something about anarchy being a wise financial move.

As I hung up the phone I wondered which clothes to pick. Remington, subtle gal that she is, would often tell me exactly what to wear. But I seemed to be on my own in this case. Airborne was looking at the back door longingly, so I let him out on my way to the bedroom.

In my closet I found a reasonably unwrinkled oxford and some even less-wrinkled khaki pants. Good enough, I thought. I put them on and went foraging for a tie. I found a blue one that seemed appropriate. I slipped it over my neck and tied it, then stuffed it under my collar.

By the time I was dressed, Airborne was ready to come back in. I put my black penny loafers on and walked to the back door.

"Come on in," I said as I opened it. I noticed he was panting; he'd been running. "And how were the bunnies?"

He didn't answer, so I assumed they'd evaded him once again. "Don't worry, those bunnies are getting older quicker than you are. You'll catch one someday."

He ignored me and found a cool spot on the hardwood floor in front of the front door. The door wasn't sealed well, so there was a slight breeze coming in from under it. I'd have to fix that before winter, I decided.

I went into the bathroom and shaved again. I did my best to make myself presentable. I was hoping to make a good impression.

I'd about done all I could do when the telephone rang. It was Martin.

"Hello, parson," I said. "We're breaking the news to Remington's father tonight. Any advice?"

"Just be yourself, Emerson," he said. "We want them to know what they're getting — what they're *really* getting."

"Thanks for the advice," I said. "I'm sure you mean it in the nicest way possible. Are we still on for lunch tomorrow, after church?"

"Of course," he said. "Lasagna. Garlic bread so garlicky even your dog won't want to talk to you. Just the way we like it."

"Wonderful. How are Meg and the kids?"

"She's fine, they're fine," Martin said. "Meg and your fiancée talked on the phone for more than an hour today. Wedding plans."

"Already?"

"Sure. It starts early, and it goes on forever. It's best to be prepared. There's one more thing we need to talk about. Pre-marriage counseling. When do you want to start?"

"What's to counsel?" I asked.

"It's standard operating procedure," he answered. "I don't think you need too much of it; I guess I've been knocking the rough edges off of you for about ten years now. And Meg's helped; you're almost husband material now."

"And proud of it," I said. "How much counseling are we talking about here?"

"I'd like to do four sessions. About an hour each. We'll talk about what the Bible says about marriage and authority and love and all that. I'd also like to get it done in the next few months, since you'll be moving to Dallas at the end of the year. When does Remington start school?"

"Late August," I said. "Less than a month from now. She's taking off at the end of next week to go look for an apartment near Southern Methodist University. At least, that's the plan."

"You know, SMU's not a cheap school."

"I know," I replied. "But Remington has some savings. She also has a father who's agreed to pay for the first year. After that, we'll rely on student loans and grants and so forth; if we come up short, her father has agreed to cover it."

"Family money isn't cheap money," Martin warned. "Realize that. I won't advise you to turn it down, but once you're married, do your best to do without it. With family money comes family involvement. That can be rough on a marriage, especially during the first year."

"Duly noted, parson."

"Well, don't worry about these things now. You'll do plenty of worrying about them later on. For now, just enjoy the engagement period. A lot of people seem to pass through the engagement time without noticing how nice it is. They're too focused on the wedding. Sure, that's important, but the engagement is the time when you really get to know someone. The relationship changes, and what might have been a minor thing when you were dating could seem major now that you're looking at marriage. And vice versa. Some of the little things will shrink in significance once you're committed to marrying somebody."

"She doesn't know me already?"

"She does, but she'll be looking deeper now. And so will you."

"You know, I think she's already doing that — at least, she's looking deeper into herself. She's a little worried about the fact that her parents are divorced, and that in the back of her mind she might still consider that an option."

"And that it might become a self-fulfilling prophecy. I know. She talked about it with Meg today. But we'll get into that during the counseling sessions. So when do you want to schedule them?"

"Let me talk to Remington tonight," I said. "We'll figure out a time for maybe an hour once a week for a month."

"Fine. Let me know tomorrow. And, Emerson, be nice to her brother and stepmother tonight. She might say she doesn't like them, but they're family just the same."

"Martin, I'm surprised at you. You know how well-behaved I am."

"I know. Take care of yourself and her tonight."

"Good-bye."

I hung up the telephone just as Remington was driving up. I walked quickly to my bedroom and checked myself in the mirror. Passable. I went back out to the living room as Remington was walking up the steps to the porch. I opened the door and smiled at my love-pumpkin.

"Passable," she said. "I'm not sure I would have picked the blue tie, but it's not too bad. Come on, we're already running late."

She passed by me long enough to pet Airborne, who was standing behind me, his tail wagging slowly. "Good-bye, sweetie," she said to him. To me she just said, "Let's go."

"I think you treat him better than you treat me," I said as we walked down the steps and she handed me her keys.

"Sure, I do. What of it?"

I was stumped. "Just making a point."

"Consider it made."

I nodded and opened her car door for her. She didn't say anything as I closed it slowly but firmly. I didn't want my love-pumpkin falling out, even if she did treat the dog better than me.

"Martin called. He told me to behave," I said as I got in on the driver's side.

"Hmmm."

There was no more response. That wasn't like her. I started the car and pulled out of the driveway. As I drove, I sneaked a look at Remington. Her face was mostly cloudy, with a strong chance of precipitation.

"What's wrong?"

She just shook her head. Dames. But being the sensitive, caring sort of modern man I am, I knew just what to say.

"What happened to your hair?"

She turned wide eyes to me. "My hair? What's wrong with my hair?"

"Nothing. Just getting your mind off whatever it was that was about to make you cry."

"By telling me that my hair is awful?"

"I didn't say that."

"What else could that mean, besides 'Remington, dear, your hair is awful'?"

"It means I'm worried about you. What has made you upset and, if I may say so, a little edgy?"

"We're going to see my father. You're going to ask him for my hand."

"Well, essentially that's true. But this isn't a risky thing; he's known about it for a while now. Most people we know have known, with the minor exception of me."

"Sure, he's known. That doesn't make it easy."

"Is this a daddy-and-daughter thing? Because if it is, I'm out of my league. I can't help much."

"You're asking him to let me go."

"Sure . . . I guess. A woman shall leave her family, and cleave to her husband, and all that. Remember, though, it says 'cleave' to her husband, not 'cleaver,' as in meat. I think that's an important distinction."

"You're not taking me seriously."

"I'm taking you, though, to have and to hold forever and ever and so on. I think I know what you're feeling: you've always looked to your father for fatherly stuff, which includes taking care of you when you've needed it. Now that's going to be my job. Except, of course, that when you're a lawyer, you'll do a lot more taking care of me; with your pay, you'll be able to buy and sell the likes of me, a lowly reporter. But that's beside the point. Remington, I know this isn't easy for you. He's your dad."

"Right."

"So do you think you're ready for this?"

"Yes. I think so. It won't be easy. But if he agrees too quickly . . ." Remington almost smiled.

"We'll just tell him to see it as gaining a son, not losing a daughter," I said.

"And frighten the poor man? That's not nice."

I grinned. Remington had loosened up. She was no longer in imminent danger of crying.

We drove through town, to Highway 6 — a two-laner that leads to real highways and interstates. We found our way to U.S. 59, which goes through downtown Houston. Before we got downtown, we took the Shepherd Road exit, then went south into a neighborhood of older, stately homes. Her father lived on Wroxton, one of the most fashionable streets in the city. She directed me to the curb in front of a restored home facing north. We parked, and I started to get out. Remington paused. Maybe she was waiting for me to get her door. Maybe she was about to cry again.

"Don't worry," I said reassuringly. "What's the worst that could happen? He could rend his clothing, put ashes on his head, throw us out, and say that he no longer has a daughter."

She almost smiled again. "That would get him out of paying law school tuition, wouldn't it?"

"Come on, Aggie my dear, let's you and me go talk to Dad."

This time she smiled. She got out of the car, checked to make sure the door locked, then took a deep breath. She then marched up the stone walkway to the front door. I followed. She banged her fist on the ornate walnut door a couple of times. After a moment, the Stepbrother of Death appeared and opened the door.

"Hey," he said in a subdued voice to his stepsister. He looked at me in a studiously bored manner. "This him?"

"Yeah," I answered, "it's me."

"Ronnie, are you going to stand there or what?" Remington asked, sounding like a big sister. "We can always go around to the back door. Maybe someone would let us in there."

"Oh, yeah," he said, stepping back. "Come in. Sorry. They don't let me answer the door much. For the most part, they keep me locked in my room. Chained to the radiator."

"No, they don't," Remington said. "That was me. And I only did it once; you were six, and it was only for a few minutes. So get over it." She let out a bored sigh as she marched past him. "Where are they?" she asked.

"In the kitchen, arguing about dinner. Mom burned something. Bet it's gonna be Chinese takeout."

"It usually is," Remington said to me. "Disappointed?"

"Nope," I said. "Chinese is fine."

"Good. Follow me."

I didn't know if she was talking to me or to her stepbrother; apparently, neither did he. So we both followed. We crossed the threshold (which had a real zebra-skin rug) through the dining room, which had an already-set table and walls adorned with modern art. We entered the kitchen, which had stone tile and a marble island in the middle. Remington's dad — looking tall, handsome, and a little confused — was trying to keep up with what a bleached-blonde woman in a black business suit was telling him.

"Kim Son is open, and they're better than the Chinese Palace, but Kim Son doesn't deliver. Since this is a special occasion we should have Kim Son, even if we have to go get it. Or we could eat there. But it really would be better to eat here, since this is a special occasion. Why else did we buy a microwave oven if we're not going to use it? Oh, A. C. . . . Hello! Is this Emerson?"

The woman had noticed our presence; she appeared to be about forty and in good shape. She was pretty enough, with green eyes and a professional demeanor. She didn't look wicked at all. She actually looked — well, efficient. In the fairy tales, the wicked stepmothers never wore business suits.

"Good to see you again, Emerson," Remington's dad said, holding out his hand. I shook it, then took the stepmother's hand.

"So nice to meet you, Emerson," she said with a broad smile. "A. C. has told us so much about you."

I smiled. "I've heard a lot about you too. And she didn't mention anything about you leading her out in the woods, and her having to leave a trail of bread crumbs. I promise."

Remington's dad looked a little confused for a minute, then laughed. So did the stepmom. I always figure I'm going to be okay if I can make someone laugh right off the bat.

"We're ordering out," he said. "Chinese or Vietnamese, whichever you prefer. There's a good restaurant called Kim Son."

"That sounds fine, Mr. Remington," I said.

"Call me Roger," he said.

"And call me Donna," the stepmom said.

"Now that everyone's introduced, let's decide on supper," Remington said. "Donna, let's call Kim Son and order, and the guys can go pick it up. That will give them a chance to talk and get to know each other a little more."

Roger and I obviously had little say in the matter, so he just nodded. "She was always like this, you know," he said to me.

"Pushy," I said. "I know."

"I'm not pushy," Remington said. "I'm forthright — candid — frank."

"I'm afraid she comes by that honestly," Roger said. "She has a lot of her father in her. Emerson, let's take a drive."

It had been a long, thrill-filled day, and I could tell I had miles to go before I slept. I was glad it was Remington's dad and not my friendly neighborhood mobster Fuzzy Ciotti asking me to "take a drive," so I agreed. Apparently Ronnie wasn't invited. I followed Roger through the kitchen and out the back door onto a redwood deck. At the corner of the deck was a set of steps leading down to another stone walkway, this one trailing to the garage. The garage door opened as we neared it; there must have been a button inside that Donna or Remington or maybe even Ronnie hit.

The door opened up to reveal a black Mercedes 300 SD. It

appeared to be a fairly late model, but since Mercedes sticks with a single body design for several years running, it was tough to tell. I walked around to the passenger's side and waited for Roger to unlock the car. He did, and I got in, sitting on a leather seat that alone cost as much as my car was worth — if not more.

"I do love the diesels," Roger said. "They run forever. This car is twelve years old, believe it or not."

"It's in great shape," I said.

He waited for the diesel to "pre-glow" before he started it; after about thirty seconds he hit the starter, and the rattling, powerful-sounding engine cranked. We backed out of the driveway and out onto the street. Roger aimed the car east, presumably toward the restaurant, and then turned his attention on me.

"We know why you're here," he said. "And believe me, we're all thrilled. Really. I don't know you well, but I've seen changes in my girl. You're partly responsible for them."

"Hasn't been just me," I said. "More than anything, I've just been around to enjoy the changes."

"You knew her before."

"Yes, we knew each other for a few months before we started dating. When she was still working for the competing paper."

"You know that I never really backed her in that field," he said. "I was wrong; it's been good for her. I wanted her to go straight into law school. Now that she's going, I can see the value of her having worked for a couple of years."

I wasn't sure where Roger was going with this line of conversation, so I simply nodded instead of responding verbally.

"I guess what I'm trying to say is that I'm glad she worked, I'm glad she met you, but I'm also glad she's going back to school, specifically law school."

I nodded again.

"Her going back is important to me."

"To me, too," I said, venturing a verbal response.

"I'm not doing this very well, am I? Okay . . . Let me just say it like this: we're happy to have you in the family, but I need —

want, hope for — your assurance that she'll have every opportunity to do this — become a lawyer."

I paused. Martin talked a lot about submission to authority — or maybe he just talked about it a lot to me, because maybe I needed it more. One thing he said was that there's a delicate balance between independence from parents and still honoring thy mother and father. I felt a twinge of pride somewhere deep inside me; was this man telling me I couldn't marry his daughter unless I promised him that I'd nail her to a desk in a law school lecture hall? I suppressed that thought; I knew it wasn't right. Roger was worried about his daughter. He'd even offered to pay for her to attend school. All he wanted from me was my word that I'd do my part to keep her in school. I took a deep breath.

"You have my word," I said slowly. "She seems to want this — she wants to be a lawyer. She's good at journalism, but it never really was enough for her, was it?"

Roger smiled. "Law won't be, either, Emerson."

"What do you mean?"

"My daughter has the dual distinctions of being a first child and coming from what they used to call a 'broken home,'" he said.

I stiffened up a little. His divorce wasn't something I was really ready to talk about. It looked as if he was, however.

"A. C. Remington will never stop trying to prove herself," Roger said. "Little by little she's coming to accept herself more, but she'll never stop trying — hard. Do you understand what I mean?"

"I think so. That's something that Christianity has done for her: given her another way to measure her own worth, besides her accomplishments. She knows what she's worth to God. But that still doesn't break the old patterns of feeling that she has to measure up by worldly standards as well."

Roger nodded. "Emerson, we've never talked about God much in my family. You're a religious man, aren't you?"

"That's getting to be a common question," I said. "But yes, I guess I am. I'm a Christian. Not a great one, not even a good one most of the time, but a Christian nonetheless. How about you?"

Roger sighed. "I'm a lapsed Methodist, Emerson. But if you ask me if I believe in God, the answer is yes. If you ask me if I believe in Jesus, the answer is yes. But something tells me it's more than that for you, and now for my daughter."

We were on the outskirts of downtown Houston now, in an area I didn't recognize.

"It's a little more than that," I agreed. "But you've got the basics. What counts is what you do with them."

"What has my daughter done with the basics?"

"She's trusted Christ — believed in Him, in sort of a more active sense of the word; but the semantics aren't important. The point is, she's following Him."

"Hmmm." He sounded like Remington. "I said I'm a lapsed Methodist, but I guess I'm not so lapsed that I don't know I made a mistake."

"Mistake?" I asked.

"Divorce. It was wrong. I can't say that around Donna, of course, but I feel it strongly now. A. C.'s mother and I weren't unhappy; we were just bored. Or maybe just I was. By the time I got my head straightened out, I was married to Donna and trying to be a father to two families. I don't think I did a great job with either one."

"I'm certainly not in a position to judge that."

"I am. But all I'm going to say is that I know in my heart that divorce was wrong in my case, and I think probably in most cases. How do you feel about divorce?"

"I guess it's never been much of a factor for me," I said. "My parents are still married, my grandparents stayed married. My pastor, Martin — he's been a big influence on me — has told me it's wrong, so I guess I've operated under that assumption, and I will continue to do so."

"Marriage is work. Are you willing to work at it — work through the problems, the boredom if there's any, the anger that comes along with it sometimes?"

"I'm willing."

"I can't ask much more than that, can I?" Roger was smiling; I think he was relieved to have covered all the bases. "Now, do you have any questions for me?"

I thought for a moment. Roger was concentrating on the road; we were at a stoplight on a one-way street. I again noted that Remington had inherited a lot of his features — his height, his dark hair, his blue eyes. He had the same strong jawline. Her hair would probably gray early, as his was doing.

"No questions," I said.

He nodded. A few blocks later we pulled into the parking lot of a large oriental restaurant. Roger locked the car, and I followed him into the restaurant, to the cashier's counter. An order was ready for us, sitting behind the counter in white bags marked "Rojer." Roger paid the lady, who spoke and smiled and nodded and made change but failed to utter a single word of English. After another nod or so, she handed us the bags and said, "Come again soon." Roger promised he would.

Back in the car I asked Roger about his ex-wife. "Remington — A. C. — talks about her less than she talks about you," I said. "Any idea how she's taking the idea of her little girl getting married?"

Roger sighed again. There seemed to be a lot of that in this family. "I don't know. She's been emotionally dependent on A. C. for a lot of years. My guess is she'll be a frequent visitor for the first few years. That's not to say she doesn't have her own life — she's always busy with something — but what's important to her is what's left of her family. My other daughter — I guess you haven't met Sandra yet — has been in New York for some time, but before that she was more comfortable spending time with me. I didn't want it that way, for the girls to be divided. But they each seemed to pick a side. I didn't even want there to be sides. I think Jean — their mother — was the big loser in the whole thing. I didn't want that, either."

He paused again. "I think, Emerson, she'll actually like the idea of having another family member. Family is important to her. But watch yourself; don't let your in-laws' problems become your problems. Know what I mean? If she comes to visit too often, don't be shy about telling her you need some time alone together. And the same goes for me. Don't be shy about telling me to back off. I'm free with the advice, Emerson; I always have been. That doesn't mean that A. C. is accustomed to taking it. We have a deal on law school tuition: she goes, and I pay for it. She can pay me back later, when she's a real live working lawyer. Or even in just free legal work for my firm; I'm sure I'd get my money's worth out of her within a few years at the rates I'm paying my lawyers. But just because I'm kicking in some money, don't think you have to do everything my way. Not that A. C. ever does anything anyone else's way." Roger smiled again.

I nodded.

We were approaching Wroxton again; we rounded a corner and found the driveway. We parked, but before we got out of the car, Roger asked if everything was said.

"I think so," I replied. "But if not, now's the time."

Roger shook his head. "I've said everything I'd planned to. And I've been planning this for a lot of years. When she was engaged before, I knew — or at least I felt — it was on shaky ground. I never went into any of this with him. So all this rehearsing and planning was just for you."

"I've avoided planning anything like this," I said. "I figured it would probably be hard on the nerves."

"It is," he said. "But in some cases it's inevitable. I knew I'd have to give her up sooner or later."

"Is this where I make the speech about you not losing a daughter, but gaining a son?"

"Not if you can help it."

"Fine with me," I said, grinning. "Now about that will of yours
— who gets this car?"

11

Dinner was quick and painless. Donna stayed true to my first impression of her — efficient. She seemed to know the boundaries, where she could ask questions and offer suggestions, and what things Remington might consider real-mother-and-daughter territory. She commented several times on Remington's ring and asked all the right questions about the gradually forming wedding plans. By the end of the evening I'm positive that Donna knew more about the wedding than I did.

Ronnie, the infamous Stepbrother of Death, wasn't such a bad kid. He was a little confused about a few things, but salvageable. Remington didn't have much patience with him, but I discovered that if you actually listened to him, he was sort of funny. He did talk about some friends of his who had been in a car accident, but they'd lived, and he didn't seem too disappointed. He said he was interested in photography, and I promised to introduce him to David sometime. He also asked a few questions — studiously nonchalant questions — about my dog. What was his name, what breed was he, did I let him in the house . . . that sort of thing. I looked around and realized that Donna had probably never gotten him a dog — the closest thing he'd ever had was probably that zebra skin by the door. Poor kid. I promised to introduce him to Airborne too.

We left before 10 P.M. Remington and I had a Sunday school

class to teach the next morning, and Roger had actually mentioned to Donna that they might hit the service at a nearby
church in the morning. Remington looked a little surprised, but
she didn't comment. Once we were in the car, she asked how I
thought it went.

"Fine," I said. "Everyone seemed agreeable to the idea of having me in the family."

"What did you and Dad talk about?"

"Just the normal stuff. He asked if I had any tattoos and if I
planned to ask you to get any."

"He did not."

"Okay, I made that part up. I promised him I'd do my best to
keep you in law school."

"That's important to him," she said. "I guess it's important to
me, too. But I don't think spending a few years working like I did
was wrong."

"He agrees."

"He does? He's never said that to me."

"There's probably a lot he's never said to you. No need to
worry about all that now. He's given his blessing, and that's what
was important tonight."

We drove southwest on U.S. 59 toward home. "When are we
going to talk to your mother?" I asked.

"Later this week, I guess. I don't know. I'm kind of putting that
off."

"Whenever you're ready."

"What did you think of my stepmother?"

"She was nice enough," I said. "You could tell she didn't want
to step on any toes, but she seemed interested in the wedding
plans."

"I think she was just being polite."

"Maybe she likes you."

Remington didn't respond.

"I liked Ronnie, too."

"I figured you would. That's what Martin says about you. You pick up strays. He is definitely a stray."

"He's not a bad kid."

"What's a bad kid anymore?" Remington asked. "I did an article last week on a kid who hired another kid to shoot his father. That kid wasn't bad, according to the school counselor — he was just under a lot of pressure from his dad. I guess since Ronnie hasn't hired any hit men, he's downright nice."

"That's funny," I said. "I made arrangements today to see a guy who used to do just that — hire hit men. At least, I assume he did."

"You're going to talk to the Old Man?"

"Verini, yeah. At least, the priest is going to ask Verini to meet with me. The priest was nice."

"Are you nervous?"

"No. What Harry told us was pretty accurate. Verini is reformed; regretful maybe. He really has changed, according to Father O'Donnell."

"Do you think he'll help?"

"Maybe. I'll know more when I meet him."

Remington nodded. She reached over and took my hand. I love automatic transmissions. We drove for half an hour without talking. We didn't need to.

Remington dropped me off at my house with a kiss and some mushy talk. I won't go into that. But when I walked into my kitchen and greeted my dog, I saw the light blinking on my answering machine that meant I had messages. I hit the Play button and heard Father O'Donnell's light, soothing voice.

"Mr. Dunn, Mr. Verini will be happy to meet with you tomorrow night. He lives just a few blocks from the church, at 465504 Avenue J. He'll be expecting you at about 8:00. I hope that's not too late, but he always has been something of a night owl. And I'll be there as well. We'll see you then."

I scribbled the address on a notepad by the telephone. Incredible! I was going to meet a godfather-gone-good.

12

I met Remington at the church at 9:28 on Sunday morning. We were cutting it close. The kids were already in the classroom. Our junior high class was a usually rambunctious group. "Usually rambunctious" is a nice way of saying the class was composed of horrid monsters from the seventh and eighth grades. Maybe that's overstating the case though. As junior high kids go, ours weren't so bad, really. Amazingly, as junior high kids go, I was surprised that ours didn't go and not come back, considering the amateurs they had for teachers.

We taught at a small Bible church; Martin was the pastor. He'd drafted me into teaching the junior high class, and in that same proud tradition I drafted Remington. The girls liked her better than me. Come to think of it, so did the boys. Not to mention my dog.

But that's beside the point. At 9:30 Remington and I took our posts: I was in front of the class, and she was sitting in the back. When the bell rang, fifteen kids looked expectantly at me. They were quiet. It was eerie.

"So what about it?" asked Dennis, a favorite of mine. He was short and round and redheaded, and he did much to advance the cause of religion. At least, I heard that all his teachers got religion after getting him.

"What about what?" I asked.

"You know," said Samantha, a bright thirteen-year-old sitting to Dennis's left. "The engagement."

I looked at the room full of attentive faces. They'd rarely been attentive before. "Well, Ms. Remington and I are engaged."

"Why?" Dennis asked, turning and addressing his question to Remington.

"Because I love him," she answered. "Besides, if I don't do it, who will?"

"Sam would," Dennis said. Samantha punched him.

"Really, I don't mind," Remington said.

"Thanks," I responded. "I'm touched. Can we get on with the lesson?"

"No," Samantha answered. "We want details."

For the next fifteen minutes or so Remington answered questions, and then threw me a transition beautifully suited to today's lesson. "And that's why we're getting married, and why we think it's God's will that we do. And that's what we're talking about today, right, Emerson? Determining God's will."

"Right." I led into the lesson, and the kids were actually interested. A few minutes later I concluded, "So it's pretty clear that we have some basic guidelines. If the Bible is against it, it's not God's will. If our spiritual leaders — people like our parents and Martin and the leaders in the church — are against it, we ought to reexamine it pretty closely."

"What if they're not around to ask?" Dennis said. "Like if it's something when we're at school, and no one is around to ask? And if we don't have a Bible with us?"

"Good question. Well, then we rely on what we already know about the Bible. For example, some kid wants you to skip school with him."

Dennis blushed; he'd been having attendance problems since kindergarten. I went on. "You know the Bible says to obey the rules, and skipping school is definitely against the rules."

"It's not always that clear," Remington added. "But the principle holds true. If you go to a friend's house and spend the night on a Saturday evening, and there's a movie on cable that your parents might not want you to see, do you do what his parents say or what your parents would want?"

"If you're in someone's house, you follow their rules," Dennis said.

Samantha shook her head. "No, your parents are your parents, and what they say goes, no matter where you are."

"You're both right," I said.

We continued the discussion for another few minutes, until the bell rang. Most of the girls immediately went back to Remington and asked to see her ring. The boys bustled around for a few moments before heading into church.

Within a few minutes the girls had seen all they wanted to see and left to catch up to the boys. Remington came up to the front of the room. She was wearing a beige blouse over a black skirt. Her hair was pulled back; she looked kind of elegant.

"I got a message on my machine last night," I said.

"The Old Man?"

"The priest. I meet the Old Man — Verini — at 8 P.M."

"Tonight?"

"Tonight."

"Are you taking David?"

"I've thought about it," I said. "But I guess I'd better not. I asked for a meeting, not a convention — I want Verini to trust me. Besides, I don't think there's anything to worry about. I don't think Father O'Donnell would lead me into the valley of the shadow of death — or even the valley of the shadow of maiming. He's a nice guy. Verini sounds like a nice guy, too . . . for a reformed gangster."

She made me promise to call as soon as I was home from the meeting, and then she led me out of the classroom and into the sanctuary of the church. The old, dark wooden pews were beginning to fill. Martin was greeting people. Meg, Martin's wife, was over in a corner conferring with someone, and there was no sign of their kids. They had three.

Gene, the one-armed greeter who had stood at the door smiling at everyone for years, gave us a bulletin. We found a seat near the back, and I started reading through it. Before long a group of women had gathered around Remington to see her ring and ask questions about the wedding. Word travels fast. I smiled and nodded and said "thank you" at all the appropriate times, but I was relieved when the organ sounded and people started moving to their own seats.

"Is it getting on your nerves?" Remington asked.

"Not really," I said. "I just don't like the attention."

Martin walked by in the aisle, just to my left. I felt his hand on my shoulder briefly as he passed. He winked at Remington, then made his way up to a chair behind the pulpit. Joe was already at the pulpit, waiting to lead the music. At Martin's nod, he asked us to open our hymnals to No. 237.

Remington leaned toward me. "It's not so easy for me either," she whispered.

"What isn't? No. 237?"

"The attention. Everyone wants to know everything, but I don't even know everything yet. I feel like I don't know anything about this wedding or any other wedding. How can I know everything when I don't know anything?"

"I know the feeling."

She nodded. We broke into No. 237. Joe missed the key as cleanly as if it were a Nolan Ryan fastball. God probably didn't mind.

At the end of the service we filed past Martin. "See you in a few minutes," he said to Remington. To me, he said, "Grab a kid, then set the oven on 350. Meg will take it from there."

"I don't think the kids are that bad," I said. "Is the oven thing really necessary?"

"Garlic bread, Emerson. Garlic bread."

"Oh. Okay."

I scanned the yard in front of the church for Ricky, Martin's son. I saw him talking with a group of about four other boys, most of whom were a little older. I called out to him. He looked up and nodded at me. A moment later he trudged over. "Hello, Emerson. Hello, A. C."

"Hello, Ricky," Remington said sweetly. "Do you want to ride with us?"

"Sure," he said. "In your car, not Emerson's, right?"

"I resent that, bucko," I said. "My car is a great car. But since the air conditioner is not at present working, we'll take Remington's car. And you can ride in the trunk."

"Can I?" He sounded hopeful.

"No," Remington said. "You may not. You can sit in the front with me, and we'll visit. Emerson can ride in the backseat."

Ricky grabbed Remington's hand, and they started for the car. I followed. Dennis was standing by his mother's truck, and he waved as I passed. He also gave me a thumbs-up sign, either for landing Remington or for that great Sunday school lesson I'd taught. I didn't know which. I smiled at him.

Remington's Volvo was parked a few rows down, probably twenty-five yards from the church's front door. When we reached it, she unlocked the doors and I got in the back. Ricky got in on the passenger's side; I made sure he buckled up. He then reminded me to do the same.

"Righto," I said.

"Dad says you guys might be getting married," Ricky said to Remington as she started the car. "Are you really?"

"Yes," she said. She pulled out into the slow line of cars exiting the parking lot. "We are. But you'll hear all about it at lunch."

He nodded, then turned back to me. "How's work?" he asked. "Working on any good stories?"

"Work is fine," I said. "I'm not really doing any fun stories right now, but I am going to meet someone tonight. A bad guy who I think has turned into a good guy."

Ricky looked interested. "Yeah?"

"His name is Al Verini. He used to be a mobster. Like on TV. But not anymore."

"What changed him?"

"I think God got to him."

Ricky nodded. By now we were at the edge of the parking lot, waiting for traffic to clear so we could turn right onto the four-lane road. At a break, Remington gunned it and pulled out onto the road. I didn't think anything of it until a couple of seconds later when I saw flashing blue-and-red lights behind us.

"Remington, that turn might have been a little fast," I said. She looked into the rearview mirror.

"Great." She slowed, then turned into the driveway of a closed garden supply shop that was next-door to the church. The cop followed us. When he got out of his car, I could see it was Ramirez, a cop we both knew. He walked quickly to Remington's window, which she was rolling down. She started to apologize for the traffic maneuver, but he cut her off.

"Ms. Remington, there's been some trouble," he said. "At the restaurant. Detective Sergeant Singer told me to grab Emerson."

"Trouble?" Remington and I asked together.

"Everyone's going to be fine," he said. "Nothing to worry about. Emerson, please come with me. Singer wants you in on this."

I nodded and looked at Ricky. "Save some of that lasagna for me, kid. I need to go see if I can help."

"Okay."

I got out of the car and followed Ramirez to his patrol car. He didn't make me sit in the back like Singer does. A few people from the church were driving by and looked over curiously, but I didn't worry much about that. Instead I worried about what Ramirez had said.

"What do you mean everyone's going to be fine?" I asked when I had entered the car.

"Some sort of a problem at the restaurant. Some breakfast customers got rowdy. Tore the place up pretty good, then left quick. The Schmidt boys weren't beat up or anything. It could have been worse. But the thing is, they're scared, and they're not talking. The perps apparently waited for the breakfast crowd to thin out, so there weren't any witnesses but the Schmidts. That's why Singer needs you."

13

Percy was humming a song I recognized: "Take Me Out to the Ball Game." He was reading the sports page.

"You a baseball fan?" I asked.

"Who isn't?"

"Lots of folks, these days. Isn't like it was when I was a kid."

Percy laughed. "No, I suppose it isn't. My grandson don't care a thing about baseball. Everything's basketball these days. You like basketball?"

I smiled. "Can't stand it. I grew tall early; in junior high I started getting close to my final height. So since I was tall, everyone assumed I'd be a great basketball player."

"Not so?"

"Not so. Takes a lot of coordination to run, dribble, change directions, throw that big ol' ball at that little ol' basket. I wasn't very coordinated. I fell down a lot when I tried those moves. I still can't bear to watch a basketball game."

"Baseball takes some coordination too."

"I didn't say I was any good at that either. To tell you the truth, I was a runner — cross-country. I started doing it based on the theory that if I was running out in the woods, no one would see when I fell down or hit a tree or something."

Percy laughed. "Well, now that's a good one. You still run?"

"No, I don't. My knees gave out sometime in college."

Percy nodded. "My feet went flat sometime after the war — the big one. Don't that figure? After the war."

"Were you in it?"

"Sure was. But I didn't go overseas. I spent most of my time in Las Vegas." He grinned. "Not gambling, mind you, but at the Army base. I was a rifle instructor. Why I didn't go overseas, I don't know. Luck of the draw, I guess. They needed someone over here to teach the boys to shoot. I was in for three years, then we came right back here."

"You and your wife have been together a long time."

"Yes, sir, we have. We've been blessed, but I don't think there's a secret to it. Just have to be willing to work at it. Most people aren't, these days. Maybe that's why they don't like baseball so much. It's a thinking man's sport, even for the spectators. Takes work to figure out things like ERAs, stats, box scores."

"That's true. Tell me something: if you were my age, and you found a girl who can actually read a box score, would you marry her?"

"Son, she'd be one worth grabbing," Percy grinned. "I don't see how God couldn't bless a match like that."

14

Five police cars were in the parking lot of the restaurant; one was Singer's unmarked. I followed Ramirez into the building, expecting to find broken windows and carnage. Instead I found Walter and Gunther sitting at a table, looking a little dazed and a little angry. The place was a wreck, but not as bad as I'd imagined. The cops — with the exception of Singer — were milling around, going over the crime scene. The ID officer was standing by with his camera, waiting for directions from Singer. Singer frowned at me when I entered. He nodded to the Schmidt boys, then shrugged, then left for the kitchen. Loosely interpreted, what he meant was, "I can't seem to get any information out of these guys. See what you can do, will you, pal?"

I went to the table and pulled up a chair.

"How bad?" I asked.

Walter just shook his head. Gunther glared at me, then said so quietly I could barely hear him, "We'll have to close. We can't cook without an oven, without plates, without glasses."

"That bad?"

"You should see the kitchen," I heard a female voice from behind me say. It was Sally Nix, Singer's top investigator. She was back recently from an interdepartmental investigation in Nueces County. I turned to look at her. She was wearing pants and a pullover top; her gun, a 9 mm Glock, was at her side in a clip-on holster. She was tall and blonde and serious.

"What's wrong in the kitchen?" I asked.

"They were efficient," she said. "They destroyed everything needed to run a restaurant, as far as I can tell."

I looked back at the boys. "You know who did it?"

"We didn't know the men who destroyed things . . ." Gunther said.

"But you know who sent them."

Gunther shrugged. "What does it matter? If he wants the place now, let him have it. It's worth nothing."

I felt Nix's presence behind me; her breathing was becoming measured. I knew what to do — let her take it from here. "Boys, it's not that simple," I said. "Sally here wants to help you. So do I. So does Singer."

"Do you really think he'll let you walk away from the debt?" Nix added. "Even now?"

Walter looked up. "Isn't this what he wants? The restaurant?"

"No," I said. "Who would run it? Jim and Tommy? What he wants is for you to be indebted to him for the rest of your lives. This is his way of telling you he's not happy with you bringing in the cops."

"We didn't."

"I know," I said patiently. "And in a way I guess this was my fault. But, guys, I don't feel bad about it. I'd feel bad if I let some crook like Ciotti hurt you. You didn't get into this mess overnight and without a little pain. You're not going to get out of it overnight and without a little more pain."

Walter stared at me for a moment. "You have the answers, of course. You always do. But your answers aren't as good as you think they are."

From behind me Nix spoke. "You're angry at the wrong person," she said. "Emerson didn't come in and bust up the place. That was some of Ciotti's people. You can identify them, and you can link them to Ciotti. But you've got to talk to me."

Instead of glaring, this time Gunther shrugged. Nix was often the "Good Cop" to Singer's "Bad Cop." Singer was purposely brusque; she was gentle and coaxing — and often successful. I felt her hand on my shoulder; there was a little pressure to her touch. She was coaxing me out of my chair.

"I'll go see the kitchen," I said. "It's probably not as bad as it seemed at first."

Nix was in my seat and talking with the boys almost before I was out of it. I walked past an overturned table and on back to the kitchen. I found Singer conferring with the ID officer. "Don't bother," he said. "Wouldn't do any good."

"But customers don't come back here," the ID officer said. "That would leave us only two sets of elimination prints — the prints belonging to the brothers."

"I'm not saying you wouldn't come up with something; I'm saying it wouldn't do any good. The Schmidt boys know better than to identify Ciotti's people, or even press any charges if we identified them ourselves with prints. And I think this incident shows there's only so much the PD can do to protect them."

"Nix is out there with them now," I said. "Maybe she can convince them to talk."

"Dunn, all I need from them is confirmation that Ciotti sent these guys," Singer said. "I don't want the boys to talk any more than that, at least not yet. I'm dead serious about the PD not being able to protect their property. My warning the other day was effective — Ciotti knew better than to hurt the boys — for now. But look how two men just walked in this morning, ate a nice meal, and then when it cleared out, trashed the place. Next time it might not be the fixtures. They might come in and pop the Schmidt boys."

"But Ciotti knows we're watching," I said.

"He would only need two things: an alibi and a shooter who couldn't be found," Singer said. "And he'd walk right out of any courtroom. At some point, the slight risk of getting implicated in two such murders is going to be outweighed by the heavy burden of losing face. When we stepped in, Ciotti lost face. If the Schmidt boys pressed charges against his people, Ciotti would lose even more face. Do you understand what I'm telling you? This guy has played on this field for years. He knows what he's doing."

I surveyed the splintered kitchen. Dishes and glasses were smashed on the floor; an oven door was pried from its hinges; pots and pans were strewn about the room. "Do we give up?" I asked. "What would your dad say to do, Singer?"

Singer smiled. "He would ask for a badge and a few fresh rounds of ammunition."

"And he'd say, 'Billy, my boy, did I ever tell you about the time I stared down Al Capone?'"

"Something like that."

"Well, we've got Harry Singer on our side. I'm meeting with Verini and the priest tonight. If I can get God and the Old Man on our side as well, do you think we'll be a match for a guy named Fuzzy?"

15

I t was growing dark when I drove across the causeway onto Galveston Island. I stayed on the highway until it became Broadway Boulevard, then took a left at 25th Street. Near the intersection of Avenue J and 25th, I found the dark Victorian two-story house where Alberto Verini lived. I pulled to a stop in front of it; I parked and checked my tie in the rearview mirror. It was the same tie I'd worn the night before; it looked better in the dim light of the street lamp.

The house was ornate; steps led up to a porch and the front door, which was carved wood and beveled glass. I knocked on the door. Father O'Donnell answered it a moment later.

"Good evening, Father," I said.

"Come in, Mr. Dunn."

I entered the home; the foyer was dark and aged. The wallpaper looked at least as old as me, and the Persian rug was faded into a few muted colors. Father O'Donnell looked much the same as he had in the church the day before.

The priest led me down a hallway lined with photographs; not a single picture appeared newer than forty years old. The dominant image was that of a young, dark, thin woman. Verini's late wife, I imagined. I almost commented on that when I realized the priest had veered off into a dark room. I followed.

Again it was the smell I noticed first. It was the smell of age;

the smell of rugs with the dust of decades imbedded in them, furniture made of wood and varnish and leather, along with smells that brought back memories. I could detect the scent of old tobacco and older whiskey. The Old Man smelled like my grandfather, who had died when I was still a toddler; my only memories of him were the rich smells.

The Old Man was sitting in a broad leather chair facing me. His worn face looked at me with mild interest; his gray hair was very nearly not there at all. He put down a small black book he'd been reading and stood. I judged his age at between eighty-two and eighty-five, his height at about 5'10".

"Al, this is Emerson Dunn," Father O'Donnell said.

"Nice to meet you," he said, holding out his hand. I took it; it was thick and cumbersome. Briefly I wondered how he could manage the whisper-thin pages of the small book he'd been reading. Up close, I could see that his eyes were bright and sure. He'd not been wearing reading glasses, I noted.

"It's a pleasure to meet you, too, sir," I said.

"Sit, sit," he said, motioning to another chair, similar to his. He held my hand a moment longer, then dropped it and returned to his own chair. "The father tells me you're a reporter, and a religious man."

"Yes," I said. "But I've got a situation I need to discuss with you."

Father O'Donnell found a third chair and sat. I looked to him for guidance, but he just smiled at me. I was on my own.

"Situation, yes," I said. "That's a good word for it. It's not me, really — it's friends of mine — Walter and Gunther Schmidt."

Verini's face was passive. "And?"

"And they've gotten themselves in trouble with an old associate of yours, Francis 'Fuzzy' Ciotti."

Verini's mouth twitched at the corners. "I gave him that name. Didn't mean to. But it stuck. Poor kid."

"He's not a poor kid anymore," I said. "He's a man who hurts people, who takes advantage of them."

Again the Old Man's face was passive. He waited for me to continue.

"My friends are in hock to Ciotti for a lot of money, and I'm out of my league," I said. "I don't know how to help them."

"Gambling?"

"No — a loan. But they've more than paid off the amount they borrowed. Seems it's all been interest, though."

Verini nodded. "Manners, son."

"Excuse me?"

"Manners. It's good manners to talk with your host first, to visit . . . not jump into business so soon."

"I'm sorry," I said. "I didn't mean to be rude."

"No offense taken," he said with a wave. "It's the world these days. No time for conversation, for visiting. Everything is done in a hurry. Well, Mr. Dunn, I'm not in a hurry. You've outlined your 'situation,' and I'll think on it while we visit. Now back to my question. Tell me about yourself. And would you like a drink? Some scotch perhaps?"

"No, thank you," I said. "Tell you about myself . . . Well, I guess I'll start with what I do. I work for a newspaper. It's not that exciting. I teach a Sunday school class for junior high kids; that can get a little too exciting, if you know what I mean."

Verini nodded approvingly.

"And I just got engaged," I added.

"Congratulations," he said. "And the young woman?"

"She's also a reporter, but for a different newspaper. Only she's going to law school this fall."

"Very nice. Did the father mention something to me about Harry Singer? He's a good man."

I nodded. "He's the one who sent me to you. But that's business. Harry himself is doing great. His son is a cop now, too. Harry's retired, living a mile or so from his son."

"He lost his Christy, what, about twenty-five years ago?"

I paused. "That sounds about right — when Singer — Bill Singer, his son — was about ten."

"I lost my Holly a few years before that," Verini said. "When I heard about Harry, I called him on the telephone. First time, and last time. All I said was, 'I'm sorry for you, Harry.' He thanked me. That's the only commerce Harry and I have had that wasn't in terms of law and order."

I nodded, hoping he would continue. After a moment he did. "That doesn't mean we don't have our connections. A few old-timers at the Galveston police department drop in on me from time to time, just to visit. Oh, for the first thirty years I think it might have been to check up on me — to see if I'd gone back to my old ways. Now it's just social. I hear a little now and then about Harry, and I'm sure he hears a little now and then about me."

"He seems impressed with the fact that you haven't gone back to your old ways," I said.

The Old Man's face darkened. "He was a doubter at first — and for good reason. It was 1949, you know. Right before I turned — that's what I call it now, my turn; there was a little fracas outside a nightclub. A man was shot. Actually, it was a man named Nicholas Ciotti . . . Francis's brother. A bad, bad night, Emerson. More pain that night than I ever thought I could stand. It was that night, you see, when my Holly took ill. I spoke to her before I went out. Do you know the last thing we talked about?"

"No, I don't."

"Home. She wanted to go home, for a visit. She was a New York girl. Grew up in an Italian neighborhood . . . a nice Italian girl. Her sister had just had a baby, and Holly wanted to visit. I told her we could. Then I left. When I got home the next morning, she was taken with the fever. Influenza. Lot of people died of it back then."

"I'm sorry."

Verini smiled. "Thank you. I think you mean it. But I didn't tell you why Harry Singer was a doubter. You see, it was me who shot Nicholas. He'd been arguing with Francis, and they started shoving each other. Nicholas was drunk, and he wasn't thinking straight; he went for a gun, and I had to drop him."

I nodded.

"He died in his brother's arms," Verini continued. "Harry Singer drove up in a squad car a few minutes after the shot. At first Harry believed my turn came because of the heat that was coming down — he thought that I wasn't sincere, that I was just trying to avoid a murder charge. But I was never indicted, of course. Everyone at the bar saw Nicholas leave drunk and angry; then Francis backed up my story about Nicholas reaching for his gun. They confiscated the weapon, then held me for questioning all night. When I got home, like I said, Holly was sick. I stayed with her for days; it didn't do much good. She never really knew I was there. I *was* there, though. No one should die alone in a hospital bed, with no one else to sit beside them and talk a bit and pray and then mourn. Especially not someone as selfless as my Holly. When the good Lord took her, He did it because He knew better than me how to care for her. That's what I've told myself."

"Is that her in the pictures in the hallway?"

"Beautiful, isn't she?"

"Very. A nice smile."

"She loved to smile," Verini said softly. "But enough about that. Tell me more about your fiancée. That baby — the one Holly's sister had just had? *He's* a lawyer now, too. Your girl's in for a time, I know. Law school isn't easy. Tell me — your fiancée, where does she want to study?"

"Dallas, at Southern Methodist."

He nodded. "Is she, then, a Methodist?"

"No; we belong to a nondenominational church."

"What brought you into the church, Emerson?"

I smiled. "I guess it was just the realization that a person can't live like I was and live long."

The Old Man nodded. "That's what the father here told me for years. But I didn't listen, until after my Holly passed. And then I listened. He told me about her novena — she'd been praying for me, that I would return to the church. It broke my heart, Emerson. I honored those prayers; at first for her memory, and later because I knew she was right. There's no life elsewhere. Father O'Donnell helped teach me that."

The priest had been silent until now. "Well, Al, it wasn't an easy mile for you, but you made it."

Verini shook his head. "No, Father, I don't know that I have — yet." Verini turned a smile to me. "Emerson, tell me about your life before."

"I guess it was just your average adolescent rebellion. I hurt some people, some people I loved. I hurt myself with narcotics."

"And what happened?"

"I hit the bottom. I was eighteen, a high school dropout, with no job skills and no future — I was even out of drugs. Then I met a man who showed me a better way. His name is Martin; he's the pastor of my church. He's more than that. He's my friend — a kind of spiritual father to me."

"Like Father O'Donnell has been to me."

I smiled. "If Father O'Donnell has shown you the kindness that Martin has shown me, you've been in good hands."

"He's shown me great kindness, Emerson. I'm an old man; I've outlived my family, most of my friends. But I'm not lonely. Father O'Donnell has been a good friend."

"Whom else do you see?"

"A few people. Like I said, some old-timers from the police department. A boy . . . Charlie." Verini laughed. "Listen to me — 'a boy.' Charlie's at least sixty, sixty-five now. But he was a boy when I met him, and I was already old. He comes around, does errands for me, does some work for me. Also, I get a visit or two a year from Vegas — old business associates," he said. He lowered his voice and leaned toward me. "And if I might say, Emerson, I'm considered quite an available bachelor among the parish widows. I get a call now and then from one widow or another who says she worries how I eat. I tell them I eat fine, but

I still let them come over and cook for me. That's not dishonest, now, is it? I wouldn't want to lead them on."

I shook my head. "Chances are, they just want someone to talk with, too."

"But a man with my looks," he said, shrugging. "I have to be careful. Don't want to break too many hearts."

I smiled. "We do have it tough, don't we?"

"That's the truth." Verini leaned back in his chair. "Now about that business you mentioned . . . I'm interested, Emerson. I think your heart is right. Tell me about your friends."

"Two brothers — Germans. They came to this country a few years ago, worked in someone else's restaurant. They saved enough to start their own. Looking back, it was obviously under-capitalized."

Verini nodded. "In a business such as that, you can't afford to count on making a profit for at least a year or so. That's what I did for Papa Rose; I made the restaurants and the clubs viable businesses, not just fronts for the gambling. He and Sam wanted to be respectable, to have nice establishments. Let me tell you, it's not an easy business."

"I guess we realize that now," I said. "I don't know how Ciotti came into the picture, but one day we — my fiancée and I — noticed some changes. The boys had a cigarette machine, and they were serving alcohol illegally."

Verini nodded. I went on. "Anyway, we were in the restaurant when Ciotti showed up with two of his goons one afternoon. The boys were acting different, nervous. When I went to see the older one, Walter, in the kitchen, I saw that he'd been beaten up. Apparently they'd missed a payment. From what I know about Ciotti, he's used to doing business like that."

"And what more do you know of Ciotti? What more do you know of me?" Verini sounded serious. "What do you know of the old gangster you've come to visit?"

"Just what Harry's told me."

Verini shook his head. "Son, you know almost nothing.

Because you know almost nothing, I'm going to inform you. Everyone I talk to, I assume they know something about me. Every Girl Scout who comes to my door to sell cookies, I know her mother has said, 'That's the house where the old gangster lives.' When I shook your hand I knew I was facing a man who'd been told about this old gangster."

He leaned toward me. "But you don't know the reality of it. The reality of it is that there's no glamour. There are no godfathers in nice suits who live by a code of honor. There are only men who live on the pain of others. That's what I am — was. Life means nothing to these men. You heard on TV about a code of honor? So few of us believed anything like that. Some of us, yes. Most of them, no. The code means nothing to Francis Ciotti; he watched his own brother die, and he didn't shed a tear. He's grown older and harder in these forty-five years. You come to me like I'm a grade-school principal, and there's been a tussle out in the sandbox. I'm no principal. You're a bystander, Emerson, and you've walked into this like it was only a game. I've seen Francis Ciotti beat men senseless for a debt of fifty dollars. I've seen him kill men, and I've seen DA's who dropped rock-solid cases against Ciotti at the last minute because of what they said was lack of evidence. Lack of evidence? It was bribery and fear, Emerson, two things Ciotti knows. Who is Francis Ciotti? A man without rules. A man who has worked very hard all his life at not making an honest living. He takes pleasure and pride in going against the laws of God and man. If he could steal ten dollars in an hour but earn fifty dollars in half that time, I guarantee you he'd steal the ten dollars. He has no friends, he has no God. May the mother of our Lord help you, Emerson, because I don't think I can. It's a different world, son, a frightening one. Frightening to me, and if you knew any better, frightening to you."

Verini had spoken slowly, and I responded only after a pause. "I respect your position. I came to ask for your help, not to beg. But I won't be frightened by this boogeyman. Who is Francis Ciotti? A crook. I won't be afraid of a simple crook."

Verini stared at me. I wondered for a moment if I'd been disrespectful. I glanced at the priest; he, too, was watching for reaction from the Old Man. After a moment it came.

"You're not a wise man, Mr. Dunn. But I think I like you. You're not going to give up, are you?"

"No. These are my friends. What they did was wrong — taking money from a loan shark — but everyone deserves a second chance, don't they? I got one. You got one."

"He's saying something worth listening to, Al," Father O'Donnell said softly. "I won't advise you on this. You made a break with your past, but we both know you haven't made peace with it yet. Send him home, Al, and think on it some more. But don't make any decisions yet."

Verini nodded, then stood. "The father is right, Emerson. It's been a pleasure meeting you. Will you come again, so we can talk more about your problem — your situation?"

I stood as well. "I'd like that."

"Fine, then. Perhaps Tuesday night? That will give me a couple of days to think and pray. Tuesday, same time."

"I'll be here," I said. I felt the priest's eyes on me as I shook the old gangster's hand. I turned and followed the priest back through the hallway to the front door.

"You did well, son," he said softly as he opened the door for me. "But I warn you again — I won't tell Al to get involved. This may be a situation in which he can't get involved — for the sake of his own soul. Francis Ciotti understands force, he understands a bullet, he understands intimidation. And that's the language the Old Man would have to speak in order to communicate with him. Understand, Mr. Dunn, it wouldn't be easy — and it might not even be right. Oh, when you come back, bring something of yourself — a photo album, maybe, some articles you're proud of. Let Al get to know you."

I nodded and took the priest's hand. "Thank you for your help," I said. "Will you be here Tuesday?"

"I'll be here."

"See you then."

During the drive home I thought about Alberto Verini. He was right. There were no godfathers left, no codes. Was that what I had been expecting? Maybe. Instead I found an elderly, reformed criminal who was crippled by his past life — his old nature. We all have our limitations, I realized, and we hide them and fear them. I feared my own. Remington feared hers. Alberto Verini's limitations had been rudely brought before him, by me, and he'd been forced to admit that fear.

Within forty-five minutes I had pulled into my driveway and let myself into the house. My watch said it was just before 10 P.M. My dog said it was time to go check on the impending bunny invasion.

"Go ahead," I said, letting him out the back door. "Protect the innocent, you valiant beast. You have no limitations — unless you count not having thumbs."

I reached for the kitchen phone and dialed Remington's number. She answered on the first ring.

"It's me," I said. "I'm back."

"How did it go?"

"It was much less dangerous than Sunday school was. He's a tired man, Remington, and he's afraid of his past. I can't blame him for that. If he can't help, I'll understand."

"Has he turned you down?"

"Not yet. He wanted time to think and pray. I'm supposed to go back to see him on Tuesday night. And, Remington, the old priest told me to bring something of myself — something to help Mr. Verini get to know me. I want to bring you."

"About time."

"What?"

"Emerson Dunn, if you think you can just bounce around having adventures and fun and meeting interesting people all the time and leave me at home, you're sorely mistaken." Remington sounded a little, well, pushy.

"Did I hit a nerve?" I inquired carefully.

She laughed. "Maybe. But if I'm going to be part of your life, I want to be part of the exciting portions, not just the house-cleaning. Get the message?"

"Got it."

"Now go to bed. We both have to work tomorrow. Kiss Airborne for me."

"We're going to have a long talk about that someday — the fact that you treat him better than me."

"Good night, Emerson."

She hung up before I could bring up the fact that Airborne treated her better than he treated me as well. I don't think I would have won much sympathy anyway. I made one last call before I went to bed.

"Hello?" David answered.

"David, it's me. Tell me what you think the threat is to the Schmidt boys."

He let out a breath slowly. "I think this Fuzzy made his point already. They should be safe for a while. But Saturday's coming up. You told me they have a payment due."

"Right."

"So between now and then, they should be safe. Come Saturday night, though . . ."

"I know. Hopefully we can have it resolved by Saturday."

"How did the meeting with the Old Man go?"

"It went well, I think. But I don't know if he can help. Maybe we should pursue other avenues."

"There's only ever been one avenue for you, Emerson."

"What do you mean?"

"One avenue. You know one way: bring out the truth. It's a good way. Maybe we can use it now."

"I don't know, David. I'll think some. Thanks."

"Sure. See you at the office tomorrow." He paused for a moment, as if he wanted to add something. I didn't know what, so I let him flounder for a moment. After a few seconds he just said good-bye.

"Good-bye," I replied. I wondered what that was all about, but I didn't dwell on it. Call me Mr. Sensitive. When I hung up the phone I let Airborne back in. He looked up at me curiously. I told him a little about the evening, and he seemed satisfied.

When I got into bed I stared up at my trusty ceiling fan for about an hour. Airborne was sawing logs within minutes of hitting the floor beside me. Before I got Airborne I didn't know that dogs snore. They do. That didn't help me any. I couldn't sleep. If not having thumbs meant you didn't have to worry about the problems of the world, was it really a limitation? I thought of the statue of the Virgin Mary atop the cathedral. She seemed not to worry about the problems of the world either — she knew she'd outlast the things of this earth.

Limitations. Statues and statutes and glorious limitations. Major crimes, such as murder, have no statute of limitations. What had Verini told me? He'd seen Ciotti kill men. If we couldn't get Ciotti on loan-sharking, how about murder? What would it take? We'd need a Galveston County DA to exhume old case files; we'd need to find one where there's a substantial amount of evidence — and maybe with a little help and a little grace, we could gather enough additional evidence to prosecute or at least to publish. Verini had told me that in some of the cases, the state was ready to prosecute, but mysteriously the DA would call it off "for lack of evidence." If we could find one of those cases, bulk it up a bit, could we nail Ciotti in a court of law, or at least on the front pages of the newspapers?

Court cases and newspaper articles are actually quite similar; you need the same sorts of evidence in both, evidence that holds up under scrutiny. But a journalist has a little more leeway than a prosecutor. We can accuse, and as long as we balance out the story some with a denial, we're within the bounds of fairness. If a prosecutor accuses, he'd better be ready to back it up fully, in front of a jury.

It was too late to call David or Remington back, or either Singer, father or son. But I had a plan. All I'd have to do was find a very old murder and solve it.

16

Fielder entered the waiting room again, looking a little more relaxed. He put his briefcase down and straddled a chair facing me. The clock said it was 3:52.

"I just finished up with David Ben Zadok," he said. "Now it's the prosecutor's turn. He'll have to go easy; I think the jury liked David."

"Everyone likes him," I said. "He's honest, he's good-looking, and he's helpful. What's not to like?"

"Exactly. The judge asked us if we thought we could finish this evening; he's got a big murder case scheduled for tomorrow morning. So the prosecutor and I both said we could wrap it up by about 6:00 or so. We'll be ready for you sometime after the recess."

"When this all began, the point was to put Francis Ciotti on trial," I said. "I still don't understand why Bill Singer's on trial."

Fielder took a deep breath. "Dunn, he wanted it this way."

"What?"

"Do you know the grand jury system? See, every police shooting goes before the grand jury, which meets in this county once per month. The grand jury hears the facts, and if they feel the facts warrant it, they'll send the shooting to trial. Most of the time they don't. In fact, when this particular shooting was before the grand jury a few weeks ago, they were ready to no-bill him.

That means they heard the facts — most of them, at least — and they found no fault with Singer's actions."

"Then why did they charge him?"

"Because a no-bill by the grand jury isn't really an end to anything, Emerson. It's not like a regular jury standing up and saying you're innocent. If Singer let it drop at the grand jury level, it might come back to haunt him. Remember, Ciotti's people — his cronies, at least — still have some political pull. Not with the DA, not with the mayor, but with a few others. They still put a lot of money into a lot of campaign treasuries."

"So?"

"So you can only be tried by a jury once. A grand jury can hear your case over and over again. Let's say some new politico comes into power and wants the case reexamined. If it's been to trial, he's powerless, because the Constitution says you can't be placed in double jeopardy."

"I know what the Constitution says."

"But that politico could send the same case back to the grand jury again and again until he found one that was willing to charge Singer. Singer just wanted to have closure."

"Is that a word my fiancée is going to start using? Closure?"

Fielder smiled. "She's the one going to law school? She probably will use it. Emerson, I know you feel nervous. And when you get in there, it's not going to be pleasant. But I think in our prior conversations we've covered all the bases."

"I don't think you can do that."

"Do what?"

"Use a sports metaphor in the same sentence as 'prior conversations.' I really hope my fiancée doesn't learn to talk like you."

Fielder laughed. "You're loosening up. That's good. One thing — the prosecutor's going to be a little antagonistic. Part of that is his personality, and part of that's his job. Believe me, he has no animosity toward you or toward Singer or toward cops in general, although you might get a different impression. He'll be drinking a beer with cops later tonight, I bet. But don't let his demeanor throw you off — don't let it anger you. If he can get you on the defensive, he might be able to get you to change your story some. And a little of that is all he needs to dismantle you as a witness. You with me?"

"Sure."

"Great. I have a phone call to make. We'll reconvene in about ten minutes; you'll be called after we're through with David."

"I'll be here," I said.

Fielder gave me another thumbs-up and left. I heard Percy chuckling.

"Shouldn't criticize a man's metaphors, son," he grinned. "At least not in front of others."

"I know. Grammar is a private thing. I should have stuck to criticizing his wardrobe."

"You said it. You ready, son?"

"Almost."

"It'll be over before you know it, son. Of course, that's what they told me about my gall bladder operation."

"You're a big help, Percy. A big help."

17

At noon on Monday, Harry Singer showed up at my office. I'd called him first thing that morning and outlined what I wanted to do.

"Can we talk about this over lunch?" he asked.

"Sure," I said, putting down a newspaper. "Name the place."

"Well, Billy's going to be at my place in a few minutes; I thought I'd cook us something."

"Great — if you don't mind. My favorite restaurant seems to be out of business temporarily. I'll follow you over. One thing, though: would you mind if my photographer, David, sits in on this?"

"The more the merrier."

"Let me grab him." I left Harry standing by my desk and went to the darkroom, where David was processing some film from the weekend. I knocked on the door; he opened it a moment later.

"Singer's dad is fixing us lunch," I said. "I think we may have a way out of this for all of us. We're going to talk about it. You in?"

"I'm in." David turned to the film canisters rinsing under the tap. He turned off the water and drained the canisters. It took him about thirty seconds to unroll the film from the metal spools and hang it to dry from a clothesline above his head. He rinsed his hands quickly, then said, "Let's go."

I started to say something; he wasn't abrupt, exactly, not anywhere close to rude. He just wasn't himself. I saw a dark, brooding look in his eyes, but it was passing quickly, and by the time he turned out the light he was smiling. I let it drop.

He followed me to my desk; we found Harry talking to Robert about local politics.

"Enough of that," I said. "Robert, we're going to eat a real home-cooked meal. Not even a mental image of the mayor is going to spoil that for me. Any more talk like that and I'll have to keelhaul you."

"Right, Captain Bligh," he grinned. "Go ahead, take off for lunch. Take your time; relax a little. Everything will be the same on the *Bounty* when you return. We promise."

Sharon the Receptionist grinned in unison with Robert.

"Just remember what happened to Fletcher Christian when he tried this sort of stunt," I said.

"I remember something about him ending up on a South Seas island with beautiful women and no deadlines."

I gave up and marched from the room. David followed, still snickering. "Not you, too," I said.

"I'm on your side," he said. "But if he took over, think he'd give me a raise?"

"Probably not," I said. "But just for that, we're taking your car. By the way, Harry, this is David."

"Pleasure," Harry said, sticking out his hand. David shook it with a grin to match Harry's. "I've heard some tales about you, David. Tell me, are they true?"

"Probably," he said modestly.

"Well, you two boys follow me home, and we'll devise our plans then. Good to have you on the team, David. Always good to have a man along who knows what to do in a tight spot."

David grinned again.

"Lead the way, Harry, before this gets too mushy," I said.

Harry smiled and went to his car. He started the old V-8 engine and pulled out onto Commerce Street before David had even unlocked the door to his car. A moment later we were on Commerce ourselves, and Harry was sitting impatiently at a stoplight, edging forward.

"He still drives like a cop," I said.

"Lots of family resemblance," David said. "He looks like Singer. Only shorter and balder."

"I noticed that too. Funny, though — I can't picture Bill Singer as a child. Think he wore polyester then too?"

"I'm not going to ask him, Emerson."

"Chicken."

A few minutes later we pulled into Harry Singer's driveway and parked behind his Ford. We started to follow him inside, but Bill Singer's unmarked car rounded the corner, and we waited for him to park on the street. Our favorite detective sergeant grunted a greeting at us, and we all went in. As I entered I could smell something vaguely Italian.

"Have a seat, and start talking," Harry said as he went into the kitchen. "I can hear you from in here. The spaghetti's been simmering, so it will only take a sec."

"I concur," Bill Singer said, pulling out a chair for himself and settling in at the dining room table. "Start talking."

David and I sat down across from Singer. "It all comes down to greasy palms, I think."

"Get to the point, Dunn."

"There are fewer greasy palms in Galveston now. Am I right?"

From the kitchen, Harry agreed. "Sure. The department's honest, the DA's a nice fella, and the sheriff's as straight as a rifle barrel."

"Right," I said. "Now, from what you've told me, and from what I learned from Al Verini last night, Ciotti was the prime suspect in several major crimes — the kinds of crimes that don't have a statute of limitations. Killings, for example."

"And?" Singer The Younger asked.

"And he was close to being charged a couple of times, but the cases were always dropped on account of lack of evidence."

"Go on, Emerson," Harry said, entering with a serving dish full of spaghetti already in the sauce. "I like where you're going with this."

"So chances are that those cases — some of them at least — were dropped not because the evidence wasn't there, but because Ciotti or someone higher greased the right palms. But the men they paid off are all gone."

"You want to dig up a decades-old case and try to talk the DA into prosecuting it," Bill Singer said as he took the serving spoon and started dishing out his lunch.

"Well, yeah," I said. "Maybe it's a long shot."

"Maybe. And maybe it's not such a bad idea," he replied. "But it's not going to be easy."

"My son is right," Harry said, returning from the kitchen with garlic bread and a bowl of salad. "You're dealing with more than crooked politicians in that era. Shoddy police work sometimes, if Ciotti slipped someone a hundred dollar bill at the right time. I saw a sheriff's investigator drop a pistol off the pier once — said the gun slipped right out of his fingers. He also wore a new suit to work the next week."

"But we're talking about several cases, aren't we?" I commented.

"Maybe a dozen, maybe more," Harry assented.

"Then at least one of them could have enough to build on. The way I see it, the underworld is gone. Other than Ciotti, is anyone still around and actively bad? Not that I know of. So if we found a witness or two who were afraid to testify forty years ago, we could tell them there's nothing to be afraid of now."

"Eyewitness testimony from forty years ago? What court would accept that?" Harry asked.

"Israeli courts," David said softly. "Every so often an old Nazi is found somewhere, and he's tried in Israel. They rely heavily on eyewitnesses from the camps."

"He's right," I said. "Look, this is just a possibility, but a possibility I think we should explore."

"We'll need files," Harry said. "Lots of files. From the DA's office. I think I could obtain them — copies, at least. I still have a little pull around there."

"What kind of time frame?" I asked.

"I'm not a busy man," Harry said with a smile. "I could drop by the DA's office tomorrow, I suppose. Is there a hurry?"

"The boys owe a payment to Ciotti on Saturday."

Bill Singer spoke up. "He's not going to let them slide again, even though it's his doing that they're shut down. He'll either foreclose or shoot them — it depends on what mood he's in. I agree with Emerson." His eyebrows got close together. "What am I saying? Dunn, forget that last part. But don't forget about Saturday. If we're going to intercede, we'll have to do it before then."

"We do have one ace up our sleeve," I said. "Verini told me he's seen Ciotti kill men. If we come up completely dry, maybe Verini's testimony could help bring charges."

"Maybe," Harry said. "But that's a stretch. Assuming that he'd go against the code, a defense attorney could tear up the Old Man's credibility in a matter of minutes."

"He talked a little about that code," I said. "He says he believed in it, but Ciotti doesn't."

"And Ciotti's beliefs won't change Verini's actions," Harry replied. "To Verini, there are just certain rules. The one against ratting on an associate might just be one of the unbreakable ones. I don't know."

I nodded. "When do you want to meet to go over the files? Wednesday's a good day for me; we put together the Thursday paper Tuesday evening, and I have another appointment with the Old Man Tuesday night. So Tuesday is booked, but Wednesday is good."

"Wednesday should be fine," Harry said. "Is that good for you, son?"

Bill Singer nodded. "Garlic. You were heavy on the garlic this time, Dad. But you toned down the basil. That's better."

Harry Singer held out his hands in apology to me and David. "I have no taste buds left — I was a smoker for thirty years. Billy helps me keep track of how much spices to put in my recipes. It's a good system, really. When we're done, I'll write on the card that I should cut the garlic by a third. Will a third do it, son?"

Bill Singer nodded.

"Fine, then — by a third. And next time it will be better. Sure, I could turn to Betty Crocker for everything, but that's not how I do it. What I do is I go to the front-lines troops — working chefs at restaurants — and I make notes about what I eat. Then I try it at home. Billy helps me with the fine-tuning. Plus, he gets a nice evening out once a month or so at a nice restaurant. Teamwork, eh?"

"It sounds like a good system."

"It keeps me busy in my old age."

"Dad, you're not old."

"Billy's kind," Harry said. "But I'm almost seventy. I feel ten years younger. I quit smoking, and that helped, and also I've tried to stay in shape."

"If you don't mind me asking, what do you do with your time?" I inquired.

"I read quite a bit. I see old friends. Actually, I find plenty to fill my days. It's not as hard as you think. You're working full-time now, and I suspect that in the back of your mind, you're aware of the things you don't get done. The new paint needed in the back bedroom, the yardwork, the letters to relatives and old friends . . ."

I nodded. "I never seem to have time for that kind of thing. I see what you mean."

"I'm able to do some of that. I have a sister in Florida. We write once or twice a week; it's almost a full-time job keeping up with her kids. They've not turned out as, well, responsible as Billy has."

Bill grunted — either in assent to what his father was saying, or in dissent — I couldn't tell which.

"Anyway, I have a lot of work to do to this old house so I can sell it; soon I'll be ready to down-size. I need less and less room. If this were a home, I think I might have second thoughts. But it's not, really. It's just a house I moved into to be closer to Billy a few years ago. It's suited my needs, I suppose. Maybe I'll get a condo."

"I think you'd like that, Dad," Bill Singer said. "Maybe a retirement condo."

"First, though, I have to finish with this place," Harry said. "I put a new roof on it last spring, and I think I'll pull up the kitchen floor soon — update the tile."

"That'll be a tough job, Dad," Bill said. "Wait for a weekend. I'll come over."

"Are you implying something, son?" Harry said with a smile.

"What do you mean?"

"First you suggest a retirement condo, then you tell me I'm too fragile to do a kitchen floor?"

"I don't mean anything, Dad, other than just the fact that you're old as dirt."

"You just said I wasn't. But don't worry, you'll be this age yourself soon enough, Billy. And as soon as we get this investigation going, I'll show you that a good cop doesn't stop being a good cop when he mothballs his dress blues."

"Yes, sir."

It was sort of heartening to see Singer — Billy-boy, that is — being so respectful. He had a deeply felt respect for me, I figured, although he was awful good at hiding it.

We finished eating, and David and I started gathering the dishes.

"No, now you boys go back to work," Harry said.

"I'm the boss," I said. "We don't have to go back just yet. We'll do the dishes. Our mothers trained us well."

Bill Singer snorted. "I've got crimes to solve, boys. Dad, I'll call you tonight."

"Okay, son."

Singer left without saying anything endearing to me or David, but I figured he was just feeling shy.

"It's funny, you know . . ." Harry said.

"What's funny?" David asked as he stood at the sink, watching it fill with warm water.

"That we're going after guys I should have gone after forty, fifty years ago."

"Times were different then," I said, repeating what he'd told me.

"That's true enough," Harry said as he opened the dishwasher and started accepting plates from David, who was giving them a cursory scrub in the sink. "But, Emerson, a cop is a cop. We all knew what was going on. It was a pragmatic decision to let the Maceo family control their side of the street and for us to just worry about our side. It wasn't a comfortable decision for many of us. Another thing funny — I never thought I'd be dealing with the Old Man again. I thought he was out."

"What do you mean? That he reformed?"

"Yeah. Plus, he never really was in that deeply anyway. Sure, he was close to Papa Rose, and Sam liked him, so he was in. But he didn't carry a gun much — he didn't walk around like he was somebody special. He did his job for the Maceo family, and then he went home to his wife. And after she died, he turned."

"That's what he calls it, too," I said. "His 'turn.'"

"That says it," Harry replied. "You could use more religious terms, I suppose. His salvation. His repentance. But I knew him, and I knew what direction he was going in. It was a turn."

"He told me that you doubted him at first."

"Did he now?" Harry smiled. "I guess I did. I dropped by his house a few times, just to check on him. He would invite me in, offer me a drink or some coffee, and ask about my work. And I'd tell him my work was going fine, and I'd ask if he was going to be doing anything that might add to it. He always said he wouldn't. To tell you the truth, I was thinking he was setting up a defense in case we charged him with the Ciotti shooting. Nicholas Ciotti — not Fuzzy. But after a few months, and then a few years, I began to believe him."

"I heard all this from Verini's perspective last night," I said. "Your stories match."

"There was one case a while after Verini changed — a doorman accidentally killed a drunk," Harry said. "It sounds uncommon, but those doormen were paid to remove the roughnecks and the rowdies, and to disturb the regular patrons as little as possible. So this drunk starts accusing the house of cheating, and he starts making a scene. The doorman grabs him, puts a hand over his mouth, and escorts him out. He hails a cab, inserts the drunk, and says, 'Take this guy home, wherever that is.' The cabbie looks back to ask the drunk where home is, and the drunk's dead. The medical examiner later said it was heart failure, but the doorman didn't know that. He was just a kid. He takes off, tries to hide out with Verini for a while. Verini calls me and asks permission to spend a few days talking to this kid about his soul. I said, 'What if I say no?' and the Old Man says, 'Then I'll bring him right to you.' I told Verini that my investigation found nothing obvious like a broken neck or a bullet wound in the head, so until the medical examiner's report was out, he could have the kid. So Verini thanks me and says he'll keep the kid around in case I need him later. Turns out I didn't need him, except to say at the inquest that the drunk seemed limp on one side as he escorted him out the door."

"Verini told me of another incident."

"Which would that be?"

"He said that when your wife died, he called to say he was sorry."

Harry nodded. "And that meant something to me when little else did, Emerson. Only because I knew what Verini had gone through. That might be when I really knew that he'd turned. He was a new man, Emerson."

I nodded. "That's a tough thing to be in a world full of old sins," I said.

The rest of the afternoon was spent dealing with deadlines and stories and such. My publisher, Louise, came and went, and my staff left before I did. I was alone in the office, working on an editorial at about 6 P.M., when Remington entered. "Have you eaten?"

"No," I said. "I was waiting here, hoping a beautiful woman would walk through that door and ask me for a date."

"Good answer. But watch how you word that. If you had said '*any* beautiful woman' instead of '*a* beautiful woman,' you'd have been in trouble. Next time try 'a *certain* beautiful woman.' It's better."

"Thanks for the safety tip, Officer Friendly. Now what did you have in mind?"

"Let's get something German."

I frowned at my love-pumpkin. "Love-pumpkin, some bad guys went in and trashed the German restaurant, remember?"

"Which is why we need to go and ask for some supper."

"Is this a female right-brain-thinking thing? Because if it is, I'll need a little more explanation than that."

"Emerson, the boys are hurt and discouraged. They need to be reminded that they're valuable, that they're capable. The way to do that is to demand that they cook for us. The oven was damaged, but the stove is fine, you said. Not every plate was broken. The pots are dented but still usable."

"I was right. Female right-brain thinking. I want supper, and you want to make someone feel better."

"Is that so bad?"

"No, my dear, it's wonderful. It's why I'm going to marry you and take you away from all of this. Let's go get some schnitzel."

Remington waited at the door as I turned off my computer and turned out the lights. I followed her out, then locked the door. We took her car to the restaurant, which had a prominent *Closed* sign hanging on the inside of the door. The fancy *Open* sign, the one that lighted up, wasn't lighted up. We parked and walked to the door; it was locked. Remington banged on it. After a moment Walter approached with a frown. He unlocked the door and let us in. "Yes?"

"We're hungry," Remington said, going to a table.

"A. C., we're closed."

"You were never closed for us before," she said, turning a beautifully innocent face to him. "Are you telling me you can't cook something just because you had a little ruckus in the kitchen? We can always go to McDonald's, if that's what you want."

Walter's legendary pride flared. "McDonald's? You will sit still and be quiet and I will cook!"

"How about that rouladen?" I asked.

Walter turned to glare at me. "You come in here, you demand that I serve you, and you expect to choose? I didn't let you choose before, so what makes you think you can now? You will eat what I prepare. I am the chef here. I have been to school — you have been to McDonald's. I have a variation on my jaegerschnitzel recipe I've wanted to try. Not that you could tell the difference, with your McDonald's palate."

From over his shoulder, I caught a glimpse of Gunther standing in the kitchen, listening to us and grinning.

"Jaegerschnitzel is fine," I said, taking a seat at the table Remington had chosen. "Tell me, Walter, does the new recipe call for quite as much cat gravy?"

18

Remington met me at my office Tuesday evening; she came
in carrying a pair of my slacks, a fresh shirt, a tie, and a
blazer.

"I've fed the dog," she said, "And I picked up these. When will
you be able to break away?"

"Now, believe it or not." It was 6:40, and the paper had been
finished for about an hour. Everyone else had gone home. Jimmy,
our courier, would be by to pick up the pages later that night. In
the olden days we'd be there until midnight or so, but now that
I had responsible reporters and a real social life, I had the
means, the motive, and the opportunity to finish my work at a
respectable hour. I was at my desk, proofing the front page again.
I took the page back to the box Jimmy carried them in to the
printer, then returned and took my clothes from Remington.

"I didn't dress up much last time," I said.

"But this time you're bringing me," Remington replied.

"In which case, there would be even less cause to dress up,
since you outshine everything and everyone in the room with
your looks," I said.

"Nice try, Dunn, but you're still wearing this tie and blazer.
Now go change."

I did as I was instructed. It's best to accept defeat with dignity.
I changed in the darkroom (it had the clothesline for hanging

stuff up), then went back into the newsroom. Remington was rifling my desk.

"Find any love letters from my other girlfriends?"

"Here's one from a girl named Eunice," Remington said. "She seems to feel you're brain-damaged if you think the city needs to create a reinvestment zone around the old downtown."

"That's a letter to the editor, not a love letter."

"Then I guess you're clean. Let's go."

Our timing was pretty good, actually. We drove down Highway 6 to Galveston, then took Broadway Boulevard. We had a few minutes to kill, so we drove all the way to the seawall and stood and watched the waves for a while. Remington held my hand tightly. The breeze from the Gulf took the edge off the summer heat, and the sun was setting off to our right.

"It makes you think forever's not such an impossible idea," she said over the patterned white noise of the waves.

I simply nodded. I had no idea what she was talking about.

"If God can make this go on forever, what's one marriage?"

Ah. As a trained investigative reporter, I picked up on the subtleties. She was talking about marriage. Particularly ours.

"Wait until you meet Verini," I said. "He's loved his wife, even though she's gone, for decades. Now there's a love story. See, it can be done. People don't have to be miserable."

"Theresa's on her third husband."

"Who?"

"My first editor at the UT newspaper. I've kept in touch with her some. She's on her third, and she's only two years older than me."

"Let's go," I said. It wasn't safe to hazard any guesses as to why Theresa couldn't keep a marriage going. I wasn't going to trust Theresa's wisdom to keep mine together; I was trusting God. Remington knew that, so I let it drop.

We walked back to her car, still holding hands. She brushed the sand off her shoes, and I did the same. We got back in the car and drove back toward Verini's house.

"It does sound like a love story," she said.

"Verini? Yes, it does. It has shaped his life. He loved her, and when she was gone, he decided to love what she loved."

"That's beautiful."

"So was she. When we go through the hall, slow down and take a look at the pictures. She has a nice smile."

We drove to Verini's house, and I parked where I parked before — on the street in front. The porch light was on, although it wasn't quite dark yet. I opened Remington's door for her, and she followed me up the walkway to the front door.

"The house is beautiful," she said.

"Yeah." I rang the bell, and a moment later Father O'Donnell answered the door. He smiled when he saw Remington. "Wonderful," he said. "Exactly what I meant. You've brought something of yourself, something important to you. Only it's a *someone* — all the better. Despite what he says, Al does get a little lonely. He likes new faces and new people to talk to."

"Father O'Donnell, this is my fiancée, A. C. Remington."

He took her hand and bowed a little. "My pleasure. Come in, come in. Al's in the library again . . . Through here."

Remington slowed at the pictures in the hallway; Father O'Donnell noticed. "That's his wife, Holly. She died some years ago."

"I know," Remington said. "Emerson was right; she was beautiful."

"We think so. And such a voice. Such an addition to the choir."

We followed the old priest as he led us to the room I'd found the Old Man in two nights before. Verini was sitting in the same chair, thumbing through the same small black book. He wore a dark suit, with the coat unbuttoned but the tie tight at his collar. When he saw Remington and me, his eyes grew bigger and brighter.

"Emerson, good to see you again. And this is, I presume, the fiancée you spoke of?"

"Yes. This is A. C. Remington."

"Alberto Verini," he said, taking her hand and grasping it. "Call me Al. Such an honor. Emerson spoke highly of you. You're going to law school; SMU, isn't it? Listen, I have a little real estate up that way. An apartment complex or two — Highland Park, University Park. I've made a list; I would have given it to Emerson, but now I can give it to you directly. If you've not found a place there yet, call some of the names on the list." He produced an envelope from his coat pocket and handed it to her.

"I'm overwhelmed," Remington said. "I'll be looking for a place next week. I don't know anything about the area, so this will really help. Thank you."

Verini looked pleased as punch at being able to help someone. "Sit, sit," he said.

Father O'Donnell moved a couple of chairs around so that we were all in a sort of semicircle. I had told Remington on the ride over about my blunder; she knew to spend a little time visiting before we got down to business.

"If you don't mind me saying it," she started, "I think your wife was beautiful."

"Mind?" Verini smiled. "How could I mind? Those pictures, they're just snapshots. I tried to convince her to make a portrait, but she was too shy. She thought it was prideful to sit in front of a painter for days. I should have insisted. But who knew?"

Remington nodded. "How long were you married?"

"Only about nine years, before she passed," Verini said. "Best nine years of my life."

"It sounds as though you recommend marriage."

Verini laughed. "I recommend it so highly that my nephew starts out his letters and his phone calls with 'No, Uncle Al, I'm not seeing anyone in particular right now.' But he's out of law school now, and maybe he'll settle down."

"Maybe he'll have time for a social life," I said.

"This is true." Verini nodded. "Can you imagine what it would be like to have an extended family of Italians watching your progress in school? A dozen relatives calling every week, asking if he's spending enough time studying? When he wasn't studying, he was answering the phone. Poor kid. But you, Miss Remington, tell me about you. Do you have an extended family of Italians?"

Remington laughed. "How did you guess? My mother's a Tortelli."

"I knew it, Father," Verini said. "I could tell."

"Tortellini? I didn't know that," I said

"Tortelli," Remington said. "And you never asked. But I forgive you."

"What kind of hosts are we, Father?" Verini asked the priest. "Miss Remington, and Emerson, can I get you something to drink?"

We both said no.

"Let me know if you change your minds," he said. "Miss Remington, that's a lovely suit. And Emerson is wearing a jacket tonight. Must be your doing."

She giggled. "He didn't complain too much."

"Good. Some are easier to civilize than others. For years our mothers break their backs and their hearts making us fit for some nice girl. And then once we find one, it takes more years for that nice girl to make us fit to live with."

This theme was haunting me — it must be a global conspiracy. "I'm fairly fit to live with," I said.

"Emerson," Verini said patiently, "do I know you well enough to say this? I think I do. Emerson, you hold your keys in your right hand. When you walked in, you were holding your keys in your right hand. Your right hand."

He emphasized the last two words.

"I'm not following you," I said.

"That's the hand you're supposed to reserve for her," he said. "That's the hand you hold hers with, the one you open the door for her with, the one with which you take her arm and help her up the steps."

I cleared my throat a little. He noticed and laughed.

"You thought I was going somewhere else with that?" he asked. "That maybe your right hand is your gun hand?"

"The thought occurred to me."

He and Father O'Donnell chuckled. "Not him," the old priest said.

"If I have a gun in the house now, it's only because the neighborhood isn't what it once was," Verini said. "I've never cared much for them."

"I'll remember that about my right hand," I said. "I never thought of it that way."

"Well, it's not something you're supposed to just know, just think of," Verini said, lifting his hands. "It's not your fault. No one knows these things anymore. You go to school, and you learn to belong to a gang and to shoot anyone who's not your friend. You know, Galveston County still has an Organized Crime Task Force. It has nothing to do with the kind of people I knew; they worry about gangs and dope dealers. Say what you will about the Maceos, they were never dope dealers."

"But what they did was bad enough," Father O'Donnell said with a hint of reproach. Verini took it in stride.

"The father's right, I suppose. Sin is sin; wrong is wrong. In the '20s, rum was an illegal substance. We still imported it."

"Smuggled," the priest said with a hint of a smile.

"Smuggled . . . right," Verini replied. "I was a driver, but not at first. At first I was muscle; they called us the Beach Gang. I rode in the back of the truck with a pistol, in case we got hijacked. That didn't last long. One night we did get hijacked, by some outfit from New Orleans. We were still on the beach, still loading from the rowboats. Well, the shooting starts, and I duck behind the truck and start firing. But my first shot goes right into our own engine block — a .45 will do that, you know. Once the shooting stopped, we had to steal their truck just to haul our hooch. From that point on, I was a driver. They let someone else shoot the guns. Ciotti was a shooter."

I glanced at Remington; she was listening closely.

"Which brings us to Francis," Verini said. "To business. I have thought about what you're asking, but I don't know that *you* have. Tell me what you're asking, and then I'll tell you what I am thinking."

I paused. "I guess we're asking that you use your influence to get Ciotti to leave our friends alone."

"Is this your understanding?" Verini asked Remington. She nodded. He sighed. "Let's look at it closer," he said. "First, you want me to use my influence. What is influence?"

"I guess I'm not really sure," I said.

"It's a threat. Nothing more. It's saying, 'I have more power than you, and I want you to do this.' In your world, Emerson, you have influence over your workers, am I right?"

"Yes."

"And where is that influence derived from? From the fact that you're the boss — you have more power. The threat is that you could fire them. So when you say, go cover a story, they go cover a story."

"I'll concede that there's an underlying threat," I said after a moment. "I guess I've always thought of it just as motivation."

"In Francis Ciotti's world, there's no talk of motivation. Influence to him is the threat of something more than just the loss of a job. If I went to him and said, 'Francis, I would like for you to walk away from these boys,' what would I be saying?"

Remington spoke up. "I see what you mean. Influence must be backed up with power."

"And power to Ciotti is violence. So if I used my influence, I would be threatening him with violence."

"What if you did it because he owes you so many favors?" I said.

"You understand favors," Verini said gently. "I understand favors. We all understand goodwill and good faith. But Francis Ciotti doesn't understand that. So many years ago I took him under my wing, Emerson, because I saw the darker side of me, and I wanted to reform it through reforming him. I thought I could make him a new man. But I couldn't. Yes, I loved him and still do, but I see him for what he is. He's just what you said — a crook. Now, Emerson, you understand that I have the juice to put him down. I could back up any threats I made — or even implied. There are men in Houston, in Vegas, in New York, in New Orleans whom I could call and no questions would be asked. But is that a Pandora's box you want me to open?"

Remington spoke slowly. "No . . . you're right. You have more wisdom than we showed in even asking you."

I nodded. "I agree. It was wrong to ask."

"No, it wasn't wrong," Verini said gently. "Because I'm not saying no. I can help perhaps. But not in that way."

I hesitated. "There is a Plan B," I said.

"And?" Verini said, looking interested.

"We might not even need your help, except for maybe some background information. You see, there's no real law against being a low-life loan shark. But there are laws against murder, and those laws don't have statutes of limitation."

Verini nodded encouragingly.

I continued. "Harry Singer is getting some old files from the Galveston DA's office. You know — in fact, you told me — that none of Ciotti's shootings in the '40s and '50s went to trial — probably because of bribery. So if we find enough evidence in even one of those files, then the DA — who by all accounts is clean — might try a case. Then Ciotti will be out of the picture, and our friends will be safe."

Verini thought for a moment. "That's not a bad plan," he said. "But it has pitfalls."

"I know. The age of the cases, for one thing."

The Old Man nodded. "And also, the DA is clean, but a lot of people are still beholden to Francis Ciotti. They could bring a lot of pressure down on the DA to let sleeping dogs lie."

"That's true, but that's where I come in."

"How so?" he asked.

"I'm a newspaperman. I could run an article — better yet, a

series of articles — on how Francis Ciotti is walking free when they have all this evidence to try him on murders — even old murders. Remember, it's awfully close to election time."

Verini thought about this for a moment. "Tell me, don't newspapers have territories, jurisdictions perhaps? Like law enforcement agencies?"

"Sure. We call it our coverage area. To make the story local, all I have to do is point out that he's operating in my county, Brazoria County. And the restaurant is right around the corner from the newspaper office, which puts it in my coverage area."

"Oh, he's operating in your county, all right," Verini said. "More loans, mostly. Contributes to some of your county's politicians too. In the late 1950s he moved inland and just spread like a disease."

"Then I can use my own influence."

Verini nodded in approval. "You're a smart man, Emerson. I'll give you what help I can."

"Emerson," the priest spoke up, "be careful with your facts."

"How so?"

Verini picked up the father's thought. "If you publish information such as that, you'd be showing your hand. If your gamble didn't work, Ciotti would still be walking the streets, and he'd be a little annoyed that you'd smeared his reputation. Remember, never show your hand if you can help it."

"I'll remember that."

Verini's last bit of advice was somehow a signal that the evening was over. Remington knew it also. We stood, and she took his hand. "It was a pleasure meeting you," she said.

"The pleasure was mine, young lady," he said. He turned to me. "Tell me, do you feel your friends are safe?"

"We think so. If there's any indication otherwise, I have another friend, an Israeli, who will stay with them."

"An Israeli? You know, we had a man, a man named Rosenberg, maybe? Rosenbaum? Anyway, he left in 1948 to fight

for Israel. He was an interesting man. Next time you come, bring
your Israeli friend. I would like to meet him."

"I'll do that."

"Good. Now, do you think you will have files soon?"

"Tomorrow."

"And you'll need my memory when?"

"Maybe tomorrow night, if you're free."

"Tomorrow night is fine. I'll see you then. Same time."

I shook his hand again, and Father O'Donnell led us to the
front door. "You're doing him a wonderful service," the old priest
said softly as he opened the door. "He hasn't made peace with
his past yet. This may be a way . . . to bring a bit of good out of
it. It's what he needs. He doesn't feel he's right with our Lord yet.
Maybe you can help."

"I'm not a theologian," Remington said just as softly, "but I
think he's about as right with God as anyone can get."

"I *am* a theologian." Father O'Donnell smiled. "And I agree
with you completely. But his soul needs peace. That's something
he hasn't found, something he won't find until he's dealt with his
past."

I left work at noon on Wednesday. It was usually a slow day anyway, and I knew Thursday night would be a long one, with both a school board meeting and a City Council meeting. When I left, Robert was eyeing my chair longingly. I insulted his hair.

I drove to Harry Singer's house; Bill Singer was meeting us there for lunch and for information. He arrived a moment after I did. Harry was waiting at the door for us.

"Billy, did you bring the oregano?" he asked as we entered.

"In my coat pocket," Bill said. "Did you get the files?"

Harry nodded as he closed the door behind us. "An old friend came through. I have six viable cases, I think, out of nine shooting incidents. There were maybe a dozen more in which Ciotti was implicated, but these six are the strongest. I figure that gives us each two cases to check out."

We followed Harry to the table, which as usual was already spread. This time it was tortellini. It could have been a coincidence, but . . .

"You're going to have to change your ways, Dunn," Bill said as he sat down in his usual chair. "I know you've done investigations before, but this is different. You'll have to think like a cop. No unnamed sources, no allegations. Just hard evidence — stuff that won't embarrass the DA."

"I can do that," I said, still humbled by the tortellini.

Harry brought out the bread, and he said the blessing. We talked as we ate; Harry asked about Verini.

"My impression is that he's a solid old man," I said. "He has legitimate investments, a good community record for the last forty years, and a real conviction that he needs to do what's right."

"Is he slowing down any?" Harry asked gently. "You didn't know him before, but can you see signs? He's older than me, you know."

"That's not old, Dad," Bill interjected.

"His eyes are clear, and his mind seems sharp," I said. "He's very analytical. His trains of thought don't make too many side-trips."

Harry nodded. "And he's volunteered to help us with the investigations, should we need background information?"

"Right."

"But you didn't mention that you might need him to testify."

"Not yet. Let's let him get involved in the cause," I said. "He's still Alberto Verini; any talk of going before a jury probably still makes him a little edgy."

"He's still Alberto Verini," Bill agreed. "And he still might have some loyalty to the old code: you don't rat on business associates. It was true then, and it might be true for him to this day."

Harry nodded. "If you get any resistance, it won't be because he wants to do wrong. It will be because the Old Man won't know how far to go to do what's right." He shook his head. "But, boys, this is speculation. We have six cases here, six good chances to get Ciotti on our own."

"Let's go over them, Dad," Singer said. "I've got to get back pretty soon for a meeting."

Harry nodded and produced six file folders from a briefcase beside his chair. I stood and gathered the dishes, then put them in a sink that was already full of soapy water. I went back to my seat, and Harry handed me two files.

"We'll go over mine first," Harry said. "Mine are the oldest ones — 1935 and 1941. In July of 1935, one George Musey was gunned down in front of a restaurant on 24th Street. Ciotti was a young buck then."

"Musey," Bill said. "Wasn't he a bad guy, too?"

Harry laughed. "George Musey was before my time, son, but I've heard the stories. Sure, Musey was a bad guy. He was a Syrian, if I recall correctly, who started a rival gang in Galveston. He started with bootleg whiskey and ended up with a syndicate all his own. The Maceos suspected that during Prohibition he was behind a few of the truck hijackings. He was also behind some assassination attempts. See, there was a Customs agent back then, a stand-up guy named Al Scharff. Of course, just like a lot of the Customs agents then, he'd been a counterfeiter and a smuggler himself until he saw the light, so to speak. He started out his law enforcement career in 1924 and quickly became a thorn in the side of the Galveston bootleggers.

"But for some reason the Maceos took a liking to him. I hear they once offered him twenty-five thousand dollars, and he refused — politely. They liked that. But not Musey. Musey hated Scharff. So Musey calls in some hitters from Chicago to put Scharff out of the picture. But luck was on Scharff's side — as it usually was. The two hitters stopped in a bar before the job and had a drink. A Maceo employee — all I remember him being called was 'Big Jim' — was at that same bar and got a little suspicious. He called Sam Maceo, and together they convinced the Chicago boys to go back north without making any trouble.

"A couple of months later, Musey tries again, bringing in some talent from Kentucky. Again Maceo muscle convinced them to leave — they even put a tail on Scharff themselves to keep him safe. Well, Musey left town soon after that. He wound up in Lake Charles, got busted, and did six years in a Louisiana prison. When he got out, he went back to Galveston and opened up a gambling hall. I figure the Maceos would have let him do his thing — they let a number of smaller operations go on during the time they were on top — but he got greedy. So he died of lead poisoning — the kind you get from a bullet. A man named Windy Goss was charged but got off."

"What links Ciotti to that one?" Bill asked.

"Good question, my boy," Harry said. "Two eyewitnesses. They were going into the restaurant and gave officers a description of a short, balding young man. Goss had a full head of hair."

"So the cops pick up Goss instead of Ciotti, and of course Goss is acquitted," Bill said. "I like it. What about these eyewitnesses?"

"We'll just have to hope they're alive," Harry said. "Their statements could be used as evidence, but it wouldn't be as strong as having the two geezers on the stand."

"Dad, that's not nice," Bill said. "What about 1941?"

"Right," Harry replied, opening his other folder. "19 February 1941. In an altercation over a race result, one Julian Newman is gunned down outside the Turf Club — that was where the Maceos headquartered their operation. The building housed the Studio Lounge, the Turf Athletic Club — I saw my first live prizefight there — and the Western Room. There's little information in the file, except that everyone knew that the race results broadcast in the Turf Club and the Western Room were legit. Anyway, we've got statements in here about how about a dozen people saw the altercation and remembered the cause, but couldn't remember what the shooter looked like. One gambler — is this smart, or what? — was trying so hard to keep from saying Ciotti's name that he would only refer to him as 'the bald guy.' You know, like this quote: 'Then the bald guy punches Newman a good one, which he deserved.' Of the dozen names in here, at least a few have to still be around."

Bill nodded. "What about my cases?"

"The top file is a promising one," Harry said. "It was 1952 — a long time ago, but not so long ago that everyone's going to be gone. In 1952 Sam was dead — he'd passed the year earlier, of cancer. Papa Rose wasn't well. Other Mafia syndicates were sniffing around, getting a little pushy. They knew Galveston was good territory, and they wanted in on the action. With Sam gone and Rose sick, a few tried to come in and 'invest.' You had some of Capone's gang come in earlier, and Albert Anastasia from New York. Papa Rose knew the Maceo empire was on its way out, but he wanted to keep the jackals away for as long as he could. When he heard about a Chicago 'investor' and his bodyguard showing up at the Balinese Room, he sends in Ciotti. Ciotti pals up to Mr. Chicago and buys him enough rum to get him and his bodyguard plastered. Now, you wouldn't catch a Maceo bodyguard drinking on the job, nossir. But Mr. Chicago — his name was Lubrano — had let his judgment slip. See, that's the thing about the Maceo clubs. Did you know they were all kept at 69 degrees? That was so you could drink more and not feel it. That was Sam's theory, anyway. I don't know if it's medically sound. Anyway, Lubrano and his guy get drunk out of their heads, and Ciotti offers to get them a cab and take them back to their hotel. They all three get in the cab, and only Ciotti gets out at the hotel. He uses the room key, gathers up the luggage, and tells the clerk that the Lubrano party has checked out — charge it to the Maceos."

"And I assume Ciotti didn't put the ailing Mr. Lubrano and his assistant on an airplane back to Chicago," I speculated.

"I assume you're right. They never showed up anywhere. My guess is they're in the ship channel."

"Still waiting for a ride," Bill said. "What do we have? I see statements from the hotel clerk, statements from Lubrano's wife and employer that he never returned. We need the cabbie."

"That's the first thing you should check, son," Harry said. "He might be here, but my source in the department says he might have been given a first-rate job in Vegas as a reward for his lack of testimony. Check out there, too."

"I will," Bill said. "What's my second case?"

"Another shooting, 1954. The month after Papa Rose died. It wasn't on the island; it was in Kemah, up on the bay — near where NASA is now. The Maceos had some interests up there, and Ciotti was trying to get what he could on the mainland. He clashed with a transplanted Cajun; he won. The Cajun, a man named Mathias Rombeaux, had a little restaurant with crawfish and slot machines. Ciotti went in, December 12, and told him that he wanted 50 percent of the take from the slots. Rombeaux said he owned the slots outright, that he'd bought them from Papa Rose. A week later Rombeaux was shot dead as he took out the trash."

"Anyone see the shooting?" I asked.

"No, but a couple driving up to the restaurant said they could identify the car. No one ever asked them to. The case was never even fully investigated."

"Okay," I said. "Now what do I have?"

"Open your first file, Emerson, and you'll see a rather detailed photograph of one Mitchell Ryan. In 1959 Ryan owned a little bar in Galveston, a few blocks off the Strand, and seems to have gotten himself in some financial trouble. He was a recent immigrant, you see, and the banks were reluctant to loan to him. So he goes to Ciotti. This is well after the heyday of Galveston's sin district was over — remember, Galveston was cleaned up in 1957 — and Ryan just couldn't make a go of it. He was picked up by the police on October 12 for armed robbery. He was the driver for a job at a small jewelry store — and the only one identified. He wore a mask, but a store clerk was a regular at Ryan's bar and recognized the barman's voice when he shouted at his partners to hurry — a distinct Irish brogue. So the department picks him up that same night on that charge and tries to convince him to say who his two friends were. He didn't, of course, and after Ciotti generously posts his bail the next day, he walks out. Two days later, on October 15, his body is found on West Beach. His hands were tied behind his back, and he had a single gunshot wound to his forehead."

"It all sounds like circumstantial evidence," I said.

"It is," Harry admitted. "But don't forget Ryan's widow. A tough one, I can tell you. I remember her well. Mary, I believe. Even though the police dropped the investigation after a day or so, she kept it up. She showed up at the DA's office a week later with a letter that she said Ryan had mailed to himself as soon as he got out of jail. She said — and mind you, no one else ever saw the letter — that Ryan wrote that Ciotti was planning to kill him to keep from being implicated in the jewelry store robbery."

"Why wouldn't she show it to the police?" I asked.

"She didn't trust us, Emerson," Harry said. "She was angry, fearful — and remember, she was still new to the country, too. She wanted to talk to the DA, and the DA alone. We scheduled a time, but she backed out and later said there was no letter."

"What was your feeling at the time, Dad?" Bill asked.

"I believed her with all my heart," Harry replied. "Still do. I think Ciotti got to her."

"Is she still around?" I asked.

"I think so — at least she was a few years ago. I remember seeing her walking along the seawall one day. I slowed my car, said hello. She smiled at me, then nodded hello. She looked well, that's all I can say. That was maybe ten years ago."

"What's my other case?"

"An aberration, Emerson. A drowning. Ciotti had numerous business associates and business rivals. It was usually tough to figure out who was which. Well, he fancied himself a sport fisherman, and he owned a boat — a trawler. He took friends out; they'd drink some beer and drown some bait. It was a reward for those who did what they were supposed to do. Ciotti had one associate who ran a courier service — a man like Ciotti just doesn't call a Pinkerton armored car to take his holdings to the bank. So Hank Henry, Jr. would send a couple of big old boys around to Ciotti's various business interests, collect the money, and take it to the bank. Ciotti, of course, did the hard collections himself. Well, it turned out that Hank Henry, Jr. was upping the percentage rate on a few of Ciotti's loans without Ciotti's knowledge. Not that Ciotti was against increased interest rates; it's just that Hank Henry, Jr. was getting all the extra money."

"Let me guess," I said. "They went fishing, and Hank Henry, Jr. fell off the boat."

"And the next day he washes ashore near Freeport. After that Ciotti hired more reliable — and less independent — thugs to do his collecting."

"Who do we have?" I asked.

"The captain of Ciotti's boat was a loyal employee for years and died of amazingly natural causes not long ago. But there was a deckhand, a Lou Carlton, who was on board. He was seventeen at the time; he's captaining his own charter fishing boat out of Galveston now."

"Got it," I said. "Now tell me how you got these files."

Harry grinned. "Someone kindly left me alone with a copier for about two hours," he said. "I spoke to the DA about all of this. He's willing to take something to the grand jury if we come up with something solid."

"Great," I said. "I've got the rest of the afternoon to start in on this. I'm visiting Al Verini again tonight at 8 P.M., so I thought I'd just spend the whole day in Galveston. I'm taking David with me, too. Verini wants to meet him."

"Dad, how tight is the DA's office these days?" Bill asked hesitantly.

"Zipped up nicely," Harry said with a smile. "Those are honest folks, son. If anyone tips off Ciotti that we're after him, I'll be surprised. Even if they do, where's the harm? With us three on the job, Ciotti will know to lay low. If he had any brains at all, he'd think this was a good time for a trip abroad."

20

I was back to watching the clock. It said 3:54. I still had a few minutes until I'd be called to the stand, and I couldn't decide if those minutes were too long or too short. Percy had apparently decided they were too long; his eyelids were getting heavy. He'd stopped reading the paper and was now just holding it to his chest.

"You can't go to sleep and leave me to worry all by myself," I said.

Percy smiled without opening his eyes. "I'm not asleep, son. Ever-watchful, that's me. It's taken years of training for me to be ever-watchful with my eyes closed."

"Sounds like a good talent to have."

"It's not bad," he said, opening his eyes. "Now what's this about worrying? I thought we were through with that."

"Nope."

"Well, don't. It's going to be over in a few minutes. And just like the lawyer said, this is the way your friend wanted it — a clean ending, a clean break."

"Those are rare in this life, aren't they?"

"Clean endings? I suppose they are. Look at my boy's divorces. Those weren't clean breaks. He still hears from both of those ex-wives all the time. Still so many issues left unresolved."

"I wonder if I've ever made a true clean break from anything.

I guess when I joined the church, I tried to put most of my past behind me. But that doesn't always work, does it?"

"No, I suppose it doesn't."

"My friend David has much more to break from . . . Born and raised an Israeli Jew. Joining the church would have to mean more to someone like him; it would mean giving up much more than I did. I left some friends who weren't doing me any good anyway. A Jew would have to risk offending some members of his family."

"Is your friend close to a decision?"

"He's made it. Maybe that's something good that's come out of all this. He got a nudge or two."

21

David met me at my house about thirty minutes after I left Harry's. That gave me time to change and to put a tie and a jacket on a hanger to take with me. I checked my cash flow and found that I was actually able to buy David a seafood dinner. I also took the time to call Galveston information and get an address and telephone number for both Mary Ryan and Lou Carlton. Mary Ryan would be well past retirement age, I knew, so she'd likely be at home. Lou Carlton would probably be out in the Gulf until this evening; I could try to catch him at the Galveston Yacht Basin when the fishing boats came in just before sunset.

Airborne's tail started wagging when David walked in. I read somewhere that dogs are pretty dumb. They think that people are just big, ugly, hairless dogs and we've let them join our pack. That's how they think, which explains why a dog will obey one person in the house but sometimes not another person. It has to do with rank within the pack. That theory would also explain why Airborne was so happy to see David — they looked. more like each other, in my opinion. I explained this theory to David.

"That's the dumbest thing I've heard in months," he said.

"But qualified animal psychologists say it's true," I replied. "And besides, you're hairier than I am."

He said something in Hebrew to Airborne; I think they were talking about me.

"Let's go," David said after a moment. "I've only got one day off left. If we're going to investigate these cases, we'd better get started."

I told David everything I knew about Mary Ryan and Lou Carlton during the drive to Galveston.

"What did Mary Ryan do after her husband died?" David asked.

"The file doesn't say. We'll have to ask."

We drove across the causeway onto the island at about 2:30; we had about five and a half hours until our appointment with the Old Man. Hopefully, we could uncover enough to ask intelligent questions of him.

Mary Ryan's address was listed as being on a street bearing a pirate's name. I knew the subdivision, out on the western part of the island. We drove down Seawall Boulevard for a few miles until we found a convenience store. We stopped and asked directions to that particular street, and a clerk with a detailed map told us right where to find it. We drove for a few more blocks, through streets of shabbily built homes, all painted pastel colors. David commented on how pretty some of the colors were. I kept my mouth shut.

We found Mary Ryan's house backed up to a small canal. Her driveway faced the road, but the home faced the canal. Like most of the other homes in the subdivision, the house was on stilts. The driveway led to a carport sheltered by the house itself. We parked under the house, then went around to the stairs leading up to the door, looking out over the canal.

Before we mounted the stairs, we heard a voice.

"She's not home," an old woman said. "She's on the jetties today. Like most days."

I looked to my right. A woman with a sun hat, long sleeves, and sunglasses was sunbathing next door.

"You know Mary Ryan?" I asked.

"I've known her for years," the woman said. "And I know that almost every day, for years, if the weather's nice she'll go and fish the jetties."

"There are a lot of jetties," I said. "Any idea where we'd find her?"

"Look on the jetties around the end of the seawall," the woman said after a moment. "Last night she was saying that she'd heard they were biting there."

"Thanks," I said.

The old woman frowned. "Who shall I say was calling, if you don't find her?"

I took a card from my pocket. "Here," I said. "Just give her this."

The card didn't pacify her. "And what shall I say it's in reference to?"

"I'm doing some fishing myself," I said.

The old woman's eyes narrowed, but she let it pass.

"Take her some lunch," she said. "She hasn't been back today, and she rarely thinks to pack one herself. She'll get out there, get distracted, and go all day without eating."

David smiled. "We'll do that. Does she like hamburgers?"

"I suppose that will do."

"Thanks," I said. "You've been a big help."

The woman nodded and laid back down in the chaise lounge. As far as I could tell, there wasn't a single square inch of skin exposed to the sun. I was a little confused, but I didn't ask.

David and I drove back through the subdivision, then found a burger joint on Seawall Boulevard. We drove through and ordered a burger, fries, and three soft drinks.

The seawall, built after the 1900 storm that killed hundreds of island residents, is a little more than ten miles long. We drove to the far end of it and parked near where Remington and I had stood the evening before. Out on a jetty a few yards down the beach, we could see a lone woman with a fishing pole. She stood out from the groups of families who dotted the beach, and from a group of fishermen who occupied the next jetty over. She was alone, whether the beach was full or not.

"That's her," I said.

David nodded and gathered his camera bag while I gathered Mary Ryan's lunch. David didn't plan to get any photos of Mary Ryan; he was just hoping for a sailboat or two and a nice sunset.

We walked out onto the jetty, hopping from rock to rock, for more than thirty yards. As we approached Mary Ryan, it was clear from the roar of the surf that she couldn't hear us, but she seemed to sense our intrusion onto her jetty. When we were almost upon her, she looked up. Mild surprise registered on her face when she realized we were heading for her, not for a spot to fish.

"Mary Ryan?" I asked.

"Yes?"

"Hi. We brought you some lunch."

She smiled. "And why should I be accepting lunch from strangers?"

"Because your neighbor said you probably hadn't eaten yet," I said.

"What interest is that of yours?" She was still smiling. Her gray hair was long, but tied up in back. Her face was deeply tanned and slightly wrinkled. Her hands, holding a fiberglass fishing rod, were strong and unadorned. She wore canvas pants and a blue cotton top.

"It's just lunch," I said. David grinned. "If you don't want it, Mrs. Ryan, I'll eat it."

"Now, I didn't say that, did I?"

"Here," I said, handing her the bag. "A hamburger and something to drink. Do you mind if we sit?"

She accepted the bag somewhat hesitantly; hesitant not out of fear, but out of uncertainty, it seemed. "I'll not mind you sitting if you'll answer my question: of what interest am I to you?"

David was already sitting cross-legged, facing out to the Gulf, searching the waters. I sat down a little closer to Mary Ryan and breathed deeply of the wet, salty air.

"I have some friends, Mrs. Ryan, who own a little restaurant. They're in debt with a man named Francis Ciotti."

Mary Ryan's expression didn't change. She was studying my face, looking for honesty, I suppose. "Go on."

"There's no law against lending people money," I said. "But there is a law against murder. We want to put Ciotti away, and there's a chance we can do it if we resurrect an old murder case."

"What's that to do with me?"

"In 1959 your husband owned a bar, he got into debt with Ciotti, and he died because of it," I said gently. "I don't want the same thing to happen to my friends."

Mary Ryan nodded. "Who are you, boy?"

"My name is Emerson Dunn. This is David Ben Zadok, another friend."

"Are you even thirty years old yet?"

"Not quite."

"You weren't even born, boy." She didn't say it harshly, just matter-of-factly. "What do you know of men like Ciotti?"

"Enough to know that he should be in prison."

She laughed. "He'll be in Hell soon enough, Emerson Dunn. What do you want from me?"

"I want to know about the letter."

She nodded. "If you were from Francis Ciotti himself, you'd know not to ask that question. The letter. We were new to the country, boy. Shipped into Galveston Bay, stayed on Pelican Island, began our new lives here. Sure, we had some money from home. All our families could spare. We were to come here, build a business, then send for brothers and sisters and cousins and maybe, someday, for my mother. But in 1959 America wasn't quite the land of opportunities she had been, was she? Sure, there were opportunities, but everything was changing then. Galveston was a royal jumble; it was chancy to start up here in the first place. But Mitchell was a Corkman, and he said wherever there's sailors, there's a sure spot for a bar. It wasn't much of a success, though, was it?"

I waited.

"It wasn't mismanagement," she continued. "It was more that Mitchell didn't know his way around yet. When Francis Ciotti came and offered to give him a hand in running the place, and even invest some capital, my husband accepted. He didn't know what Francis Ciotti was going to want. First, it was a slot machine or two in the back, then Mitchell was driving that car . . ."

"I'm sorry . . ."

She smiled. "Yes, boy, there was a letter. It came in the post a few days after he died. He'd mailed it to himself, knowing I'd read it if anything happened. Ciotti was afraid he would talk, but if he knew Mitchell, he wouldn't have been afraid at all."

"And you were going to take that letter to the district attorney."

"Yes, I was. But it wasn't mine for long. Soon after the police knew about it, my home was broken into and ransacked. I still lived above the bar. They knew right where to find it, of course — in the safe. Where else would it be? And the safe wasn't blown apart or jimmied or stolen outright; it was opened nice as you please and closed and relocked. Who else but a business partner would have had that combination, I ask you? Ransacking my rooms was just a diversion, I think, so I wouldn't know it was him."

I nodded. "What did you do after that?"

"I knew all was lost; I'd have been back to Cork myself if it hadn't been for the bank. They came 'round a few days later and said Mitchell had paid off the loan on the building. I went to the church, after that, you see, and I prayed. I felt that maybe God was wanting me to stay a little longer, to see if I couldn't make a go of it."

"Did you?"

She laughed. "Not me, boy. But my brother did. He came over, and we decided that if we were to stay the course, we'd best be concentrating on the tourists instead of the drunk sailors. We started selling trinkets and T-shirts, renting bicycles and beach umbrellas. It's done pretty well. My brother still runs it; whenever I get involved he gets a little nervous. I never did have a head for numbers. So I can do as I please all day. What I please just happens to be fishing."

"That's what I would do," David said.

Mary Ryan turned a smile to him. "Who wouldn't?" she asked.

David smiled, then turned back to his camera bag; he took out his favorite — a Nikon — and started staring through the lens at the four or five boats on the horizon.

"Have you seen Ciotti since then?" I asked.

"No. He's stayed far away from me," she said. "I think he knows better than to come too close. I never remarried. For me it's always been Mitchell. Not that I'm bitter; I'm not, mind you. But I don't think Francis Ciotti has a mind to try my temper."

"Would you be willing to testify in court that you had that letter and then it was stolen?"

Mary Ryan laughed. "I was willing then, but we all knew what kind of help that would be. A distraught widow — a senile one now — talking about something that doesn't exist, that no one else ever saw. Think like a lawyer, and you'll see the fun you'd have with that one. There just wasn't enough to it then, and there's less to it now. It's not worth my time, or yours."

I paused. "Maybe you're right."

"You know I'm right, boy. Here," she said, turning to David and handing him her pole. "Take this while I eat. You know what to do with it, don't you?"

David grinned in reply. He put down his camera and took the pole. He cast gracefully out toward the sea, then slowly started reeling the lure in.

"Slower, boy," Mary Ryan said. "Slower or you'll scare them away. They're a bit skittish this afternoon."

David nodded.

She took a handbag from beside her and found some of those moist, disposable washcloths. She cleansed her hands and opened the bag from the burger joint. "This was kind of you," she said. "Kinder than I've been to you."

"You've told us what we needed to hear," I said.

She shook her head. "But you came and offered me food and a way to make peace with my past."

"Peace with your past . . . Everyone needs that."

"It's peace your friends are looking for," she said. "But with Ciotti walking God's green earth, they'll not find it."

"Probably not."

"I'm sorry for what I said before. I'll do what you ask. If you want to let an old woman ramble on the witness stand about an old letter, you'll find me willing."

"In and of itself, your testimony probably won't do much," I admitted. "But if it went toward showing a pattern, a way of doing business, it could help."

Mary Ryan ate in silence; some gulls began to get interested in her meal, but she ignored them. David fished for another twenty minutes or so, then surrendered the pole to our host. She smiled.

"Do you have my number?" she asked.

"Yes," I said. "I'll call you with any developments."

"Do that," she said softly. "It's not an easy task you two have picked out for yourselves."

"We have help," David said. "Lots of help."

Mary Ryan smiled. "And you have my prayers."

We left Mary Ryan on the jetty, humming softly to herself. We made our way back to David's car. "It's about 4:30," he said. "Let's go by the docks and look for the other guy. And if he's not there, we'll find some dinner."

"Great," I said.

Instead of starting his car, David hesitated. "She wants to make peace with her past. Well, who doesn't?"

He started the car decisively and gunned the engine. We

pulled out onto Seawall Boulevard and drove toward the other side of the island, where the yacht basin was.

About twenty minutes later we slowed in front of the yacht basin's security gate. The tanned blonde girl at the booth waved us on; maybe we looked like yachtsmen. But instead of going through, David rolled down his window.

"We're looking for a boat," he said. "The captain is Lou . . ." He looked at me. "Carlton," I said. "Carlton," David repeated. The girl consulted a list.

"Oh, Louis? He's in slip 247. Down there, take a left, then about halfway down."

"Do you know if he's in?"

"He's doing some repairs," she said. "Had to turn away a charter this morning. Engine trouble. He should be there."

"Thanks," David said with that silly grin of his. I tried to ignore the fact that not only did my dog respond better to him, so did tanned blondes.

We parked and followed Goldie's directions. We walked along the floating dock until we found a sheltered slip with a forty- to fifty-foot trawler. A tall, bulky, tanned man of about forty-five was on the deck, looking down into the engine compartment. He was pacing, and he seemed to be growling.

"Lou Carlton?" I asked. He looked at me with a little of the anger he was feeling toward whatever was down in the engine compartment.

"Yeah?"

"I'm Emerson Dunn. This is David Ben Zadok. Can we talk?"

He softened a bit. "Come aboard. The cabin's air-conditioned. Want a beer?"

"No, thanks," I said as I stepped from the dock onto the deck of the boat. It was a gorgeous craft, well maintained and orderly. David stepped onto the boat after me; we followed Carlton forward into the cabin. Inside we were greeted with cool air in our faces and soft couches lining the bulkheads.

"Have a seat," Carlton said, taking one himself. He was wear-

ing shorts and deck shoes and a T-shirt from a fishing tourna-
ment that had occurred about ten years earlier. "What do you
want to talk about?"

"A man named Francis Ciotti," I said.

Carlton grinned. "He send you? Well, the discount stands, but
I'm not going out for another couple of days. Blew a head gas-
ket. You in town for long? I can take you this weekend."

I felt David start to tense.

"No, that's not exactly why we're here," I said. "We're not
really *friends* of Ciotti's. We want to talk to you about something
that happened a few years back."

Carlton didn't lose his grin. "You boys ought to know better
than to be asking about things that happened a few years back.
Where will that sort of talk get you?"

Carlton was leaning back on his side of the boat, his arms
spread wide. He looked relaxed, as if he spent more time on his
boat than he did on dry land.

"Mr. Carlton, we're trying to help some friends," I said.

"And that's a nice thing to do. Will this help *my* friend, Francis
Ciotti?"

I smiled. "Probably not. I guess we've taken up enough of your
time."

Carlton shook his head, still smiling. "I'm a little curious. What
were you going to ask me about?"

"About a man named Hank Henry, Jr. who didn't have nice,
non-slippery deck shoes like yours."

"That was more than a few years back," he said, standing. He
made a stretching gesture, then sat back down a couple of feet
from where he'd been originally. I was watching his face, but
from the corner of my eyes I saw his left hand start to slide
toward a drawer in the bulkhead. From beside me I heard
David's soft voice.

"If I lose sight of your hand, Mr. Carlton, I'm going to break
your arm." He said it without malice. "Then I'll think about your
other arm."

Carlton stared at him. "You think you're that quick, boy?"

"I know I am."

Carlton never lost his smile, but he started inching his hand back away from the drawer. "What exactly did you want to know about Hank Henry?"

"Was he murdered?" I asked.

"It was ruled an accidental drowning."

"But you were there, Carlton," I said. "You know better. Hank had been skimming off the top, and Ciotti found out and decided to let him swim with the fishes."

David looked at me. "Swim with the fishes?"

"David, it's not polite to criticize my idioms in front of the criminal element."

"Sorry."

"Was there a question in there?" Carlton asked.

"Was it murder?" I repeated.

"You want to know all about Hank?" he asked. Then he made his move. In the time it took him to reach the drawer and open it, David had a hand on Carlton's left arm and his other fist in Carlton's stomach. Carlton's free hand made a wide swing, but David ducked inside of it. Still gripping Carlton's right arm, David threw the larger man across the cabin — straight toward me.

"What am I supposed to do with him?" I asked. David probably didn't hear me because of the thumping noise Carlton's head made on the bulkhead next to me. Carlton sank down slowly, but David yanked him back up and threw him to the floor. Carlton covered his head with his arms; after a moment he seemed to realize that neither of us was going to kick him when he was down.

"David's kind of cranky today," I said. "I don't know what it is. But you never answered our question."

I helped Carlton up, with David watching warily. As Carlton slumped onto the couch, David reached into the still-open drawer and took out a pistol. It was a nickel-plated revolver.

David opened the cylinder and checked to see if it was loaded; it was. Carlton's forehead was red where he'd hit the bulkhead. I wasn't feeling sympathetic.

"Now about our question . . ." I said.

"I'm not talking. I don't know who you are, but you can't push me around like that. I'm connected."

"I can connect him," David said amiably. "You have 110 volts coming into this boat? Or 12 volts with an AC/DC converter?"

"Mr. Carlton, please," I added, "all we need to know is whether Hank Henry, Jr. was really as clumsy as they say he was."

"I'm not telling you anything. Thanks to your friendly visit, you're dead. But if you walk out of here right this minute and leave me alone, I might call off a few dogs."

"I've been threatened by scarier men than you," David said. "I'm not impressed."

"And I've had punks tougher than you killed," Carlton replied.

"Yeah, and my dog is bigger than your dog," I said. "This isn't getting us anywhere. Carlton, we're obviously not going to get any answers out of you without doing more than we're willing to do."

"I'm willing," David said.

I ignored him, but I hoped Carlton wouldn't. "We're leaving now, and I'm sure that within a few seconds Francis Ciotti's going to hear about our visit. Let me warn you, Mr. Carlton — when he goes down, you could go down too. For all I know, it might have been you who threw Hank overboard."

Carlton just glared. David held on to the pistol. "I'll just keep this for now," he said. I exited the cabin, and David followed a few paces behind. We hopped onto the dock and walked quickly back up to David's car. After a few minutes I knew Carlton wasn't following us with a spare shotgun.

"David, you want to explain that?" I asked as we got into his car. "You've always been good at that, but you've never seemed to enjoy it so much. And come to think of it, something's been on your mind lately . . . since our mystery-solving adventures in Dallas. What's going on, Dave?"

"Something you said. Or something she said."

"What are you talking about?"

David started the engine and gunned it again. "I'm talking about making peace with your past. I am who and what I am, Emerson. You can't ask more."

"I'm not asking more."

He seemed not to hear me. "I am good at what I do," he said. "I am proud of it. Not everyone has a past they must make peace with."

"I realize that."

"What have I done? When I have hurt people, it has been for good reason."

"I'm sure it has."

"Fine." He pulled from the parking spot and roared out of the yacht basin, not even pausing to talk to his blonde friend at the booth again.

David sighed, then went on, "I mean, all this Jesus stuff you've told me — I . . ."

"The theology of it doesn't bother you, does it?" I asked.

"I don't know what you're talking about."

"You can handle the part about Jesus being the Messiah. You've been reading, and the miracles don't seem to cause you any problems. It's the dying to yourself part, isn't it?"

"What do you know about my life?" He sounded angry.

"I know more than most people, and that's still not a whole lot," I said. "And I know you've been looking for a way to make your own peace. This has been eating at you for a while — but it's been more and more intense since we went to Dallas. You're looking for a peace you didn't find in Beirut. And it's a peace you didn't find in Jerusalem during the riots. You came here, to America, to a safe, secure environment, and you still haven't found it. Maybe you've been looking for the wrong kind of peace."

"Just words. 'Dying to myself.' What's that mean?"

"It means you assume that David Ben Zadok is dead, that anything past this point is on God's time and on God's dime."

"I'm good at what I do."

"I know that. Dying to yourself doesn't mean repudiating everything you've ever done; it just means that you recognize that what you did wasn't enough, that it never could be enough."

David was silent for a moment. "It never was, you know. I was never a good enough commander, never a good enough soldier, never a good enough person. People have died because of my decisions."

I nodded; I knew it was true. One afternoon in 1983, while patrolling Beirut, a mortar shell rained down on David's position. The crew members of his tank, with his permission, were out stretching their legs. The activity must have caught the enemy's eye; that mortar shell wounded two of David's men. One died of complications, but only recently — nearly a decade after the shelling. David felt responsible, although no one else felt he was to blame for anything. I knew this had been eating at David for a few weeks; I should have seen this coming. I was taken a little by surprise, but I knew what to say.

"There's a way out," I said. "Trust Christ to be good enough for you. It's not that complicated."

"Do you know what that means? To my family?"

"No, David, I don't. I've wondered."

"It means, to some, that I am dead. Not to my mother, I think, or to my Uncle Mordechai. But my mother's mother — it would hurt her very, very deeply."

"It would hurt her for you to turn away from your people's ways, David. You don't have to do that. Your culture is still your culture. Your traditions are still your traditions. There are congregations of Jews like you who have trusted Christ. We could talk to some of them."

David didn't respond. He was driving down Port Industrial

Boulevard; it was only about 5:15. We had some time before we were to meet Verini.

"Let's go down to the beach," I said. "Walk a little. It'll do us good."

David nodded and turned left at the first major intersection; after a few more blocks we were approaching Seawall Boulevard again.

"Let's park and walk here," I said.

We found a parking place across the street from the seawall; we locked the car, then waited for the light to change so we could cross. The beach and the seawall were starting to clear of the weekday summer crowds; when we walked down the stairway onto the beach, there were only a few families in sight. David ambled toward the surf; when he reached the high-water mark, he paused and looked down. Then he turned to the right and started walking. I followed.

"It's not so simple," he said when I caught up. "Judaism is more than celebrating the right holidays."

"So is Christianity," I said. "Listen, David, I'm not going to push you. I'm not the one pushing you now. But if you know what you need to do, why wait?"

He laughed. "You don't know my grandmother."

"I know *you*. Something is throwing you off-balance; something has upset your legendary equilibrium. You're not detached and distant now. Something's going on."

"What is it, then?"

"God sometimes gives us little pushes — little proddings. The Holy Spirit is on your case. You've read through the New Testament I gave you; you know what's going on. You've seen it in me, in Remington, and in Maggie."

He didn't respond. We walked slowly, breathing in the sea and the noise and the visual rightness of a beach. After a few more yards he spoke.

"If Jesus is the Messiah, then there's no question, is there?" he asked. "Everything I learned as a boy in Hebrew school leads up to this."

"Yes."

"And He *is* the Messiah."

"Yes. Not the one an occupied Jewish populace was looking for at the time; He came and offered freedom on an individual basis first. And He'll be back with the other kind."

"Then there's no question." That calm, slightly interested expression I knew so well reappeared on David's face. He had decided.

"Is there a special prayer?" he asked.

"Not really. You don't even have to close your eyes if you don't want to. Just ask God to forgive you, and accept Christ's offer of salvation. Accept Him as your own Messiah."

David nodded. "Let's stop."

I did as he asked. I watched his face; for a moment he looked at me. "Let's pray, Emerson."

For about half an hour we stood on the beach. David found his peace with God, and I felt a peace about David that I had wanted for as long as I had known him. Salvation is a private sort of matter at first; it was between David and God. Later, I knew, it would need to be made more public. Martin, the pastor of my church, was clear that God wants us to make a public expression of our faith, and he liked to do it fairly soon after a conversion. Personal preference, he told me; it was by no means a deal-breaker, if you'll pardon the expression. But Martin liked clean endings and clean, public beginnings. That seemed fine by David; he didn't mind getting dunked.

"Another thing, Dave," I said, "you'll need to consciously put yourself under Martin's spiritual authority. It's called discipleship. When you have questions, you go to him; when you need leadership, you go to him."

"What about when we go to Dallas?"

"Then we'll find someone there, I guess. But it's important to always be learning, growing. Martin calls it 'knocking off the rough edges.' I seem to have quite a few left."

We were walking back toward the car; it was nearly 7 P.M., and we were getting hungry. "How about some seafood?" I asked.

"Fine."

"You've already done the tough part," I said. "From here on out, you'll do nothing alone. He'll never leave you."

"Nor forsake me."

"Right. You've been reading. And you know I'm always around. Only now we're talking in terms of eternity. You really can't get rid of me now."

David smiled. We found the steps leading up from the beach to the seawall; we crossed back over to David's car and drove back toward the Strand area, where we'd seen some decent-looking restaurants. We parked at one, out on a pier, and went in. A waitress with a pirate's eye patch (flipped up so she could see better) asked if we wanted dinner. I started to ask if I could borrow her ship's plank for a few staff members I had in mind, but instead I just said yes, we wanted dinner.

By 7:15 we had plates of mediocre (at best) red snapper. The cole slaw was warm, the fish was cool, and the prices were meant for tourists. David didn't seem to mind; I rarely saw him turn down food of any nature. I ate a little of mine and filled up on the hard bread the waitress served us.

By 7:45 David had finished his dinner and mine. He was helpful like that. We paid the waitress, including enough of a tip so she could go out and buy some sort of hat that didn't have a skull-and-crossbones on it; then we went to the car. We drove to the Old Man's house, arriving at 8 P.M. sharp.

"He's a nice guy," I said. "Be sure to talk a little first, instead of getting right down to business. It's the polite thing to do."

But when we knocked at the door, it wasn't Father O'Donnell who answered. It was Verini himself, and he got right down to business. "Inside," he said brusquely.

We followed. Father O'Donnell was standing in the hallway,

waiting for us. "Come into the library," the old priest said. "We all need to talk."

David shot me a look of curiosity; I shrugged. We walked past the photos again and into the library. The priest gestured at two chairs, and we sat. He sat down as well. Verini entered, but he remained standing. He paced a little, found absolutely nothing to do with his hands other than clench and unclench them, and finally spoke.

"You boys have been in town today for what, four hours now?"

"A little longer," I said.

"A little longer. Maybe five hours. You're here five hours, and already someone wants to hit you. I get a call from an old friend in New York; he says a man in Galveston has called, looking for someone to drop by and do a reporter and a photographer, meaning you two. See, I had mentioned to my old friend that I had a new friend, a reporter. That's a lucky break for you, that he called me. Very lucky."

"A hit? Do they do that anymore?" I asked.

"They don't, but you get a schmuck like Louis Carlton, who thinks he's a mobster like Al Capone when he's really nothing but a dock rat, and he'll try to do things like he sees on TV."

"So what did you tell him?" David asked.

"What did I tell him? I told him to tell Carlton that we can find some talent closer to home."

"You have anyone in mind?" I asked.

Verini ignored me. "Father, what shall we do with these boys?"

Father O'Donnell shook his head.

Verini looked back at me. "This is your friend?"

"David Ben Zadok, meet Alberto Verini and Father O'Donnell."

Verini shook David's hand almost calmly. The priest stood and did the same. Verini sighed and shook his head. "Boys, you impress me. If you have a choice between the truly connected and the truly stupid, always tangle with the truly connected. But no, you two went straight for the truly stupid."

"Tell me what happened," I said.

"That's what I should be asking you," Verini replied. "All I know is you roughed up Louis Carlton, and five seconds after you were gone, he was on the telephone. You helped out a lot by giving him your name. Within an hour he had your addresses, your place of employment, and everything else there is to know about you. Then he goes out looking for some talent, like he's John Gotti. Chances are Francis Ciotti is financing this venture, by the way, since Louis now knows you're looking into Francis's past."

"So someone's going to get paid ten thousand dollars or so to kill us?" I asked.

Verini laughed. "You two? No way — five hundred dollars apiece, probably. If they find out you're a friend of Harry Singer's, then maybe twenty-five hundred dollars for the both of you. If they find out you're a friend of mine, then maybe more. Depends on how much trouble killing you is going to cause — how much heat they'll have to duck. The only reason Louis called out-of-state is that Ciotti already knows Harry Singer's boy is watching him."

David laughed. "Dying to ourselves, Emerson; this could take on a new meaning."

Verini's eyebrows went up, and he looked at David. "You're Israeli, yes?"

"Yes."

"Served in the army, I assume?"

"Beirut, Golan Heights."

Verini nodded; it was enough information. "You can probably do an okay job of taking care of yourself and your friend. But I think I have a better idea. Let me work on it tonight."

I nodded. "We're sorry to have caused you this trouble."

Verini smiled. "You haven't caused anyone trouble but yourselves, and Louis Carlton — not that he doesn't deserve it. Papa Rose would put up with a schmuck like him for a total of two minutes."

"He was a little annoying," I said.

"Annoying? He's also trigger-happy. He's shot holes in his own boat."

"Not anymore," David said. "I took his gun away from him."

"You still have it?" Verini asked.

"Yes."

"Give it to Harry Singer — the ballistics people might want a look, see if they can come up with any matches."

"I'll do that."

"Boys, I feel it's best that you go home," Verini said. "Get out of Galveston. Right now Louis is steaming; in the next hour or so he'll wind up at a bar, getting drunk and getting brave. He might get impatient, wave some cash around, and who knows who'll take it? We'll talk more later. Emerson, I'll call you."

I nodded. As before, Father O'Donnell led us to the door. This time he had no parting words of wisdom for us. He just shook our hands and closed the door.

"I guess this complicates things," I said to David.

"A little, but not much. I've done security jobs before. You just have to know which situations to avoid."

"I'm glad you're on my side."

"You should be."

"Staying over tonight?"

"Sure," he said. "I get the bed — you get the couch."

"It's my house; why should I get the couch?"

"Because there's not enough room for Airborne on the couch, too," he said. "I get Airborne."

"And you'll want breakfast, too, I suppose?"

"Sure."

Soon we drove through the small towns up Highway 6, then wound our way through the farm-to-market roads until we found my farmhouse. Airborne was at the door waiting for us. I unlocked the door, and we went in; David grabbed the telephone, called his mother, and explained that he was with me tonight. He then let Airborne out for his evening bunny patrol, while I checked the answering machine. There were messages. I hit the button below the flashing light.

"Bang, bang," Louis Carlton's voice said. "You're dead."

The second message was a little more pleasant. It was Remington.

"Call me when you get home," she said. "I've had such a boring day. Tell me about yours. I hope it wasn't as dull as mine. Give Airborne a kiss for me."

I started to dial Remington's number when I heard a knock at the front door. David, waiting at the back for Airborne, glanced at it. I grinned. "How quick do those planes from New York fly?" I asked in a whisper.

"Verini said something about local talent," he said softly. From his pocket he produced Carlton's shiny revolver. "Go stand to the side of the door, then ask who it is."

I walked softly over to the door and stood to one side of it.

"Yeah?" I said out loud.

"It's Nix," I heard through the heavy wooden door.

I glanced at David. He nodded. I opened the door from the side. No one shot anything. Instead, Sally Nix walked through the door with a broad grin. She closed it behind her as David made his gun disappear.

"Say hello to your hit woman, boys," my second-favorite cop said sweetly.

22

arry Singer and some old mobster from Galveston set it up,"
Nix said. "I'll meet with this guy Lou Carlton tomorrow
night. He'll offer me money to shoot you boys, and I'll
record every word he says. Then we'll bust him. Nice and simple. Hey, what did you do to make this guy mad, anyway?"

I shook my head, then pointed to a seat. Nix sat down on the
couch. David let Airborne back in, then sat on the floor, scratching my dog's ears.

"Well, it was really David's fault," I said.

"It wasn't my fault. It was your idea to go see him."

"You threatened to break his arms."

Nix sighed. "Boys, I'm getting the picture. So you threatened
him?"

"Well, it started that way. Then David bounced him off his own
boat cabin."

"He went for a gun," David said. "And I didn't break anything."

"That's true," I said. "He didn't break anything."

"That's nice," Sally said. "But from what Harry Singer tells me
about this Carlton, maybe you should have. It would have saved
you some trouble. But then again, you know how I love this
undercover work. I've never been an assassin before."

"What's he getting for us?" David asked.

"Harry was told a grand apiece. Apparently this gangster told another guy — someone in New York — to tell Carlton that he would provide a local shooter. Then the gangster called Harry."

"He's not a gangster," I said. "At least not anymore."

"Yeah, that's what Harry said. Anyway, I'm going to sleep over tonight — at our detective sergeant's explicit instructions — and there's a cruiser outside, just in case Carlton decides to do anything by himself. I'll stick around you two during the day tomorrow until we get this creep in the can. Are you covering any fun stories tomorrow? I've always wanted to be a journalist. Maybe I can go undercover as one someday. Think I'd be good at it?"

I ignored her question. "Wait a minute," I said. "You're proposing to protect my life, right?"

"That's why I'm here." She smiled, brushing some blonde hair away from her pretty face. "What's on the tube tonight?"

I ignored her question again and reached for the telephone. I dialed Remington's number and held the phone out to Sally Nix.

"You'd better explain this to Remington — and you'd better make it sound believable. Forget assassins — I'm more afraid of *her*."

Nix grinned and took the telephone. "A. C.? It's Sally Nix. I haven't seen you in so long. I'm at Emerson's place. No, I'll be here all night. Guard duty. You won't believe what these boys got themselves into. Sure. I've got plenty of time to talk."

I closed my eyes and shook my head. I was doomed!

23

It was as bad as I thought. Remington stayed on the telephone with Sally Nix for over an hour. They discussed my many failings, of course, but they seemed to agree that Airborne made up for a lot of those. Then Nix handed me the telephone, and I was given detailed instructions on how to be a nice host for our bodyguard.

After a few moments, though, I felt David's hand on my shoulder. I turned, and he asked if he could talk to her.

"Hold it," I told Remington. "David wants to talk."

"I'll take it in the bedroom," he said, turning on his heel. A few seconds later he picked up the extension on my nightstand. "Is this private?" I asked.

"No," David said. "Remington, I have some news. I am a Christian now."

Remington didn't respond for a second. Then she spoke softly. "That's wonderful . . . When? . . . How?"

"Today . . . On the beach. It's been coming for a while now, I think."

"I've hoped," Remington said. "But I've been scared to hope too much. Christ has done so much for me, David — I'm really *really* happy."

She had that hesitation in her voice that said she was about to cry, but I knew she wanted to talk more. "You two are doing fine without me," I said. "I'll go entertain Nix."

Remington said good-bye and that she'd call tomorrow. I hung up the telephone, then went to the couch where Airborne sat looking at me expectantly. His tail thumped twice. I capitulated to his wishes, sat beside him, and began absently scratching his ears. My mind was on something else: my best friend's soul. It was whole now. I smiled and thanked God silently.

Nix took the couch for the night, of course, and I slept on the floor of my bedroom while David took the bed and the dog. At about 6 A.M., the patrol car outside took Nix home for a quick shower; another cop sat in the kitchen, reading my newspaper and drinking my coffee until Nix returned at about 7:30.

As David and I ate some breakfast (bagels), Nix went over the evening's exciting agenda. She helped herself to a bagel and some coffee.

"There's a little bar in the old Turf Club building," Nix said. "It's dark, it's quiet, and no one goes there. I'll meet Carlton there at 9. He'll give me half the cash tonight and the other half when I plug you two."

"Just arrest the guy, okay?" I asked.

"First I'll make him talk," she said, taking another bagel. She'd had two already. For such a trim woman, she sure ate a lot. "I'm young, and I'm pretty — he's not going to suspect I'm a cop, and he'll try to impress me. Once I get him going on how important he is, maybe I can get him to drop a few names."

"Names like Fuzzy Ciotti?"

"That's the one we're looking for," she said. "Singer — Bill Singer — has brought in the Galveston sheriff's office on this. They're interested in Ciotti if we can get something on him. I hear you boys are trying to do just that?"

"Yeah, but we're working with ancient history," I said. "In fact, the two cases we looked into yesterday both came up bust. There was Carlton, who might or might not have witnessed a murder in 1964, and I doubt he's going to want to cooperate with us now. Also, we talked to a widow who had a letter from her husband that Ciotti might try to kill him. He died a few days after he mailed that letter to himself, back in 1959. Only, the letter's gone, and all we have is the woman's word that the letter ever existed."

Nix nodded. "Maybe we've got a chance to implicate him in this. So don't consider yesterday an unproductive day."

The telephone rang. When I answered, I heard the cheery voice of Detective Sergeant Bill Singer.

"Still alive? Well, that's something. Let me talk to Nix."

"Sure," I said. "She's been a delightful houseguest. Who knew she could eat like this?"

I handed the phone to Nix, who glared at me. "Nix," she said. After a moment she grunted. Maybe Singer's speech disorder was contagious. "He wants them there, in the city? With him. Fine. I'll drop them off before the meet. I'll pick them up after."

She hung up the telephone. "That old gangster wants you boys with him this evening. Since we'll need his testimony, Singer's feeling cooperative."

"We can do that," I said. "You'll like meeting him. He gives a little hope that some of the bad guys you bust can actually turn good."

Nix snorted — which wasn't particularly ladylike, but then neither was her Glock 9 mm pistol, which was on the table beside her plate. It didn't seem to bother David, so I ignored it as well.

"We'd better get in to work," I said. "It's Thursday."

David nodded at that irrefutable truth. "It's Thursday," he said. "Emerson, do we actually work on Thursdays?"

"Not much," I admitted. "That's what we have staff members for. Remember when I gave you that title last year?"

"Photo editor? Sure. I got that instead of a raise, you cheapstate."

"Cheap*skate*," Nix corrected him. "He's a cheapskate, not a cheapstate."

"Thank you both very much," I said. "Anyway, I have a few things to write and a few crises to deal with. You have any photo shoots you know about, David?"

"The cheerleaders have their new uniforms for next school year," he said. "They have practice at 10 A.M. at the football field."

"You have it rough," I said. "What else?"

"Nothing. Let's hope for a nice house fire."

Nix snorted again. "You two are ghouls."

"We're newsmen," I said. "Now kiss Airborne good-bye and let's go to work."

I was greeted at the office by a stack of fourteen pink phone messages. I was learning to hate the color pink. Exactly eight of the calls were complaints or criticisms, while four were "hot tips," and the other two were personal. One was from Remington, the other from my mother.

I called Remington first. "Hello, darling," I said when she answered.

"Which one are you?" she asked. "Bruce, Ron, or Emerson?"

"I think I'm offended."

"I'm not the one who had a beautiful blonde cop spending the night."

"It wasn't by choice. She ate half a package of bagels."

"She saved your life."

"How could she save my life when she's the one being hired to kill me?"

"I don't think we should be talking about this. Suffice it to say that I'm going to milk this one, Dunn. Fair warning."

"Fine," I said. "Have you scheduled anything with your mother yet?"

"No, I'm still putting it off. I need to do it, though."

"Make it next week. This week is filling up fast."

"I can see that. You seem to be getting popular with the women."

"If I'm so popular, why is someone trying to kill me?"

"Jealousy."

"Right. Well, anyway, any news on the law school front?"

"I gave notice today. I'll work two more weeks, and then I'll have two weeks to get settled in Dallas before classes start."

I felt my stomach sink. I hadn't really thought about it before in those terms; Remington was going to be in Dallas without me until January — for almost six months.

"I know," she said, in response to something I hadn't said. How did she do that? "It started hitting me this morning, too — when I gave my notice. You know, my city editor even asked about you, whether you might be interested in my job. I told him you had some other things going on."

"Not going on soon enough," I said.

"I know. But really, this might be best. This will let me concentrate on law school for that first semester. I won't always be worried about making time to see you."

I didn't respond.

"I didn't mean it like that," Remington said. "I mean, I'll want to see you and I'll miss you, but it won't be a question of should I go see you or should I study. You'll be six hours away, so I'll study."

"You're right," I said. "This really is working out well. It's just not working out comfortably. I'll miss having you around."

"Me, too."

From there, the conversation got a little mushy. That was becoming a habit with us. Afterwards I called a few of the complainers just to get out of the mood Remington had put me in. One lady told me I was illiterate if I thought that the banner headline on Sunday's paper was grammatically correct. I told her I wasn't illiterate, I knew exactly who my mother was. One guy said that Robert's article about the tax increase was hopelessly biased on the side of the City Council. The next call was a woman who said the article was hopelessly biased against the City Council. When I got to the hot tip stack, I was my usual surly self again. An elderly woman told me that the police were shooting stray dogs. I said I'd check it out. A young woman said her neighbor was a dope dealer. I said I'd ask the police to check it out. A man told me his water bill last month was $24,978. I asked if he took long showers. He said no, it was some kind of a computer error. That's always interesting (plus I was in a surly mood), so I sent Robert out to interview him, then interview the city utilities director. I beeped David, and when he called I told him to swing by and get a shot of the man with his water bill. The last tip was from a man who thought the school board was actually a secret society dedicated to an agenda of teaching our children about communism. I agreed with him, but I pointed out that if they couldn't even teach our children to read, how successful would they be teaching them about Karl Marx, much less the Marx Brothers — Groucho, Zeppo, Sneezy, Doc, and Dopey? That seemed to satisfy him.

The rest of the day was pretty much the same. Sherri wanted some help with the bulky school budget; we broke it down into a few categories and determined that with the salary increases the administration was giving itself, there wouldn't be any money left over for copies of the *Communist Manifesto*, so I felt even more secure about the future of our nation. Sally Nix rode along with David while he was out, and she sat in a desk across the room when they were back at the office. She was reading a forensic science textbook. I didn't ask to see any of the pictures.

About 5:30 David had finished running his film, and we had two good front-page photos and plenty of inside art. Remington showed up at the office a little before 6 P.M., and we called the Schmidt boys to see if they'd feed us.

"We are still not open, but we have a new oven we've been testing," Walter said after a pause. "Yes, we have some things you can try. We're experimenting, you might say."

I hung up the telephone and grinned. "We're on," I said.

The four of us took Remington's Volvo to the restaurant. Nix sat in front with Remington, and David and I behaved ourselves in the back. When we got to the restaurant, the neon sign wasn't only turned off, it was taken down. I smiled. Nix turned to look at David and me before we got out of the car. "Don't say anything about tonight," she said. "I know they're your friends; they're my friends too, but they're financially beholden to Ciotti. We can't afford a leak. I'm going in with a wire tonight, not a Kevlar vest."

We nodded. Remington looked a little worried. "But you'll have backup, right?"

"Sure," Nix said. "The bar's going to be full of cops dressed as drunks. Not that there's much difference anyway. I'll be fine, as long as we don't get sloppy."

We all got out of the car and walked to the restaurant's door. Remington knocked, and a moment later Gunther unlocked the door. We entered the restaurant, which was beginning to look like new.

"*Guten abend*," Walter said, coming out of the kitchen. "Coffee for all? Yes? Fine."

"Sit down," Gunther said, pointing to a table with a cloth on it. There were six chairs. We sat, and Gunther sat with us.

"And all is going well?" he asked.

"Everything is going fine," I said. "No major problems. How are you boys doing?"

"We're well," Gunther said. Walter approached from behind him with the coffee on a tray, with six cups.

"We may open tomorrow night," Walter said. "We need to. We think we have repaired the oven; it took a little work with a hammer. We have some dishes still not broken. The money situation, though . . ."

I shook my head. "Let's not talk about depressing subjects — there's no use brooding. We're all doing everything we can. You're working hard to reopen, and we're working on things from the other end. Let's leave it at that and enjoy ourselves."

Gunther nodded. "Yes. Why worry when we're doing all that is possible? Now, A. C., tell us more about this law school you're leaving us for."

Two hours later we were parking in front of Alberto Verini's house on Galveston Island. Another car was in front of his house — an old black police car, the kind you buy at an auction. David and I were in the back of Nix's unmarked; she was alone in the front. She noticed Harry Singer's car as soon as I did.

"I didn't know he'd be here," she said.

"I didn't either, but it doesn't surprise me," I replied. "They've never mixed socially, but there's a bond between these two old guys. They're more alike than you'd think."

Nix nodded, then got out of the car. We followed (her back doors did open from the inside, unlike Bill Singer's). Father O'Donnell answered the door when we knocked. We introduced him to Sally Nix, who was dressed in lots of denim and a western hat. The priest bowed a little and took her hand gallantly. He then led us through the hallway to the now-familiar library. Inside, we found more Singers than we knew what to do with. Bill was standing; Harry was sitting, laughing, across from Verini.

"So we had these Little League shirts made up with 'The Turf Club' printed on the back, and you know who Sam asks to coach? Me!" Verini hooted. "And you know what the newspaper says? It says we're the odds-on favorite!"

Even Bill Singer was starting to laugh.

"So I come to Sam one day, and he asks if we've won any games," Verini continued. "I told him no, that we stink. He asks why. So I said, 'Why do you think? You put this group of kids together — our own kids — and give them baseball bats, and what do you think happens?' Sam didn't ask about our win-loss record after that."

Verini noticed our presence and stood when he saw Nix.

"Alberto Verini," he said, taking Nix's hand. "So very pleased to meet you. You're the undercover cop? Sally Nix?"

"Yes," Nix said shyly. I'd never seen her do anything shyly before.

"You're very brave," Verini said. "Very brave. But don't you

worry — you'll be fine. That bar is going to look like a police convention. Such a pretty young woman."

"He's right," Bill said. "I mean about the backup. Let's go, Nix.
We've got to get you wired for sound."

Nix nodded and mumbled something about how nice it was
to meet such a charming man. Verini beamed and didn't release
her hand until he absolutely had to.

"She's very pretty," Verini said when she and Bill Singer left.
"Isn't she, Father?"

"Yes, she is, Al."

Father O'Donnell had taken a seat near Verini, and he pointed
to two more chairs. David and I sat down.

"Such memories," Verini said. "I haven't thought about the
Turf Club Tornadoes in years. Of course, our opponents said the
'T' on our caps stood for 'Thugs.' Maybe they were right."

Harry shook his head. "Not like the kids today, Al. Not like the
kids today."

Verini motioned to David and me. "And what do you think of
our young friends here? Efficient, right? They don't mess
around, no. They get right to business, making the wrong people mad at them. These boys must have a guardian angel or two,
seeing things have worked out like they have."

"I know Emerson does," David said. "I've met her. Big hair. She
dates my uncle."

Father O'Donnell smiled. "I've read nothing in the Scriptures
about angels having big hair, but I suppose it's possible."

"All I know is what she told me," I said. "She said she was my
guardian angel. Am I supposed to dispute a claim like that?
Besides, she was packing an automatic."

Harry nodded. "That's what I would want my guardian angel
to be packing." He turned to Verini. "My boy told me about that
incident, the one involving the lady with big hair. These two" —
he indicated David and me — "have had their share of misad-
ventures."

Verini sighed. "What can we do? Well, let's get down to business. It's time for our history lesson, right?"

"Right," Harry said. "We've got six cases we're investigating. We've got some preliminary impressions we want to bounce off you — that is, if Emerson and David had time to form any impressions before they convinced Louis Carlton to put a hit on them."

"We have some impressions," I said. "None of them very promising, though."

Harry turned back to Verini. "First, there's the George Musey killing. Remember that one?"

Verini smiled. "George Musey. I haven't heard that name in many a year."

"Gunned down on 24th Street. Witnesses described Ciotti, but the police arrested some guy named Windy Goss."

"Goss was thrown to them like a bone," Verini said. "The cops didn't really mind that Musey was dead, you know."

"And Goss was acquitted."

"Of course — because he was innocent."

"Then Ciotti did the shooting?" Harry asked.

"I believe he did. I didn't see it, but I know he was the one given the honor of doing it. Musey wasn't a popular man among the Maceo people."

Harry sighed. "If you had seen it, we'd be home free. Anyone still around who might have seen it?"

Verini shook his head. "No one. Francis was a loner then. It was before I took him under my wing."

"Okay, that's one down," Harry said. "Five more to go. Now, do you remember anything about a Julian Newman?"

No hint of recognition came to the Old Man's face.

"A gambler who was shot outside the Turf," Harry said. "It was 1941, February. It was over a race result."

Verini nodded. "I always suspected that Francis might have had someone in Louisiana delay the results for a few minutes —

long enough for Francis to shave the odds. This Newman fellow had a good watch and knew when the races were run."

"Then you remember it?"

"I remember hearing of it. I wasn't there. They got into a fight, then carried it outside? Francis says Newman went for his gun, so he shot him. Am I right?"

"That's the one," Harry agreed. "Francis must have been quick."

"Oh, he was, Harry," Verini said. "He would practice, as if a Sicilian kid like him could become an Old West cowboy just by moving to Galveston, Texas, and carrying a gun."

"There were a dozen or so witnesses to the altercation, but Ciotti took Newman outside to shoot him. No one followed. Of the witnesses, three are still alive and lucid. None of the three says they saw anything more than a shoving match. Any leads for us on that one?"

Verini shook his head. "I'm sorry, Harry. Francis never spoke to me of that incident either. I know less of it than you do."

"All right. Two down. Next is one my boy looked into. He's good, isn't he?"

"He's a fine boy," Verini said. "He holds himself well, like his father. Luckily he has his mother's looks."

Harry beamed. "Amen to that. Anyway, this happened in 1952, March. The case deals with a certain Mr. Jude Lubrano."

Verini nodded. "A jackal. Worked for the Chicago outfit, but more as a freelance thug. He wasn't important to Nitti, who was in charge at the time."

"Frank Nitti?" I asked. "You mean as in Al Capone's enforcer?"

"That's the one," Verini said. "You know, Nitti didn't start out as Frank Nitti of Chicago. He was born Francisco Nitti, but called himself Frank Noonis here. He went into partnership with Dutch Voight. When the partnership went sour, he went off to Chicago — still owing Dutch about twenty-four thousand dollars. He repaid it later, I hear, after he linked up with Capone."

"He was in charge of the Cicero syndicate," Harry added.

"After Eliot Ness put Capone in jail for tax evasion. He probably told Lubrano to come down here and check things out — see if Papa Rose was still strong enough to make muscling into the Galveston operation a bad business move. When Lubrano failed to return, Nitti just took it as a sign that Papa Rose still had some juice. Now, if it had been one of Nitti's key men, there would have been war. But Lubrano was disposable. The question is, who disposed of him?"

"It was Francis," Verini acknowledged. "I remember it well."

"My boy has found the cabbie who dropped Lubrano, Lubrano's bodyguard, and Ciotti off at the wharves, then returned an hour later and picked up Ciotti alone. The cabbie is eighty-six now, living in Vegas — surprisingly healthy; I think it must be the desert climate. He's not willing to volunteer his testimony, but we could subpoena him."

Verini nodded. "It was after I turned," he said, "but I knew all about it. Papa Rose told Ciotti to sink the Chicago gentlemen, and that's exactly what he did."

"But he did it alone?"

"Alone. That's why he got the men drunk first; he probably led them into a boathouse, shot them both, then loaded them up and weighted them down. Probably used one of the bootlegging boats to take them out into the Gulf."

"Did you hear Rose tell Ciotti to kill them?"

"I didn't," Verini said. "Like I said, it was after my turn. I was out of the middle of things. There's the rub. But everyone knew about it."

Harry nodded. "But we still have the cabbie. That's something."

"What's next?" Verini asked.

"In 1954 a man named Mathias Rombeaux was shot in Kemah, just up the bay a ways."

Verini nodded. "Good restaurant. Good food."

"Ciotti tried to get the same percentage off the slots as Papa

Rose had gotten — 50 percent. Rombeaux said he'd bought the slots from Rose outright, just before he died."

"That was a lie," Verini said. "Rombeaux was a good cook, but that doesn't make him honest."

"He was shot a week later. Was it Ciotti?"

"No, actually it wasn't," Verini said. "By that time Francis was starting to hire people. He had a couple of boys — they're both gone now — who did that job for him. Used his car, though."

"We know. We have a description of the car, even the first couple of letters on the plates. It was never investigated."

"Rombeaux was bringing over prostitutes from Louisiana," Verini said. "I'm sure your people weren't so sorry to see him go."

"Wasn't my people investigating this one," Harry said. "It was the sheriff's office. It wasn't followed up on, and I guess that could be why."

"The description of the car — is that enough for a prosecutor to link Ciotti to the shooting?" I asked.

Harry frowned. "I doubt it. Especially if he set himself up an alibi, as I'm sure he did. That leaves us your cases, Emerson."

"Then we don't have much hope, other than that cabbie," I said. "You know how our discussion with Lou Carlton went. But earlier we talked to Mary Ryan."

Verini's eyes widened. "Mary Ryan?"

"Her husband was killed in 1959."

"I know," Verini said. "Go on."

"She claimed she had that letter, remember, but later said it was gone? And the DA couldn't go any further without it. We talked to her yesterday, and she says Ciotti stole it. He probably destroyed it."

"How was she?" Harry asked.

"Quite well," David answered. "She looked healthy, not too bitter. Her husband paid off the building where the bar was, just before he died."

Verini shook his head. "No, he didn't. Mitchell Ryan was in debt to everyone in town."

"But she said a banker came by and told her the building was hers."

"What do you think, Harry?" Verini asked. "Thirty-odd years ago, could I pass as a banker?"

"I wondered about that," Harry said. "I knew the banks wouldn't touch a recent immigrant like Ryan. So you bought the place for her?"

"Ryan was paying me rent; at least he paid me rent twice. I wasn't going to evict him, but his other creditors weren't as patient as me. That's what got him in trouble with Francis. He panicked, accepted money. When he couldn't pay it back, Francis asked him to be the driver in a robbery. Poor idiot."

"You gave her the building?" I asked.

"It wasn't making me any money; the boom had ended, and Galveston Island just wasn't the place to sink a lot of money. I just signed a few papers, is all."

"You did more than that," I said. "She's done well for herself, and for her family."

"I'm glad to hear that. Of course, it caused the final rift between Francis and me. He came to my house, waving that letter, saying that she had nothing on him, and why did I feel it was necessary to pay her off? I tried to make him understand that I wasn't paying her off — I was being charitable."

"Wait," I said. "You saw the letter?"

"Sure; he waved it under my nose. I took it and read it, then gave it back to him. 'Francis,' I said, 'get out. You murdered a poor soul, and now you want to extort money from his widow. God will make you answer for this, Francis.' He left, and I haven't seen him face to face since."

I turned to Harry. "That's two people who saw this letter. Think the DA will like this one?"

"Maybe," Harry said. "There's still no actual letter, though, nothing we could enter into evidence."

"It's something," I said. "And there's always hope that Lou Carlton might implicate Ciotti tonight."

Verini shrugged. "Maybe. He's giving stupid a bad name."

I looked at my watch; it was about ten minutes until 9 P.M. Verini noticed what I was doing, and he looked over at the old priest.

"Father, how about a short prayer for the officers?" he asked.

Father O'Donnell agreed, then bowed his head. We all did the same, and the priest prayed for the safety of all involved. When he was finished, I heard David say a soft "Amen."

"Not a bad feeling, is it, Dave?" I asked. "Someone to watch over us and ours."

"Not bad," he smiled. "I read this morning, while you were in the shower . . . Some psalms, in Hebrew. I also read some in the New Testament . . . About us being new creatures."

"Second Corinthians," Father O'Donnell said, glancing at Verini. "That's a favorite of ours. Chapter 5, verse 17. 'Therefore, if any man be in Christ, then he is a new creature: old things have passed away; behold all things are become new.'"

"That's the one," David said. "Before, I think it would have been impossible for me to trust a prayer. I trusted only my abilities. That's why I worked so hard to develop them. Emerson understands."

I nodded.

David continued. "I became a Christian yesterday."

"God bless you." Father O'Donnell smiled. "Another one comes home."

We talked about spiritual matters for well over an hour; we were interrupted, however, by the doorbell. David rose to answer it, and when he led Bill Singer, Nix, and a well-dressed black man into the room, we could tell that earthly matters were going to require our attention.

"We bagged Carlton," Nix said.

"But he didn't even mention Ciotti," Bill Singer added. "Dad, Mr. Verini, Father O'Donnell, Emerson Dunn, and David Ben Zadok, this is Daniel Parr, assistant district attorney for Galveston

County. He was in on the bust, and he's been assigned to look into our investigation of Francis Ciotti."

Verini smiled and shook the ADA's hand. "My pleasure, young man. You're the image of your father."

Harry grinned and took the ADA's hand next. "I was about to say the same thing. Served with Alex Parr for twenty years, I did. Oh, did we have some adventures. Made enough as a cop to send his boy to law school, did he? That explains all those egg sandwiches."

I shook the prosecutor's hand in turn, as did David. Parr was beaming a bit, showing that he was glad these men knew and respected his father. Bill Singer and Sally Nix remained standing, but Parr accepted the seat Father O'Donnell found for him.

"Let's get right to it," he said. "I understand your PD is investigating Ciotti; that's not our jurisdiction, but we don't mind one bit. You nail him here, you nail him there, it doesn't matter."

I didn't know our investigation had become so official, but I kept my mouth shut. Parr continued, addressing his comments to all of us.

"Now, we will honor your request to reopen any cases that have a snowball's chance of winning." He paused, then looked at the priest. "Sorry, Father, but you know what I mean. We can't spend great amounts of manpower on a case that's thirty years old unless it has at least an outside chance of getting past the grand jury. In the meantime we'll prosecute Carlton. You two gentlemen are the ones he wanted to kill?"

"That's us," I said. "We seem to have that effect on people."

Parr didn't even smile. "We'll need statements from you about the initial incident — aboard his boat, I believe. I don't think you'll need to testify; we have so much tape he'd be an idiot to want to take this to trial. He should plead out. The problem is that he didn't implicate Ciotti in this, although we agree Ciotti probably put up the cash."

"He bragged, just like we expected," Nix said. "But he was trying to impress me so much that he forgot the money wasn't his.

He wanted to convince me he was a big shot, not just the boat captain for a big shot."

Parr nodded. "So Ciotti's still walking," he said. "That's not because anyone here didn't do their job; it's just the way this one worked out. Ciotti's a bad actor, and he'll do something sloppy sooner or later. If we stay on him, we'll get him."

"When do you want our statements?" I asked.

"I'll need you to come to the courthouse early next week. I'll set up a time and call you later. Sorry I can't be more specific than that."

He looked over at Harry Singer. "My father said you were a good cop," Parr said. "So be straight with me. On these old cases you have, is there anything worth taking to the grand jury?"

Harry looked at me, the instigator of all of this, and shook his head. "No, Daniel, not yet. I wish I could say differently. But we've come up with no hard evidence. To tell you the truth, I was hoping this one would work out. It would have served our purpose. But don't give up hope yet."

Parr sighed. "Like I said, Ciotti will make a mistake sooner or later. We'll keep on him. For now, let's just concentrate on who we have — Louis Carlton."

"What's the charge?" I asked.

"Solicitation of capital murder," Parr said.

"Is that strong enough to get him to roll over on Ciotti? Maybe for some degree of immunity?"

"I don't know," Parr said. "Right now he's still bragging about how Ciotti's lawyers are going to have him on the street in twenty-four hours. I can tell you right now that's not going to happen."

"This might help," David said, producing the revolver from his photographer's vest. "I took this away from Louis on the boat."

"Just took it away from him?" Parr asked, accepting the weapon.

"He wasn't practicing firearm safety," I explained. "David is a real stickler about that."

"I'll take this back to the office and give it to the evidence boys," Parr said. "In fact, I'd better get back now. Mr. Verini, Mr. Singer, Father O'Donnell, gentlemen, it was nice to meet you, and I hope something comes of all this."

Verini was on his feet again, shaking hands and smiling. When Parr left, both Singers and Sally Nix followed. "We're just going in to wrap up a few things," Bill Singer said. "You boys are safe now — as long as you don't make any more low-rent mobsters mad. But since making people mad seems to be a talent of yours, Dunn, let me know if anything happens."

"Right," I said. "You'll be the first one I call."

Nix grinned at us and got her hand squeezed gallantly again by the Old Man and the priest. She liked that. "It was a pleasure being your assassin, boys. Hope to do it again."

We didn't respond.

Nix was almost at the door before I remembered that she'd driven us to Verini's.

"Wait," I said. "What about a ride home?"

Nix frowned. "No problem, of course, but we'll be up at the ADA's office for at least a couple of hours."

"Not to worry," Verini said. "I'll have someone drop them."

Father O'Donnell nodded. "I'll call Charlie. He'll be glad to do it."

"We don't want to be a problem," I said.

"No problem for Charlie. A real servant's heart, he has," Verini said.

Father O'Donnell walked the Singers and Nix to the door, and then we heard him on the telephone. Verini was getting droopy-eyed, and we knew he wouldn't last much longer into the evening.

"Charlie's a good boy," Verini said. "He runs some errands for me; he also watches over some of my properties. Sort of a handyman. *He* turned, too. Worked as a doorman at the Balinese for years. Came to me when he was in trouble once, and we spoke about our Lord. Charlie had been an altar boy as a kid, so he knew right from wrong. It was just a matter of getting him to do what was right — to turn to Christ for forgiveness. And when he did, everything changed."

The priest reentered the room with a smile. "Charlie will be right over," he said. "What an evening, eh?"

Verini sighed. "What an evening. I tell you, if we're ever successful in putting away Francis Ciotti, I think I'll miss these boys. They add a little excitement, don't they, Father?"

"Some excitement, indeed, Al."

"And I think I give them something to think about," Verini said. "Am I right, Emerson? Have I given you something to think about?"

"You have," I said. "You've given me as good an example as I've ever seen that people can change, with a little help. My own change was significant — to me, at least. Yours was dramatic."

"That may be my spiritual contribution to the world," Verini said. "And if it is, that's enough. Making people think. If they think, 'Well, this old criminal changed, so maybe I can too,' then I've done something, haven't I?"

"Yes," David responded softly. "You have."

A few moments later we heard the doorbell. David answered it and came back into the room with a burly, dull-eyed man of about sixty-five. He had large arms, a big chest, and a receding hairline. He seemed delighted to have been called on at this hour — it was after 11 P.M. — for an errand.

"Just point me in the right direction," he said. "Do you need anything else, Mr. Verini? Need me to stop by the grocer or anything?"

"Not tonight, Charlie," Verini said. "But thank you very much. And take tomorrow off. Have a long weekend."

Charlie shook his head. "Thanks just the same, Mr. Verini, but I've got half the roof off your Avenue R house; it's just covered in plastic. It might rain on Sunday, the TV says, so I'd better get the job done before then."

Verini nodded. "Whatever you think is best. You're a good man, Charlie."

Charlie beamed. "See ya," he said, bowing to Father O'Donnell.

Charlie led us out, after Verini shook our hands (not as gallantly as he had Nix's, I noticed). The Old Man made us promise to call him the next day with any new developments.

We followed Charlie to a large van, which he obviously used for work. "I only got two seats," he said, opening the passenger's door. "But one of you can sit on my toolbox."

I climbed in and found the toolbox between and a little behind the two front seats. I sat on it; it would be a long thirty-five miles home. David sat in the front. Charlie came around, climbed in on the driver's side, and started the van.

"Let's go to the office," David said. "That's where my car is. I'll take you home from there, Emerson, so Charlie won't get lost on all those country roads."

"Fine. Charlie, you can just take Broadway to 45, then head up Highway 6 West."

Charlie nodded.

"Mr. Verini has told me a little about you guys," he said. "He likes you. He likes feeling useful. I've worked for him for more than thirty-five years now. He's a good man."

"We agree," I said. "He said you used to work at the Balinese Room."

"That, and some other places. When I was young. Then I had some trouble. Mr. Verini had always been kind to me, so I went to him. He straightened me out, took me to Mass."

"You don't have to tell us, but if you don't mind, what happened?" David asked.

"I thought I killed a guy. I didn't really. See, he was drunk and mad, and he was yelling at the dealer. Couldn't have that. My job was to keep things nice and proper. So I escorted him out the door. Only he dies."

I remembered one of Harry's anecdotes. "This is the guy who died of a heart attack, in the back of the cab?" I asked.

"Yeah, that was him. The doctor says the pain was what was making him cranky, probably. And I noticed that he was almost dead on one side when I was walking him out. Turns out it wasn't my fault. I was just the last person to touch him."

"You stayed with Mr. Verini for a few days."

"About a week, yeah. I was hiding out. But everyone knew where I was, I think. Mr. Verini was out of the business at that time, you see, but I still looked up to him."

"So you also knew Francis Ciotti."

"Sure, I knew Fuzzy. He hates that name. He's not anything like Mr. Verini. Always was getting into trouble."

"Still is," David said.

"Nothing like his brother, either," Charlie said. "You heard about Nicholas?"

"We've heard Ciotti had a brother who died," I said.

"Yeah, that was sad. He was a different sort. More like a businessman. He was a little older, maybe two or three years. He was always looking out for Fuzzy, and that made Fuzzy feel bad."

"How was he different?" I asked.

"Like I said, more like a businessman. Always wore suits — not fancy suits, not shiny suits, but nice, respectable suits. Like my dad would wear — he worked for the city before he passed in '63. Nicholas wasn't hotheaded — he wasn't violent. That's the thing — Papa Rose always told me we shouldn't have to be violent anymore. Our reputation was enough. And it was. Nobody carried in the Balinese. That was part of my job; I made sure no one — not even our own people — carried guns into the club. We were there to provide a nice evening for folks — to provide recreation. I know now that we weren't providing the best kind of recreation."

"Are you still a churchgoer?"

"Sure. I take Mr. Verini to Mass twice a week. Also, we sometimes get together during the week just to pray out of his little black prayer book. Us and Father O'Donnell. But one thing: we don't talk about the old days."

"Why?" David asked.

"I think Mr. Verini's afraid he'll start remembering only the good times and forgetting the bad things. If you tell the good stories over and over, then that's what's going to happen."

"You're probably right," I said. "We're new creatures now, like the Bible says. We probably don't need to dwell on the past."

"Amen," David said.

"I feel for Mr. Verini," Charlie said. "It's gotta be hard. He's cut himself off from his past, and he's got no one in the present to care about, or to care for him. Sure, he's got a nephew up north somewhere, and he's got me and Father O'Donnell. But that's it."

I frowned. "I understood that he has plenty of visitors."

Charlie shook his head. "He says that he does. It's just not true. It's not like he's lying; he just doesn't want people to think he's a lonely old man — even though that's what he is."

"I'm sorry to hear that," I said. "I wish there was more I could do."

"You're doing something now," Charlie said. "He appreciates it. And so do I."

We drove for about forty-five minutes. Charlie was a slow driver, always a few miles-per-hour below the speed limit. We eventually arrived at the newspaper office, but it was already midnight — which made me wonder why lights were on in the office.

"Robert?" I asked David.

"That's not his car," David said. "That's a dark sedan . . . Like Ciotti's."

"What's he doing here?" Charlie asked.

"I think he wants to talk," I said. "Charlie, there's a pay phone up the street. Drop us here, then call the cops. Tell them that Francis Ciotti is at the newspaper office. They'll send someone by."

"You sure you want out of the car?"

"Yeah," I said. "If he knows the cops are coming, he's not going to do anything. That will give us 3.25 minutes to talk."

"3.25 minutes?" he asked.

"Average response time for the department. That's pretty good, actually. Drop us here."

Charlie slowed to a halt in the newspaper office parking lot. We hopped out of David's door, then waved Charlie on. He looked worried. I checked David's expression. He didn't look worried. "We don't have to go in there," I said.

"No, we'll be fine," David said. "You're right. If we walk in and say right off that the cops are on their way, and that they know who's inside, he won't shoot us."

"We hope."

"We hope," David agreed with a shrug. "God's time and God's dime."

"Yeah." I led the way to the front door; it was unlocked. I wondered how Ciotti got in. I opened the door and saw Ciotti sitting at my desk. He was leafing through a newspaper. Two gentlemen with large biceps were standing behind him. It was the same two guys he'd had with him in the restaurant.

"Francis Ciotti," I said. "So nice to meet you. Before you plug me and my friend, let me warn you that the cops are on their way. They know who we're in here with."

Ciotti laughed. When he did, his bald head wrinkled a little. It was sort of cute, kind of like a bulldog is cute as long as it's not sitting at your desk reading your newspaper.

"Dunn, we're not here to plug anyone," Ciotti said in a raspy voice. "We're here to talk . . . To ask a question. What's with you?"

"What do you mean?"

"You're buzzing around me like a bumblebee," he said. "Very annoying — and very overrated. What's a little bumblebee sting?"

"Who writes your dialogue?" I asked. Behind me, David snickered as he closed the door.

"So what's with you, Dunn? And this must be the Israeli. I had a fishing trip planned for this weekend. You screwed that up for me. One last time, what's with you?"

"It's our friends, Walter and Gunther Schmidt."

"So why couldn't you come to me and say you were worried about your friends? I have friends. I would have understood."

"But would you have done anything?"

Ciotti shook his head. "It's business. It's also legitimate business. We have a deal. Signed paper."

"You do business by beating up Walter?" David asked.

"He fell. Now here's the deal: you need to walk away. I'm giving you that option."

"That's funny," I said. "I was about to say the same thing to you. *You* need to walk away. I'm giving you that option."

Ciotti laughed. "You hear that, Jim, Tommy? A tough guy . . . Or a smart guy. Which are you, tough or smart?"

"Doesn't matter, Fuzzy. Let's just say I'm dedicated."

"Dedicated. Dedicated to what? Seeing me break your skinny neck? I'm not so old I have to rely on these two for everything. I could take both of you punks."

David smiled but didn't say anything. I did. "Ciotti, what's it going to take for this to end without anyone taking anyone else? Is there any working room here? I'm asking in good faith."

"No room whatsoever. I walk away from this deal, what do I tell the next guy who wants to go Chapter 11 on me?"

"Tell him you forgive him his debt," I said. "You've got enough money to last the rest of your life, I bet."

"Maybe," he said. "Unless I want to improve my lifestyle, and why shouldn't I be able to do that?"

"I'm not here to argue against capitalism," I said. "I like capitalism — just not your brand of it. Look, the cops will be here in a minute or so. We've answered your question. What more do you want?"

"I want your word that you're going to back off."

"No."

"Then I can't be responsible for what happens," Ciotti said. "To you, to your friends. Too bad, really; they could have made a go of that restaurant with a little help."

"David, I think we've been threatened," I said.

"It would appear so," he replied, looking a little amused. "Not the first time."

"He's right," I told Ciotti. "We've been threatened a lot. We've even had dates threaten us. But what bothers me is your threat against Walter and Gunther. That might have worked with Mitchell Ryan, but it won't work now."

Ciotti frowned. "That's another thing. Why are you digging up the past? I don't care why. Just stop."

"Boss," one of the goons said, "let's go. This meeting is no longer productive."

"Jim, you're right," Ciotti said. "It's no longer productive. Dunn, be warned, okay? That's all I have to say."

Ciotti got out of my chair slowly, then led his two goons past us through the door. Nobody bumped us with their chest or shoulder. Without another word they left. We heard the gravel under their wheels as they drove from the parking lot. About thirty seconds later a squad car approached, then slowed to a halt in front of the door. A uniformed cop got out.

"Any trouble here?" he asked. It was Ramirez.

"Nah," I said. "But leave a message for Singer that Ciotti paid us a visit."

"Did he make any threats?"

"None clear enough to prosecute on," I said. "He's slick. He just said he can't be responsible for what happens. I think we've irritated him somehow."

"You guys want protection tonight?"

"No," David said. "I'll stay at Emerson's. We'll be all right."

Ramirez nodded. "Fine. I'll let Singer know."

It wasn't until he drove off that we noticed Charlie's van parked at the side of the newspaper office; Charlie was waiting in the shadows.

"I was here the whole time," he said. "Nothing would have happened. I used to do that for a living — make sure nothing happened."

"Thanks," I said. "Now you'd better get on home. You have a roofing job tomorrow."

Charlie nodded. "Fuzzy won't do anything for a few days. If he did anything tonight, it would be too obvious to the police. So sleep tight. I'll say a prayer for you. By the way, here's my telephone number. If you need me . . ."

He handed me a card; it had his name and telephone number, under a drawing of a ladder, a hammer, and a paint bucket.

"Thanks," I said. "We'll call if we need you."

He nodded, then returned to his van; a moment later he drove away.

"Call your mother," I said to David as we reentered the office. "I'll call Remington."

He sat at Robert's desk and took Line 1; I sat at my own and punched Line 2. Remington answered on the first ring.

"Hello," I said. "We're all safe and sound, so you can go back to bed."

"Sally Nix didn't shoot you?"

"Nope. She bagged the bad guy."

"Good. Are you home?"

"No, we're just now back at the office."

Remington paused. "You sound a little strained. What's wrong?"

"Ciotti was waiting here at the office for us," I said. "He's not such a bad guy, if you like rabid bulldogs."

"What did he say?"

I went over our conversation with Ciotti for her. She didn't respond.

"Remington, he's just trying to scare us off," I said.

"Maybe you *should* be scared," she said. Then she paused. "No, I know that's not right. You shouldn't be scared off. You're doing what's right. How are those cases coming — the old ones you and Bill and Harry are investigating?"

"Not so great," I said. "We won't know until tomorrow, when Harry talks them over with the DA. He's essentially told the assistant DA not to get his hopes up. There's a chance the DA might like one of the cases, but not a big chance."

"And the gangster fisherman you guys beat up — did he mention Ciotti?"

"No. He was too busy trying to impress Sally with his own influence."

"Well, I guess all we can do is keep at it," Remington said. "Maybe something will break."

"That's the way it's done," I said. "Persistence. Maybe something little will turn into something big," I said. "Remington, persistence has paid off in another area, hasn't it? David has become a Christian."

"I've been praying for that to happen, but I didn't dare hope. It's so much for him, so much harder than it was for me."

"David's whole life has been harder than ours," I said.

"I know. In fact, I've noticed that it's been a little harder for him lately. He's been a little, well, troubled."

"Troubled. Yeah. I wish I could have picked up on that sooner than I did. But it has all worked out fine, I think. The big part, at least. Now, tell me how you're doing, love of my life."

"I'm fine. We're on for dinner with my mother next Thursday."

"Great."

"I've finished the paperwork for SMU."

"Great."

"It's going to be a long autumn."

"No," I said. "It won't be bad."

"But distance killed your last relationship."

"I killed my last relationship by being an insensitive clod. This relationship is safe, as long as you're pushy enough to overcome my insensitivity."

"It's a deal. I'm going to bed now. Call me tomorrow."

"I will. I love you."

When I hung up, I noticed David grinning at me.

"Insensitive clod?" he asked.

"That's an important part of a relationship," I said. "Totally humbling yourself at your true love's feet. It's important to them."

"I don't think you're insensitive," David said. "Clueless maybe, but not insensitive."

"Clueless does seem to be our problem," I replied. "Let's go home and see if Airborne has any wisdom to impart."

24

The next day was Friday; that's when we put out the Sunday paper. The art was good, the stories were in, and by noon I was ready to begin paste-up. I got a call just before lunch, though; it was Martin.

"Bring David over and we'll have some casserole," he said. "We ought to talk some."

"Sure," I said. "We'll be over in about fifteen minutes."

I went back to the darkroom and knocked. David opened the door; he was wearing gloves, cleaning out his trays for the weekend.

"Martin's invited us over for some lunch," I said. "You interested? I already accepted for both of us."

"Okay," he said. "I'm pretty toxic right now, though. Give me a few minutes to wash."

"I'll be at my desk."

David emerged about five minutes later. He smelled a little of film chemicals, but then, he usually smelled that way. We drove to Martin's house in David's car. When we arrived, Susie was waiting at the door for us. Susie was Martin's kid — one of the three. She was allegedly sweet and undeniably pretty and about four years old. I knew better than to turn my back on her. That disarming smile didn't fool me anymore. At least, not often. I still had this feeling that someday, maybe twelve or so years hence, she was going to bat those eyelashes at me, and I'd hear myself saying, "Of course, of course, but what color sports car do you want?"

"Where's A. C.?" she asked in the here-and-now.

"She's at work," I said. "Remember David?"

"Yes. No girls?"

"No girls. Sorry. We'll have to do."

"Okay." What a charmer. Maybe a red sports car would do. Susie turned and went into the house, a small red brick ranch-style on a large lot; the oaks we'd planted a couple of years earlier were maturing nicely. There was a doll stuck on an upper branch of one of the trees. She seemed be wearing some sort of a parachute, which was caught on the branch. Undoubtedly Ricky's doing. I grinned, then followed Susie inside.

"We're here," I announced. We walked into the kitchen, which was bright and airy. The table was already set, so I knew it was a formal occasion. Meg, Martin's wife, usually made me set the table. When we studied the part about spiritual gifts in the Bible, Martin tried to convince me that mine had something to do with dishes.

Martin was at the table, reading the Thursday edition of our newspaper. Meg hugged me, then did the same to David. David wasn't an overly demonstrative guy, but he accepted it well. Martin shook our hands and appeared pleased that we'd made it. Susie hopped up on a chair and stared at us.

"Sit down," Martin said. We did. "A. C. told me what happened, David. Do you want to talk about it?"

David nodded. "We've been busy, or I would have called you myself."

"Yes, A. C. told me something about you being busy too. But first things first. You made a decision."

"I've trusted Christ."

"Praise God," Martin said. "That's wonderful. You've been on my heart a long time. I know how much Emerson and A. C. care about you; I knew you must be someone pretty special."

Meg brought in a casserole dish with something that involved chicken and cheese. I was sold. She handed me the serving spoon, and I started hitting the plates with big lumps of casserole.

"Do you have any questions about your decision?" Martin asked.

"Emerson answered most of them," David said. "I know what I need to do next. I feel I need to join the church."

Martin nodded. "That's a good step. It sort of helps make a clean break from your old life."

"That's come up a lot lately," I said, still serving. "Martin, how clean a break is it?"

"It differs," he said. "I've known men — alcoholics and addicts — who put away the bottle or the drugs the day they accepted Christ and never touched it again. I've known others — people I firmly believe are saved — who still struggle with old sins, old habits. You're a good example, Emerson."

"Of which one?" I asked.

"Of both. I don't mean you're an example of either extreme. You're a good example of what God does with a person. You were able to give up most of your bad habits, but you still struggle with a few things."

"Sure," I said. "I assume we all do."

"Right. There's always the push-and-pull of our old nature."

"Remington worries that her old nature — the one she fears she inherited from her parents — will prevent her from making a real, lifelong commitment," I said. "And Alberto Verini is afraid he hasn't distanced himself enough from his old nature."

David was silent. Martin spoke up after a moment. "And, David, if I'm reading you right, what you're wondering right now is how much of your past you should retain."

David nodded. "I am a Christian now, but am I still a Jew? It's all I've ever been. It's what I feel deep down. If Israel is attacked, I would go back and fight. Do I keep kosher? Do I have a Jewish wedding? Do I marry a Jewish girl, or do I look for a Gentile and dishonor my mother? There are many questions."

"Emerson was a pretty good writer before he became a Christian," Martin said. "He didn't stop being a writer. This old gangster I've heard about, he didn't change all his ways at once, I would guess. David, I don't think you can stop being a Jew, an Israeli, because you've become a Christian. There are others, you know. They call themselves 'completed Jews' sometimes."

"I know a few," David said. "They still keep kosher."

"And they still celebrate Passover," Martin replied. "The thing to remember is that the Holy Spirit is in you now. Don't worry so much about losing your heritage. The decisions you'll make will be made on a case-by-case basis. We'll help you through them; so will the Bible, and so will the Holy Spirit."

"Speaking of the Holy Spirit, can we bless this stuff?" I asked. Meg smiled at me — she usually didn't mind me calling her culinary specialties "stuff."

Martin asked me to say the blessing — I think it was more of that discipleship stuff. When I was through, I looked at David.

"You'll be doing it next, you know."

David grinned. We started eating. After a moment Martin looked up at me.

"Now tell me about this old gangster," he said. "And why someone wanted to have you two killed last night."

It was a longer-than-normal meal; we had a lot of explaining to do. Martin knew the Schmidt boys and commended us for our efforts, but he warned us to be careful. He always did that; it was sort of his job. Remington had told him everything, including about Lou Carlton. By the time we were ready to return to work, Martin was almost satisfied that we'd live long enough to show up for church on Sunday. He and David talked about baptism, about what it means and what it doesn't mean. David said he was comfortable with being baptized soon; he wasn't one to back down from a decision or its consequences, even if those consequences involved preachers in chest-high fishing waders.

"I'll have the baptismal ready," Martin said as he walked us to the door. "Be there a little early, we'll go over the process."

David nodded, then turned to Martin. "I don't want you to think the questions I have mean that I regret my decision," he said. "I know I've done the right thing. I can feel it. I'm happier than I've been in a long time. More at peace. Do you understand?"

Martin smiled. "Yes, I do. See you Sunday."

David didn't talk during the drive back to the office. When we arrived, and before we got out of the car, I paused. "Dave, it's not always going to feel good, but it's always going to feel right. You'll know the difference."

He nodded, and I followed him into the office. When I walked in the door, Sharon the Receptionist handed me a pink message slip. "Call Singer," it said.

"Which one?" I asked. "I've been spending time with the son and the dad both lately."

"The son," Sharon said. "The one who's rude to you."

"He's not rude," I said. "He's just socially challenged." I went to my desk and dialed his number.

"Singer," he said.

"It's Emerson. You called?"

"Yeah."

"News?"

"Yeah."

"You're not making this easy," I said. "What's the news?"

"We're 0 for 6 on our cases," he said. "The DA won't touch a single one of them. They're too old, too obscure, and too hard to substantiate. I can't say I blame him."

"How about Lou Carlton? Did he say anything worthwhile last night?"

"Nothing linking him to Ciotti. By the way, tell me a little about your visit from Ciotti last night."

"It was a meaningful experience," I said. "He was *mean*, and he was *full* of himself. He wants us to back off."

"Will you?"

"No."

"Didn't think so," Singer growled. "I can't baby-sit you, though, Dunn."

"I don't need a baby-sitter. I need a good dose of German food a couple of times a week, and I'm just trying to save my source."

"Right. Dunn, did it ever occur to you that these boys might not need to be in business for themselves? They're no good at it. If they went away, went to work somewhere for someone else, they'd be just as happy."

"You don't know them well. They've wanted this for a long time. And I agree they're no good at it. That means they need a legitimate business partner, not a loan shark. That's all."

"Maybe. But they've got the loan shark. I don't know how much more we can do. We're batting zero."

"At least we ruined Fuzzy's fishing trip. He'd planned to go out this weekend."

"That's one for our side," Singer said. "Look, I'm doing all I can. I've passed the word through Dad and through his old Galveston contacts to Ciotti that we're very fond of you. It's a slight stretch of the truth, I know, but it might keep you alive, if you're smart enough to back off."

"I'll take what you've said under advisement."

"Do that." He hung up. I closed my eyes and let the disappointment sink in. We had nothing on Ciotti, and meanwhile he was still squeezing money and blood out of my friends. When I opened my eyes, David was in front of me.

"Have you been in back?" he asked.

"No. I came in the same time you did," I said. "Aren't we ventilating the darkroom well enough?"

"You'd better come back here."

I followed David to the paste-up area; there on the boards were all twenty pages of the Sunday edition. Completed. Robert stood over the front page, holding an Exacto knife and grinning.

"Impressive," I said. "Three hours. What's my best time, David?"

"For eight-and-twelve? Three hours, fifteen minutes."

"Impressive. Robert, you're a wonder. Has your hairline always been that far back?"

25

We spent another hour and a half proofing Robert's paste-up job. Then there was nothing more to be done, so at 4:30 we closed shop and left for the farmhouse. I invited Robert out for some grilled burgers. David called Remington, and she said she'd be by right after work. David swung by his house to put in an appearance. His mother and his uncle were probably ready to send out a posse.

The evening was a needed respite from problems. By 6:30 David was back, and Remington had arrived with Maggie in tow. Maggie and Robert found a lot to talk about. David spent most of his time with my dog. Which left me with Remington, my Gooey Apple Strudel of Love. She hit me when I referred to her as such.

"I'm going to look for an apartment in Dallas next weekend," she said casually. "Want to come along? I'm going to try that list Mr. Verini gave me first."

We were sitting on my porch, watching the evening light recede. I was in the rocker; she sat beside me in a molded plastic patio chair. Robert, Maggie, and David were inside, talking politics.

"I'd love to come along," I said. "We can stay with my folks."

"Good. What about Airborne?"

"David won't mind coming and feeding him," I said. "It's only for the weekend. I bet Maggie might even do it."

Remington nodded. "Things are really looking up for her, aren't they?" she asked.

"Yeah. She has a good job, a car, and an apartment so she can spend all that money from her good job."

"She seems pretty interested in Robert."

"He's bright, good-looking, and fashionable. I don't see what's so interesting about him."

"He reminds her a lot of you. She told me that."

"Only I'm old and grumpy."

"Right," Remington said. "I can live with old and grumpy. In fact, I could out-grump you in a fair match any day of the week."

"Oh yeah? How do you feel about people?"

"Don't like 'em."

"And traffic?"

"I hate it when people have the nerve to be in my way. They should all just stay home when I'm driving."

"How about dogs?"

"I love dogs. Especially Airborne."

"Gotcha. I think he's a smelly, uneducated mutt. See? I'll be a grumpy old man before you know it."

"No, you won't," Remington said. "You love that dog. You talk to him. That's a little neurotic, but it's sweet."

"I talk to him? How do you know?"

"He told me."

I nodded.

Remington shifted around a little in her seat. "Emerson, you're probably wondering why I brought Maggie along."

"Nope," I said. "Hadn't wondered that at all. Should I?"

"It has to do with what we've been talking about. I was with her last night; you were off galavanting around, so we got together."

"Girl talk?" I asked.

"You're a sexist. Anyway, she told me that last time she

stopped in the newspaper office to say hello to you, you weren't there. But Robert was. They talked for a while."

"He's like that. Personable. Maybe he'll get boils."

"He asked her out."

"Okay, hold off on the boils. Those could ruin a date."

"She turned him down."

"Why?" I asked.

"Because of her past," Remington said softly. "I told her she was wrong to turn him down."

"You did?"

"Yes. I've been doing the same thing — worrying about my own past, and I was almost to the point of letting it damage my future. But it's so clear now. Look at Mr. Verini. Look at me."

"I do look at you. Every opportunity I get."

"That's not what I mean. I worried about my background, my past. But I've moved beyond that."

"You have?"

"It was news to me until I told Maggie that last night," Remington admitted. "But I have. Yes, there's always going to be remnants of our past still lying around. There's always going to be a struggle between our old nature and our new nature. But that's a conflict that's already been won, right?"

"Right."

"So what I'm saying is, forget my doubts. Forgive me, maybe. I'm sorry."

"There's nothing to be sorry for," I said. "You weren't hurting me with them, only yourself."

She was silent for a moment.

"Remington, you seem to have convinced Maggie of the same thing."

"I convinced her that there's no use making herself miserable in the present," she said. "She wasn't ready for a date, but this sort of a get-together is safe enough for her. I think maybe Mordechai was on her case a little too."

"Mordechai seems to have taken a somewhat fatherly role," I said. "I like it. It will be good for both of them."

Remington nodded.

David appeared at the back door, with Airborne close behind. "What's up?" he asked, closing the door, then sitting on Airborne's blanket.

"We're just solving the world's problems," I said. "Got any you need straightened out?"

David laughed. "Not me. Not by you two. Well, Remington maybe. She's a good help on things like wardrobe and menus with things like 'buffalo wings' on them. That bothered me for weeks, until she told me what they were."

"Thanks for your confidence," Remington smiled. "Have we discussed your photographer's vest yet? You know, you wear it an awful lot."

"Pushy, Emerson. Just like you said." David grinned as he scratched Airborne's ears. "When do you think we'll see Mr. Verini again?"

"We can go by tomorrow," I said. "We told him we'd report any new developments. There aren't any, but he'd probably appreciate a call or even a visit. You're starting to like the Old Man, aren't you?"

"Yeah," he said. "Like Charlie said, he's a little lonely. I worry about that."

"He shouldn't be," I said. "He's a good man. He's also charming."

"That he is," Remington said. "He could charm the socks off a snake."

"You should have seen Sally Nix melt like butter when he took her hand. He could have confessed to the St. Valentine's Day Massacre and she'd have let him walk."

David nodded. I rocked back in my chair for a few moments, and then something clicked. "And maybe he did. Maybe that's exactly what he did."

Remington and David looked at me curiously.

"Emerson, have you been into the flea dip again?" David asked. "I've told you to try not to breathe the fumes."

David was looking at Airborne, whose eyes were closed in canine bliss.

"Dave, you're a Jew. You are — were — a soldier. You are Israeli. Martin says that being a Christian doesn't change that. There's a new nature, but there's the old one too."

"Right. We've been over this, Emerson," Remington said. "What's your point?"

"We've been looking at Alberto Verini's new nature, and not his old nature. We've been investigating the wrong suspect."

"You're making absolutely no sense," Remington said.

I took a deep breath. "Okay, I'll slow it down. Harry, then Verini himself, told me about the incident that led him — Verini — to turn to God. It was his wife's death. What made his wife's death so much more painful was that the night she became ill, he was involved in a shooting. He says he shot Francis Ciotti's brother, Nicholas, when he went for a gun."

"Yeah," David said slowly.

"Something about that story has been bothering me for days. It doesn't mesh with what we know about Alberto Verini. He told other stories. Remember, Remington, the story about how he was a guard in the early days, when they were still bootlegging? He guarded a truck, but when shooting broke out, he shot his own engine block. After that, they used him as a driver."

Remington nodded. "And Father O'Donnell's comment when you thought that Mr. Verini might have been talking about your right hand being your gun hand. The father said, 'Not him,' meaning maybe that Mr. Verini wasn't used to guns?"

"Right. That wasn't enough, but then when Charlie told us his job as a doorman at the Balinese Room was to keep rowdies and all firearms out of the club, I knew the stories weren't adding up."

"So what are you saying?" David asked.

"I'm saying something's not kosher about the killing of Nicholas Ciotti."

26

David and I were at Harry Singer's house the next morning at 10 A.M. Harry was wearing coveralls, and he looked delighted to see us.

"I was spreading mulch in the backyard," he grinned. "Needed a good excuse for a glass of iced tea. You'll do nicely."

"Great, Harry. We need to talk to you for a few moments," I said.

Harry nodded, then let us into the house. We followed him into the dining room. "Have a seat," he said. "I'll get some glasses. Start talking — I can hear you."

I pulled out a notebook and a pen. "Go over the Nicholas Ciotti case for me again," I said.

"Okay," Harry replied from the kitchen. We could hear him washing his hands, then putting ice in some glasses. "Around midnight, January 12, 1949, I was called out to a shooting. When I get there, Nicholas Ciotti is on the steps leading down from the pier, being held by Francis Ciotti. Nicholas has a single gunshot wound to his chest. Al Verini hands me a gun, says he shot Nicholas Ciotti when Nicholas went for his own gun. He said the brothers had been arguing, even pushing each other a little."

Harry entered, carrying three glasses of tea. "Why the questions, Emerson?"

"It doesn't add up. Did you find a gun on Nicholas?"

"I found a cannon on Nicholas. A .45 caliber service automatic . . . Colt."

"Did you ever know Nicholas to carry guns?" I asked.

"They all carried guns," Harry said, but then he paused. "No, that's not fair. That's a generalization. Your question was, did I ever know Nicholas to carry guns? And the answer is no. He wasn't the type. A nice guy, in his fashion. But he had the gun on him . . . Tucked in his waistband. I went over to Francis and Nicholas, unbuttoned Nicholas's coat to see how bad the wound was, and there the piece was, staring at me."

I nodded, then looked at David. He was frowning.

"Harry, we're going to Galveston," I said. "Call the Old Man and set up a time for us to meet. This afternoon maybe. I'll call you later, after lunch, and we'll all convene at Verini's house. I think we've got something."

Harry nodded. "I think I see where you're going with this, boys. I'll make the call. I'll also call Alex Parr's boy, that assistant DA, and see if we can't get some action this weekend. If, that is, this all pans out."

David drove calmly down Highway 6 toward Galveston. "The roofing job was on Avenue R," he said. "But we don't know where on Avenue R."

"So we drive down it until we see Charlie on someone's house," I said. "No problem."

We drove for another thirty minutes until we turned right from Broadway Boulevard and headed toward the seawall; between the two we found Avenue R. Near the intersection of Avenue R and 31st Street, we saw Charlie's van parked in front of a modest frame house. Charlie himself was on the roof, pushing a roll of tar-covered felt across new-looking plywood. David parked his Toyota, and we got out.

"Charlie!" I called out. He looked down, then smiled when he recognized us.

"There are two hammers in the back of the van," he said. "I need someone to tack down the felt while I hold it in place."

We nodded, then found the two hammers in the van. A wooden ladder was leaning on the house just to the side of the driveway. We scaled it, David going first, and we soon found ourselves on top of the roof with Charlie. He was cutting the tar-soaked roofing felt with a large knife.

"The nails are in that little brown bag there," he said, nodding toward a collection of tools and bags perched on the apex of the roof. David walked up the plywood-covered roof to the bags and grabbed a large handful of roofing nails. He came back to me and handed me about half.

"Charlie, we want to talk to you a little about the old days," I said, "if you don't mind."

Charlie shrugged. "See the white lines on the felt?" he asked. We nodded. "Those have to match up. If they're not straight when the felt is nailed down, I'll never get the shingles on straight. We'll start from the bottom. Always start from the bottom."

He laid a roof-long piece of the felt along the bottom of the roof; it hung over the sides a little, but he said he'd trim that later. When he was satisfied it was straight, he told us to put in a nail every eighteen inches or so. We did.

"What about the old days?" Charlie asked.

"We're curious about Nicholas Ciotti," I said.

Charlie nodded. "Nice man. I already told you about him."

"We want to know about his death."

Charlie nodded again. "That was a terrible night."

"Were you there?" David asked.

"Not outside when it happened. I was on duty inside, though."

"Charlie, you said that your job was to keep firearms out of the nightclub," I said. "Did that go for Maceo employees as well?"

Charlie nodded. "Only gun in there was the one guarding the bank, and that night it was on my hip."

"You were guarding the bank that night, not the door?" I asked.

"Yeah. Someone else was at the door that night."

"Was there any chance that Nicholas Ciotti had a gun in the Balinese Room that night?"

Charlie shook his head. "Not when I saw him. I remember it clearly — because he was always friendly, and that's the last time I saw him alive."

"Are you sure?" David asked. "Could it have been in his suit? In his waistband?"

Charlie snorted. "Only the best Maceo bodyguards worked the Balinese," he said. "First of all, he wouldn't have gotten in the door with a piece, and he knew it, so he would have left it at home or in his car. Second, I would have noticed. Nicholas always wore nice suits, like I told you. They fit well. Spotting those things was my job, remember."

I looked at David. David frowned and looked back at Charlie. "What was he doing at the Balinese Room's bank?" he asked.

"Markers," Charlie said. "He collected about fifteen thousand in markers — paid off a very large debt. Sam Serio — they called him 'Books' — cashed him out. Funny, though, Nicholas was never much of a gambler. I always wondered how he'd gotten in so deep."

"Is Sam Serio still around?" I asked.

Charlie shook his head. "Been gone for years," he replied. "He was nice, too. Very businesslike. When I started contracting — fixing up houses and things, I mean — he helped me with my money for a few years. When he passed, Mr. Verini found me someone else."

"Charlie, you've been a big help," I said.

"So are you," Charlie replied. "Let's do the second row."

We stayed with Charlie for another hour and a half; once we had the felt down, he said he could do the rows of shingles himself. He thanked us for the help and offered to pay us. We laughed and said we might need him to return the favor later.

When we drove away, David grinned. "It's coming together," he said.

"It's still just a hunch. Find a phone, and let's see if Harry's set up a meeting with the Old Man."

At a convenience store across the street from the seawall, we called Harry. He said we'd meet at Verini's at 3 P.M. That gave us a couple of hours to kill.

"Let's find Mary Ryan," I said as I hung up the telephone. "We'll tell her we won't need her to testify. We'll also tell her that if she wants to return a favor done for her more than thirty years ago, we know of a lonely ex-mobster who could use some company."

David agreed. We drove out along the seawall looking for signs of Mary Ryan on the jetties. About two miles from the end, we found her. She wasn't on a jetty; she was surf fishing, standing waist-deep in the water, casting out into the Gulf.

We parked, then walked down to the beach. David had to yell to get her attention over the drumming of the surf. When she saw us, she waved, then pointed at her pole. She slowly reeled it in, then sloshed her way back onto the beach.

"Hello, boys," she said. She was wearing a T-shirt and shorts, and both were soaking wet. On a chair near her tackle box she found a towel, which she used to blot herself dry, or at least tried to. "What can I do for you? Did you catch your crook yet?"

"Not yet," I said. "But as for solving mysteries, we've gotten one or two figured out. Mrs. Ryan, last time we came to you asking for a favor, and you agreed. Now we need to change the favor. We don't need you to testify."

"What is it you're needing, then?"

"We need to tell you what happened in 1959," I said. "You weren't very involved with the business before your husband was killed, were you?"

"No," she said. "Would that I was."

"Well, he didn't buy that building just before he died. He was renting, actually."

Mary Ryan frowned at me.

"It was a gift to you," I explained. "From someone who had lost his own spouse ten years earlier. He bent the truth a little when he came by and said the building was paid off; actually, it was his building, and he signed it over into your name."

"Who was he?"

"Is," I said. "His name is Al Verini. He's a lonely old man now, although he hides it well. He's done so much good like that in his life, but he doesn't have many friends to show for it. If I'm asking anything of you, I'm asking you to let Al Verini enjoy some of the fruits of his kindness here on earth, not just in Heaven."

Mary Ryan nodded. "I'm not surprised, am I? I know of Al Verini. I go to a different church, but I hear he's a regular at St. Mary's. He's been the subject of some talk now and again through the years. And I've heard the stories about him. A lonely old man, is he? Perhaps I could drop in and introduce myself. Saying 'thank you,' is the least I could do."

She eyed us with an appraising stare. "And what is your interest in this, boys?"

"We like him," David said.

At 3 P.M. we were in front of Verini's house; Harry's car was already there. We parked and walked up to the front door. It was Harry who answered the doorbell.

"I haven't said anything to him yet about this," Harry said. "Be kind, now, boys. If you're wrong, you'll be bringing up some painful memories for no good purpose."

"I know," I said.

We followed Harry into the library. Verini was standing. Father O'Donnell wasn't there.

"Boys, it's good to see you," Verini said, shaking our hands. "But I must admit the good captain here has me a little wary. What's this all about?"

"Can we sit?" I asked.

Verini nodded, then gestured to the chairs.

"Mr. Verini, this is very hard," I said. "But I think you might have — well, been a little untruthful with us about something."

Verini stiffened.

"We think that you didn't kill Nicholas Ciotti," I said gently.

"Quite a gutsy accusation," Verini said slowly with a slight smile, "accusing me of not murdering a man."

"Too many things are wrong with this picture," I said. "First, you can't shoot straight. On the beach you shot your own truck. And Nicholas was killed with one shot, to the chest. Through the heart, Harry says."

Verini didn't respond.

"Second, Charlie was on duty that night," I continued. "He says that Nicholas didn't have a gun to go for. When Harry found a gun stuffed in Nicholas's waistband, it was after Francis Ciotti had been holding him for a while."

"If I didn't kill Nicholas, why would I say that I did?"

"You were trying to save Francis Ciotti," I said. "Papa Rose would have killed Francis for shooting Nicholas, especially on the steps in front of the Balinese Room. You knew that Papa Rose would accept your story if you said you did it. Papa Rose trusted your honesty and your judgment."

I looked at Verini. He was wearing either the same dark suit or a similar one; his eyes appeared just the slightest bit cloudy in the harsh daylight filtering into the room. "Mr. Verini, tell us what really happened that night."

Verini shook his head. "Were Father O'Donnell here, I don't know that I could even tell him. Think about what you're saying, son. It's horrible. If Nicholas had no gun, there was no need for anyone to kill him. But I saw him reach."

"I think he was reaching into his coat for a handful of markers," I said. "He'd just paid them off. About fifteen thousand dollars, Charlie says. I don't think they were his. I think they were Francis's — everyone's told me how Nicholas always bailed Francis out of trouble."

Verini shook his head. "You don't know what you're saying."

"But I know what I'm talking about," I said. "I'm talking about the murder that could put Ciotti away — the premeditated murder that he took advantage of your kindliness to commit. We can take this to the DA."

Verini stood. "I need to think. Maybe you should go for now and leave me alone for a little while."

I nodded.

Verini took my hand. "Go now. I'll call you later today. I have your number."

I lowered my voice a bit. "It's Saturday, Mr. Verini. A payment is due tonight. Don't think for too long."

Harry led us through the hallway and out the door.

"Harry, what do you think he'll do?" I asked nervously.

The old cop shook his head. "No telling, boys. Go home now. There's no rushing him, and there's nothing more to do until he makes a decision."

During the drive home, David was quiet. After about fifteen minutes, I couldn't stand it anymore.

"What's on your mind?" I asked. "You're thinking again. I can tell. Your eyebrows get lower."

"It's Saturday. There's a payment due. We don't know what Ciotti's going to do."

"And?"

"And I think I feel like some German food . . . And a few cups of coffee . . . And a long, relaxing evening with friends . . . At the restaurant."

"I agree. If they're going to have any trouble, I'd kind of like to be there to share it with them."

"Very considerate."

"Bill Singer knows that Ciotti might show up tonight. I'm sure he's going to watch the place."

"I hope so. What are the chances the guys have enough money to make the loan payment?"

"Close to zero," I said. "They've been open two days this week. I don't think that's long enough to make much of a profit."

We drove on; half an hour later we were at my house. I changed clothes and kissed my dog, and then we headed back into town for an early dinner. When we approached the restaurant, we could see a couple of cars in front; neither was a dark sedan.

We parked, and I followed David in. Gunther was wiping down a table in a booth near the front door, and he smiled when he saw us.

"Hello," he said. "How's this booth?"

"Fine," I replied. "Any sign of Fuzzy Ciotti today?"

Gunther frowned. "He's coming for dinner."

"Do you have the money to pay him?"

Gunther smiled again. "This time, yes. All we did was deduct the cost of the broken plates, the broken oven, and the anticipated profits during the time we were closed. For this payment, we owe him nine dollars."

I frowned. "Whose math is that?"

"Mine," Walter said, appearing from the kitchen. "If he doesn't like it, he can jump in a lake."

"Walter, it's your call," I said. "I won't interfere. But don't you think that might make him an eensy bit angry?"

Walter shrugged. "What can he do? There is no money, because we were closed. Does he want to foreclose? If he does, fine. Like you said, Emerson, who will cook? Jim and Tommy?"

I shrugged. "We're sticking around for a while," I said. "Bring us some coffee and an appetizer."

Walter bowed and left for the kitchen. Gunther paused for a minute. "Thanks for your help," he said. "But maybe it's time we stood up for ourselves."

Four hours later Francis Ciotti marched into the restaurant, followed by Jim and Tommy. I didn't know which was Jim and which was Tommy; at this point, I didn't much care. They walked past David and me to a table that had recently been cleared. They took their seats, with Ciotti facing the door. It was almost

8 P.M. exactly; the last of the dinner customers had just left. It was just the good guys and the bad guys.

"Howsabout some service," one of the goons called out.

Gunther appeared with three menus; Walter appeared in his dress whites. He even had on the hat. Gunther handed a menu to the leaner-looking goon and said, "Jim." Then he handed one to Tommy, whom he also greeted curtly by name. He didn't say Ciotti's name; he just put a menu in front of him on the table.

"Mr. Ciotti," Walter said softly, "we will serve you dinner, and we will talk business. But if you're here to collect money, you may leave now. We have no money, and even if we did, we wouldn't give you any."

Ciotti smiled. "We're not here to collect," Ciotti said. "We're here for this fancy meet you people want. I'm going to listen to what you have to say, and then I'm going to foreclose."

"A fancy meet?" Walter asked.

"A meeting. You people called it. You'd better not be wasting my time, yanking my chain."

The door opened; Al Verini entered. I was stunned.

"Al . . ." Ciotti said.

"Francis," Verini replied. "Glad you could make it. May I take the extra seat?"

Without waiting for a reply, Verini sat down at the table across from Ciotti.

"So you called this?" Ciotti asked. His bald head was slick with sweat. David glanced at me, then glanced at the table. We stood and walked a little closer.

Verini sighed. "Yes, Francis, I called this meeting. To see if we can work something out."

"What's to work out, old man?"

The tension was building. David and I were behind and to the left of Verini; Walter and Gunther were to his right. Jim and Tommy looked a little bored — well-dressed, as usual, but bored.

"There have been some bad dealings in the past," Verini said.

"Must I go into details? Must I put it into words? Such unpleasant business."

"Go ahead and put it into words," Ciotti said. "I'm listening, and I don't mind unpleasant words."

Verini nodded. "That's all it would take, Francis. A few unpleasant words — 'Yes, Francis Ciotti did it' — and this would be over."

"We were right," I said softly to David.

Ciotti looked up. His goons were already looking at us. Ciotti grunted. "Did you bring these two into this, old man?"

Verini looked around slowly, then nodded to me when he caught my eye. David and I stayed put.

"They're the reason I'm in it, Francis," he said, turning back to Ciotti. "Think of it. All these years I've spent going over and over everything that happened. Every beating, every shooting, every card game I let you throw, every race result I let you delay. And I never put two and two together. Remember 1949? January 12?"

"Pretend that I don't, old man," Ciotti said, staring through Verini. "Tell me about it."

"That's when it happened," Verini said. "The little altercation outside the Balinese Room. Remember? It was about midnight, and I was ready to go home. You said you needed to talk. I said okay, let's go back inside. No, you said, on the beach. So we walked down onto the beach and walked for a while. You talked. About nothing. Nothing at all important. You kept checking your watch. We turned around a few hundred yards down and started back. I was a patient man; I thought maybe it was something difficult — maybe about your brother. I know there was a little tension — he was rising in the organization and you weren't. We got back to the Balinese just in time to see your brother coming out of the club. He's mad. He starts pushing you, shoving you; you tried to calm him down — you made sure I was there to see that part. When he doesn't calm down, you hit him. Once. Twice. He goes into his jacket for something, you pull your gun and shoot. Bang. He's gone."

Verini spoke softly, calmly, sadly. He leaned toward Ciotti. "I took the gun from your hand, Francis. When Dutch Voight came out the door to see what the shot was, I lied to him. I said I shot your brother Nicholas when he went for a gun. We told the same thing to Sergeant Singer when he arrived in a police car. We told the same story to the police captain, and then we told the same lie to Papa Rose. Papa Rose was mad, but it was self-defense, I said.

"I was looking out for you, Francis. Papa Rose let it go because it was me. He wouldn't have done that for you. I knew you had tried to calm your brother down — at least I thought I knew that. You didn't, did you? You set him up. You knew you were going to kill him. And you set me up. Even if I had let you take the rap, you had a witness — me — to say you fired in self-defense when he went for his gun. But was he going for his gun? Sure, we found a gun on him, but only after you went over and held him as he died. I was pretty busy wiping down your .38 and putting my own prints on it. Harry Singer found a gun stuffed into Nicholas's pants — a .45 auto Colt. I remember the gun — you got it from a fly-boy who brought it back from the war. Ripped up five hundred dollars worth of markers for that little jewel. What was Nicholas doing with your gun, Francis?"

"You were there, old man. He went for it; he was gonna shoot me."

"With his coat buttoned? He went for a piece stuffed into his pants without unbuttoning his coat? I — we— think he might have been going for something else. Charlie — you remember Charlie — said that right before Nicholas left the club, he paid off a stack of markers — fifteen thousand dollars. Were they your markers, Francis? Was he angry at you because you'd gotten yourself into trouble, and he'd had to bail you out one more time? You let an awful lot of people bail you out of an awful lot of trouble, Francis — me, Nicholas, Papa Rose."

"That was years ago, old man. Who's going to believe a story like that? The shooting never even went to the grand jury. No one remembers, no one cares. What's your point?"

"My point is this, Francis: that fifteen thousand dollars was your debt, and it was wiped clean when your brother paid it off and then died," Verini said. He motioned to Walter. "These young men standing here, these German boys, also have a debt. It will be wiped clean. And we'll all walk away from this."

Ciotti laughed. "I can't do that. It's bad business. But I'll tell you what: if you're apologetic, if you're sorry for the things you said about me, I'll let *you* walk away from this."

"That's a threat, is it, Francis?" Verini still sounded calm. "If I don't apologize, you'll shoot me too, just like your brother? But you haven't heard the whole story. I haven't finished it. Where were we? January 12, about midnight. Francis, I didn't go home until the next morning, what with first the police questioning me, then Papa Rose grilling me. When I got home, my Holly was in bed with the fever; she wasn't conscious. She came out of it for only a few moments at a time after that, and even then she didn't know me. And sixteen days later, she died. Remember that, Francis? You were at the funeral at St. Mary's."

"I remember."

"You robbed from me her last few lucid moments, Francis. You didn't rob me of money, of my possessions. You took something more important . . . much more important. I couldn't tell her I loved her, Francis. I should kill you for that."

Tommy's large frame rose slowly and steadily from his seat. Jim did the same. I heard David's breathing beside me become measured; I knew my photographer and best friend well enough to know he was readying to make a move if either of the goon's hands went out of his line of sight.

"Kill me? You haven't got the firepower and you haven't got the guts," Ciotti said, leaning back and smiling. "The way I see it, it's me who should kill you. What you said about me and my brother — I find that offensive — very offensive. Yeah, I should kill you."

"You can't threaten a man who's almost dead anyhow, Francis."

"But I could help you on your way. Jim, bring those boys closer and keep an eye on them. I don't like the looks of that dark one. Reminds me of Rosenbaum — that pushy doorman at the Turf. Can't trust those Jews."

"I think he means you," I said out loud to David. "If he'd said the handsome Gentile, he'd have meant me. These gangster-types sure are perceptive."

Ciotti ignored me. Lots of people do.

Jim took a silent cue from Ciotti and approached us. "Arms up," he said.

I looked at David. He nodded. I raised my arms and let Jim pat me down. He did the same to David. Jim did it without being in a hurry; when he was through, he stood a few feet away from us.

"Now you, Schmidt, lock the door," Ciotti ordered. "No more visitors."

Walter looked at me, then at David. We both nodded. No use in getting Ciotti any more upset than he already was. Gunther stayed in place as Walter walked to the door with his head bowed. He reached into his pocket, found his keys, and inserted one into the door. We heard the bolt slide. Walter looked up. We looked back at Ciotti.

"What now, Fuzzy?" I asked. "Are you going to fit us for cement galoshes?"

"You got a smart mouth," he said, glaring at me. "I don't like smart mouths. Old man, did you bring a smart mouth here to save you? Think he can do it by wising off?"

"I didn't bring him, Francis," Verini said. "I'm sorry that he's here. I like him, and I don't want to expose him to people like you."

"He's here, though. I'll worry about him and his Jew friend later. Tell me again about how you're gonna kill me." Ciotti leaned forward with mock interest. Tommy, still standing beside him, smiled.

Verini's voice was slow and cool. "You need to get right with God, Francis. You also need to get right with your fellowman — including these German boys here. So we're back to what I told you. You wipe clean the slate, you wipe out this debt, and we all walk away from this. And you're one step closer to getting right with God."

Ciotti forced a look of boredom onto his face. "You're one step closer to getting to meet God, old man. Tell me why I shouldn't pop you now, and your friends too."

"Look in your heart, Francis. You know I'm right. What I'm doing now, I'm doing because of the old code — the code you never recognized. I could have gone straight to the cops, but I didn't. I'm giving you a second chance because I think it's right."

"I don't know from right," Ciotti said with disgust. "I don't know from Nicholas, I don't know from Al Verini. And I sure don't know what you think's going to save you. My conscience? I don't have one."

Tommy smirked. "No one's getting saved tonight," he said.

I took a breath and let it out with a short laugh. "You're wrong, Tommy."

Tommy looked down and got a grin of permission from Ciotti. He started toward me. "I'm wrong? Tell me how I'm wrong."

"It's Saturday night," I said. "Sunday already in some parts of the world. People are getting saved all over the place. Right here, tonight, I see a man making peace with his past — being saved from it. You could do the same, Tommy."

David nodded. "You're the one who needs saving, Tommy. We can show you how."

Tommy glared; he unbuttoned his coat. My heart paused for a brief moment. When he took off the coat and I saw he had no gun, my heart conveniently started beating again. Tommy unbuttoned his left cuff, then started rolling back his sleeve.

"You're gonna need to save yourself, I think," he said to David.

He finished rolling up the left sleeve and then the right one. David didn't take his eyes from Tommy's, not even to watch his hands. After another smile, Tommy let go with a right to David's face. I knew it was coming, and I knew David could roll under it and be inside Tommy's guard in a single motion, and that with another motion Tommy could be taken down.

But David didn't do that. He took the punch; it rocked him back a little, but he stayed up. My brain was slow in accepting what my eyes saw; I started toward David, but I felt Jim grab my arm firmly.

David looked back at me and shook his head. There was something going on within him that I didn't understand fully; but I understood more when I saw his eyes. He was trying to rise above something, to be more than what he'd been in the past. The old David would have made short work of Tommy; the new one offered Tommy another way out. He turned back to Tommy. "You've done wrong in your life, Tommy. Just like I've done and Emerson's done and Mr. Verini's done. But you can be saved — forgiven — set free."

Tommy responded with another right. David took it in the jaw and still managed to stay up. His mouth wasn't working properly now; he was probably tasting blood. But he continued, "People all over the world are getting saved tonight, Tommy. You can be one of them."

"I have plenty of sins left to go," Tommy said with audible anger. He threw another punch. This time David stumbled back, but he held on to the counter for a moment, then steadied himself and stood firm. "You just have to want to be saved. Do you want that, Tommy?"

Tommy hesitated in a fighting crouch. I was starting to worry he might lose control; his voice was low when he rasped, "Fight back."

"You too, Ciotti," I spoke up. "People all over the world are being saved tonight. You can be one of them. Mr. Verini knows what he's talking about. You don't want this night to end without getting right with God."

Tommy looked at me, then back at his boss. Ciotti shook his head and pulled a pistol out of his coat.

"You're wasting my time," he said to me. "I'm gonna have to close that smart mouth of yours."

The pistol started to raise when I heard four shots — four ear-slamming beats coming from under the table, from a gun Verini was obviously holding. Ciotti's hand faltered; he dropped the pistol, then looked into Verini's eyes. He fell forward onto the table.

Jim wasn't slow to respond. I felt the butt of a pistol on the back of my head, and I felt myself going down, but in the fog that began to form around my senses I heard yelling: yelling from David, yelling from Jim, and yelling from behind me, from the entrance to the restaurant. And then the shots seemed to repeat themselves again and again.

27

I took the oath and sat down in a hard wooden chair on the witness stand.

"Move the microphone closer to your mouth, please," the judge said to me. I reached over and pulled the gooseneck closer. "How's this?" I asked. The judge nodded.

"Mr. Dunn, we've heard from the other witnesses, and we just want you to clear up a few details for us," the prosecutor said. "Now, Mr. Dunn, we all understand that it was a traumatic event for you. Wouldn't you say that's so?"

"Less traumatic for me than for some others."

"Yes, well, that's certainly true. Tell us what you remember about the confrontation."

"The confrontation?"

"When Mr. Verini shot Mr. Ciotti. Tell the members of the jury what you saw."

"I watched Ciotti die. He was going to shoot me, but Verini killed him. Four shots. Under the table. It's interesting — that's something Verini said to me once: never show your hand. I guess that's especially true if you've got a gun in it."

"Mr. Dunn, what happened after Mr. Ciotti was shot?"

"Jim — he was one of Ciotti's goons — hit me with his gun and took aim at Verini."

"And then what happened?"

"It got a little foggy for a moment. I went down just as I heard Detective Sergeant Bill Singer and three uniformed police officers come into the restaurant."

"You fell to the ground?"

"Yes."

"Did you see the officers enter the building?"

"No, I just heard them. I recognized Singer's voice."

"What did he say when he entered the building?"

"He just yelled 'Freeze' and 'Police,' like they do on the cop shows," I said.

"Yes, I'm sure they do." The prosecutor looked a little troubled. "But you said everything was a little foggy?"

"Well, yes — Jim hit me in the head. Not that I minded much; it turns out that I fell right out of the line of fire."

"If you were a little foggy, how can you be sure that Detective Sergeant Singer identified himself as a police officer? Couldn't you be confusing the incident with one of those cop shows?"

I paused. "I heard him yell, 'Police.' I remember feeling sort of relieved that the cops had crashed the party. Seems Walter hadn't done a very good job of locking the door. He must have slid the bolt forward, then slid it back. I think he knew the cops were watching the place for signs of trouble."

"Well, let's move on. What happened then?"

"I heard more gunfire. A shot or two from Jim, then shots from behind me. I guess that was Singer."

"There's no room for guessing here, Mr. Dunn. Just stick to what you know to be the facts."

"All right. I heard shots from behind me."

"Did you hear the shots from behind you before or after the shots from Jim Ulmer?"

"After."

"How long after?"

"Not long at all. A split-second."

"Again, if you were foggy, how could you be sure?"

I paused, and the prosecutor jumped in. "Mr. Dunn, another

witness, Thomas Wentworth, testified that the victim, Jim Ulmer, had already fired his weapon several seconds before the police entered, in defense of his employer, Francis Ciotti. Mr. Wentworth also testified that Mr. Ulmer was in the process of raising his hands when he was shot. Isn't this possible?"

"Yes, I suppose it's possible. But that's not how I remember it."

"And isn't it possible that you only think you remember hearing Detective Sergeant Singer identify himself as a police officer before the shooting of Mr. Ulmer?"

"That's possible, too."

The prosecutor smiled at me. "Thank you. One more thing — a few moments ago you didn't like it when I used the word 'confrontation,' did you?"

"No."

"Why is that?"

"It wasn't so much a confrontation as a defensive action. Verini acted only when it was clear that Ciotti was going to shoot someone — namely, me."

"Verini is a good guy, isn't he?"

I hesitated. "I think so, yes."

"You think so. A known organized crime figure. You went to visit him after that night, didn't you?"

"Yes, until he died, four days ago. He lost consciousness on the way to the hospital and never regained it. So I never actually spoke to him again. Or at least, I never spoke to him and got a response."

"Yes, well, we're all sorry about Mr. Verini's death, I'm sure. As you said, he was a good guy. And Mr. Ciotti was a bad guy, and so was Jim Ulmer, right?"

"In my opinion."

"Isn't that the way you think of this, Mr. Dunn? In terms of good guys and bad guys?"

"I suppose."

"And you feel that Detective Sergeant Singer is a good guy?"

"Yes."

"Couldn't it be possible that your view is a bit simplistic, that this is more complicated than that — that life is more complicated than that?"

"Depends on whose life it is, I suppose."

The prosecutor frowned. "Thank you, Mr. Dunn. That's all I have."

He turned and went to his seat at one of the two long tables. From the other table, the defense attorney arose. He looked confident and casual, striding up to the witness stand and leaning against the railing. Just an old friend catching up on things. He and I studiously ignored the jury.

"Mr. Dunn, have you ever been in a car accident?"

"Twice."

"One was a hit-and-run, wasn't it?"

"Yes."

"You were banged up pretty good, right?"

"Yeah. It was before I became much of a believer in seat belts."

"You hit your head against the windshield, and you even received a cut, didn't you?"

"Yes."

"And yet you remembered the other car's make and model, and even its license plate number, didn't you?"

"Yes."

"They caught the guy, didn't they?"

"Yeah. Didn't do any good. He didn't have insurance. Probably why he ran in the first place."

"Let's get back to the night in question. Do you remember other details of the incident?"

"Sure."

"Such as what Mr. Ciotti was wearing?"

"A black business suit, with a blue tie. Looked like something I would have picked out."

"And even after you were hit by Jim Ulmer, do you remember details?"

"Yes."

"For now, let's talk about what happened after you were hit. You say Jim Ulmer fired, and then you heard Bill Singer fire. We'll take your word for now that those events happened within a short span of time. What happened immediately after the shooting?"

"I looked up, and I saw Jim falling. He fell a few feet away from me. Then I felt a hand on my arm, and it was David — David Ben Zadok — he helped me up, out of the way. But he'd already been busy. He took out Tommy. But I didn't see that, and I guess I'd better stick with what I saw."

Fielder smiled. "So I hear. What happened next?"

"Cops appeared all over the place. I went to Verini; he was hit in the back, but was still sitting upright in his chair."

"Did you speak with him?"

"For a few moments. Until the paramedics arrived."

"What did he say?"

"He said he was sorry it turned out this way. He said he came prepared because he knew it might. He said he had to handle it that way; it was the only way he knew. He asked me if I thought he'd done the right thing."

"And what did you say?"

I paused. "What did I say? I was alive. So I said yes. Then he asked me a question."

"What was the question?"

"He asked me, 'Do you know who was saved tonight?' I said I was. He smiled at me and said no, it was Alberto Verini."

"And then what happened?"

"Then the cops took over; the paramedics arrived. I was taken to a booth in the restaurant and checked out physically, then questioned. They did the same with David. He gave the police photographer some tips on lighting. He's nice like that."

"Yes, we've already heard from Mr. Ben Zadok. He is very nice. What happened to Mr. Verini?"

"He was taken away in an ambulance; but by then he was starting to cough blood. Sign of a punctured lung, I hear."

"And the others?"

"Jim Ulmer was dead at the scene — but you already know that, since that's what we're here about. Ciotti was dead too. Tommy was placed under arrest. He was slightly injured when David hit him."

"Slightly injured?"

"Dislocated jaw. They couldn't question him very well for a few days. But he got off better than Ciotti and Jim."

"Is this what you wanted to happen, Mr. Dunn? The good guys won, the bad guys died?"

"Not at all. At the risk of sounding simplistic, it's like this: good guys don't win when bad guys are defeated. They win when bad guys become good guys."

"Another way out was offered, was it not?"

"Yes. Verini said we could all walk away from the restaurant that night if Ciotti would do what was right. But that didn't happen. Ciotti chose the wrong thing."

"One last question — when Mr. Verini told you he was the one who was saved that night, what did he mean by that?"

"I think he told me what he meant right before they put him in the ambulance."

"What did he say?"

"He'd finally made peace with his past — not by denying it or ignoring it as he had been doing, but by facing it. What he said to me was, 'To live is Christ, to die is gain.' He said 'If the Old Man dies, so much the better.' I told him to give Holly my love."

28

The jury deliberated for about an hour, then found Singer innocent. I was waiting on the steps of the courthouse when Percy came out, heading for home. I thanked him; he shook my hand and told me to remember what he'd taught me about marriage. I smiled and said I would. Singer and Fielder walked out together a few moments later.

"I'm glad that's over," I said to Singer when he approached.

"You and me both."

"I don't think I'm happy with the way it turned out overall," I said.

"What's to be happy about? People died. But now we can move past it. There are plenty more where Ciotti came from."

"But Al Verini was the last of his kind, wasn't he?"

Singer nodded. "And for that, I'm sorry."

EPILOGUE

After the trial I got a call from Mary Ryan. I hadn't seen her since our hours in the hospital together, waiting to see if Al Verini was going to survive. When she called I was a little surprised.

"I never got that chance to thank him, did I?" she said. "But no matter. He probably would have been uncomfortable. He'll get his reward."

"You did your best," I said. "Besides, there was something more. He told me once that no one should die alone in a hospital bed, with no one else beside them to talk and pray and mourn. You gave him that. I would feel I'd done my duty if I were you."

Mary Ryan laughed. "But in this case, you *are* me," she said. "Or much like me. I have a number for you to call. It's a Joseph Buren, in New York."

I took the number. "What's this about?" I asked.

"You'll see. Take care of yourself, boy."

She hung up still laughing. I dialed the telephone number and was greeted by a perky female voice chiming, "Buren & Adkinson, Attorneys."

"Joseph Buren, please," I said. "I was told to call. My name is Emerson Dunn; I'm calling from Texas."

"One moment."

A few seconds later a man picked up the line. "Emerson Dunn?"

"That's me," I said.

"My name is Joseph Buren. I'm handling the estate of my uncle — Alberto Verini. He left some notes, handwritten, attached to his will. He wants you to have a piece of property a few miles north of Dallas and Fort Worth, near Denton, Texas."

"Me?"

Buren laughed. "You. The note says he wants to continue giving you something to think about. The town is called Ponder, Texas. I haven't seen the property, but it's out in the woods, and it has a little cabin on it. My uncle got it as part of a package deal a few years back and never could figure out what to do with it."

"Ponder, Texas."

"The estate has also been instructed to take care of the inheritance taxes, that sort of thing. So it's yours. He must have liked you, Mr. Dunn."

"I liked him."

"When you're thinking in Ponder, Texas, Mr. Dunn, think about my old uncle every now and then."

"I will, Mr. Buren, I will."